Maybe it's hormones...?

Tad had no idea what to think when it came to understanding pregnant women. But Doc Harlan had been married and madly in love with his wife for thirty-five years, had six kids and sixteen grandchildren and had handled every moment like a pro.

"Probably's hormones causing Abby's mood swings," Doc said matter-of-factly. "But I'm going to give you a few pointers that should help out."

Tad was willing to try anything.

"Rule number one—agree with her about everything, no matter what."

Tad leaned forward in his chair. "But—"

"No buts," Doc said from the other side of the desk. "Just agree with her. You'll both be a lot happier. Rule number two—give her presents for no reason, frequently." Doc smiled. "You'll be surprised how much that'll help her mood, if she knows you're thinking of her. And last but not least, rule number three—and this is very important, Tad—you need to let her know you love her."

Dear Reader,

Can anyone forget the excitement that pulsed through the house when you were anticipating the arrival of a new baby? The expectation, the nervousness, the preparations will always be remembered. Two beautiful sons have been brought home to my house—and I know I never will!

Well, now American Romance captures those unforgettable moments in the NEW ARRIVALS promotion. And to make these books even more irresistible, each soon-to-be "mommy" is about to meet the love of her life—the "daddy" to fulfill her dreams!

This month, Cathy Gillen Thacker delivers *Make Room for Baby*. And that's a topic she knows a lot about—she's the mother of three. After moving all over the country, Cathy and her family now live in North Carolina.

In the months ahead we'll be bringing you some more NEW ARRIVALS books. Just look for those delightful chubby baby feet on the cover!

Warm regards,

Debra Matteucci
Senior Editor & Editorial Coordinator
Harlequin Books
300 East 42nd Street
New York, NY 10017

Cathy Gillen Thacker
Make Room for Baby

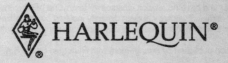

HARLEQUIN®

TORONTO • NEW YORK • LONDON
AMSTERDAM • PARIS • SYDNEY • HAMBURG
STOCKHOLM • ATHENS • TOKYO • MILAN • MADRID
PRAGUE • WARSAW • BUDAPEST • AUCKLAND

ISBN 0-373-16747-4

MAKE ROOM FOR BABY

Copyright © 1998 by Cathy Gillen Thacker.

This edition published by arrangement with Harlequin Books S.A.

® and TM are trademarks of the publisher. Trademarks indicated with
® are registered in the United States Patent and Trademark Office, the
Canadian Trade Marks Office and in other countries.

Printed in U.S.A.

Chapter One

Moonlight bathed the luxurious hotel room in irides-
cent light as Tad McFarlane made one last thorough
tour of Abby Kildaire's lips. When finally the kiss
came to an end, he lifted his head. Still feeling as if
he never wanted to let her go, he shook his head in
heartfelt regret. "I can't believe we both have to leave
here tomorrow."

"Neither can I." Abby sighed. As the spring breeze
draped them in flower-scented warmth, the last thing
Abby wanted was to return to her normal life.

Tad kissed her brow and traced his fingertip across
her lips. His arms encircled her once again. He pulled
her closer to his sinewy six-foot frame. "It's been the
best weekend of my entire life," he whispered huskily
in her ear.

And the most unexpected, Abby thought as she ran
her hands across his broad shoulders. Who would've
thought when she emptied her savings account to
splurge on a trip to Paris that she—who never did
anything on the spur of the moment—would also meet
a handsome globe-trotting reporter and have a weekend fling that would change her life irrevocably? Because Tad had changed her life. He'd taught her that

she could feel earth-shattering passion. He'd taught her that she could love a man in the most fundamental romantic way.

"It's been the best weekend of mine, too," Abby admitted wistfully, wishing their impetuous love affair could continue forever.

Tad framed her face with his hands and met her eyes. "I meant what I said before we made love, Abby. About having you with me—not just now, this weekend—but for the rest of my life."

How she wanted that, Abby thought as she inhaled the brisk citrus scent of his cologne. But like it or not, they had to be practical. They had to consider their responsibilities. "I have a job…" A good one. And so did he.

"We can work around that," Tad told her with the utter confidence she would've expected from one of the most respected reporters on the international beat. "I would never ask you to give up your profession just to be with me, any more than I would give up my life as a journalist."

Abby began to relax. Her career as the Home and Garden editor for *Trend* magazine was very important to her. She'd worked ten hard years to land such a coveted position. More important still, her work had sustained her through many a challenging time. Tad knew that. He accepted that. Just as he accepted that she lived in New York City and had for the past ten years.

Abby let her gaze drift over the arresting contours of his face and the perpetually rumpled state of his naturally curly black hair. At thirty-six, he was five years older than she was. And undoubtedly the sexiest, most easygoing man she had ever met. Everything about him—from his cleft chin, dimpled smile and deep blue bedroom eyes—appealed to her.

"What about your work?" she asked curiously, aware that at the moment he had no regular home, just a post-office box. Home for Tad was whatever city he happened to be in, whatever hotel he happened to stay in. To him, they were all one and the same. A hotel room was not a home to Abby. Her apartment in New York City was home.

Tad shrugged. "The constant traveling is beginning to wear on me. I've been thinking about moving back to the States for some time. Now that I've met you—" he paused, his expression both thoughtful and content "—it seems like the time is right for everything. Like the two of us—this—is preordained somehow."

Abby knew exactly what he meant. She had never believed in love at first sight, either, but the moment she'd encountered Tad in the Paris airport, she'd known he was someone very special. "You'd do that for me?" she asked softly, realizing she had never met a man more generous or tender. Her heart filling with happiness, she studied him. "You'd give up the international beat?"

Tad nodded, his lips taking on a serious slant. "And so much more," he confirmed with a sincerity that went soul-deep, "if it means I could be with you." Abruptly his eyes darkened with a combination of affection and mischief. "Not that I don't have dreams of my own. I do. The difference is that now I know I want you with me when they all come true." He paused before adding, "I want to share my life with you, Abby. I want to share everything."

Hope for the future filled her. "Oh, Tad…"

"Say you want that, too, Abby," Tad demanded gruffly, drawing her close.

"I do," Abby said on a halting breath. *So much.*

"Then marry me, Abby." Tad sifted his hands through her hair. "As soon as we get back to the States."

Abby shut her eyes, the desire she felt for Tad warring with her common sense. How she wished they could keep the problems of their real lives at bay and stay locked in this moment in time until she'd had her fill of him and he of her. But she knew better. Didn't she? "It's not that easy," she murmured, distraught. She looked deep into his beautiful eyes. "I have to be at work on Monday morning." *So do you.*

"Then we'll do it Sunday night. In Tennessee," Tad told her confidently. "There's no waiting period there."

Abby grinned. Somehow she wasn't surprised Tad had gone to the trouble to find that out. He was a very thorough determined man. Never more so than when he wanted something. "You *have* done your homework," she teased.

Tad grinned. "I always do my homework." Many kisses and a long bout of leisurely lovemaking later, he asked her again.

Abby knew he deserved an answer. She also knew she shouldn't be naked, her heart pounding at his nearness, when she gave it. She knew what she wanted, but she had to think about this.

"I don't know. It's so impulsive." Abby threw off the covers and sprang from the bed. Her body still tingling from their lovemaking, she snatched up the satin-and-lace robe she'd left on the chaise. Pushing her trembling arms into the sleeves, she turned and walked toward the window. Outside the moonlight blanketed the city in sparkling silver. April in Paris. Was there anyplace more beautiful or more romantic in spring? she wondered as she belted the robe around her.

"I'm not impulsive, Tad," she told him as he moved to stand beside her. And yet she was here, with him. Didn't that tell her something? About the magic of the situation and the special something they shared?

Tad put both hands on her shoulders. He turned her to face him and flashed her a sexy grin. "I know you're not impulsive. Neither am I."

"Tad…" The breath soughed from her lips as he unbelted her robe, slipped his hands inside the silky fabric and tucked them around her waist.

"What?" he said, caressing her gently.

"I can't think when you do that," Abby protested as his hands moved lower toward her thighs, then swept upward across her ribs.

"I don't want you to think," Tad told her gruffly, dipping his head to hers. "I want you to kiss me."

And heaven help her, she did.

By Sunday morning he had her on a jet to Memphis. By noon Eastern time they'd located a justice of the peace who had everything they needed right down to the witnesses, bouquet and wedding rings. An hour later they were in their hotel, making love again.

If only things could always stay this simple, Abby thought as she melted in his arms.

But of course, as luck would have it, they didn't.

Three weeks later

TAD MCFARLANE strode into the offices of *Trend* magazine, knowing the moment of reckoning had finally come. He found his runaway wife right where he expected to find her—seated behind her desk, her silky golden-brown hair spilling to her shoulders, her long-lashed golden-brown eyes focused on the magazine layout in front of her.

She turned as he approached her desk.

Tad resisted the urge to take her into his arms and kiss some sense into her. Succumbing to passion, in lieu of talking, was what had gotten them into this mess.

"What's the meaning of this?" Making no effort to hide his unhappiness with her actions, Tad handed Abby the sheaf of legal papers that had finally reached him via registered mail.

Abby arched a delicately shaped brow at him and handed the documents right back. "I would think that would be glaringly apparent."

Tad refused to take them. He cleared a space and sat down on the corner of her desk. "Well, it's not."

Abby let the papers drop. She kept her pretty oval face level with his. "I want an annulment."

No, Tad thought, *you don't. You're just angry with me right now. And considering the giant misunderstanding we had, that's understandable.*

Determined to take whatever time they needed to work this out and salvage the marriage that had lasted barely a day, Tad folded his arms in front of him. "On what grounds?" he demanded, searching her wide-set eyes. "As I recall we consummated the marriage quite thoroughly."

Abby flushed, unable to argue that, and with good reason, Tad thought. They had made love repeatedly

that entire weekend, both before and after the cere-
mony.

"That's just it, Tad," Abby snapped irritably as she
stood and began to pace. Her willowy body was ac-
centuated by a buttercup yellow jersey dress. Bone-
colored stockings and matching shoes showed off her
spectacular legs. Just watching her made Tad's blood
run hot and quick. "We were driven by hormones. We
weren't thinking clearly."

Speak for yourself, Tad thought irascibly. He'd been
thinking very clearly, then and now. He'd known the
minute he'd laid eyes on her that he had to have her.
And that desire—to make her his and his alone—had
only increased over the past two weeks.

"You're still ticked off at me for buying the newspaper," Tad guessed as he tried not to think how good
and right her soft mobile lips had felt beneath his.

Abby tossed her head, her hot-tempered movement
filling the small elegant office with the intoxicating
vanilla scent of her perfume. "You could have told
me your plans before we married!"

"I did!" Tad replied, aware they'd covered this
ground the morning after they'd gotten married—the
morning she'd walked out on him and their new marriage.

"Funny, I don't recall you saying one darn word
about the two of us moving to North Carolina."

Tad scowled. "I told you I spent summers there as
a kid."

"Visiting your aunt Sadie, yes, I know," Abby said
impatiently, obviously exasperated at having to go
through this again.

"I also told you I wanted to own my own newspaper," Tad continued patiently.

"Right!" Abby aimed an accusing finger at him. "Someday!"

Tad cocked a brow, the hint of a smile playing around his mouth, even as he noticed Abby was still wearing the fourteen-carat-gold-and-jade ring that she'd selected to serve as both her wedding and engagement ring. That could only mean one thing—their impetuous union wasn't nearly as over as she wanted him to believe it was. "You didn't believe I was serious?" he chided, refusing to let her off the hook even for a second.

Abby rolled her eyes. "Of course I did. Your plan to buy and revamp an ailing small-town paper sounded exactly like one of those irrational cockeyed retirement dreams that every man I know has. I figured you'd get around to it when you were sixty or something. And I'd happily go along with you at that point, twenty-five years from now, when I was ready to retire from the business, too!"

Abby'd never dreamed a journalist of Tad's caliber and fame would attempt to drop out of the mainstream at age thirty-six! Never mind literally the day after he'd married her. But that was exactly what had happened.

Unable to talk him out of it, unable to put the brakes on her formerly sedate but work-laden life that was fast spinning out of control, she'd promptly put a hold on everything and curtailed any plans to actually move in together, saying they needed time—at least three weeks!—to cool off and rethink what they'd done.

At first Tad had been adamantly opposed to such an arrangement. When she hadn't backed down, he'd eventually agreed to her request, but only because she'd given him no choice. Besides, he had some stories to finish and loose ends of his own to tie up before concentrating once again on her and their marriage.

Abby tried hard not to think what his nearness was doing to her or notice how fast her heart beat whenever he was near her. "Look, I'm sure what you are doing in Blossom is laudable," she said politely.

"But?" Tad said, sensing there was more.

Abby swallowed around the unaccustomed dryness in her throat. "If you'd told me you had already put a bid in on the *Blossom Weekly News* beforehand and were planning to move to North Carolina as soon as said bid was accepted—"

"*If* said bid was accepted," Tad corrected, letting her know that at that point it had been far from a done deal.

"—then I never would've married you," Abby concluded. Because that would have meant giving up her job at *Trend,* and she never would have done that.

Tad lounged against her desk. "So now it's over— just like that?"

"It has to be."

"No," Tad said heavily, looking very sexy in jeans that clung like a second skin, a white oxford shirt worn open at the throat, tweed sport coat and hand-tooled leather boots. "It doesn't."

Damn it all, anyway, Abby thought as she returned to her desk. She should have known a man like Tad, who was used to getting damn near anything and everything he wanted in life, would be difficult about this! She sat back in her chair, her forearms lying flat against the armrests. Hiking the skirt of her dress slightly, she crossed her legs at the knee.

"You're saying…what—that you're going to fight

the annulment?'' she asked tensely, wishing she wasn't still so attracted to him. Wishing she didn't recall in such exquisite detail what it had been like to make slow wonderful love with him.

He leaned across her desk. ''I'm saying I want you to see what you're giving up before you actually give it up.'' He took two airline tickets out of his pocket and placed them in front of her.

''I can't go to North Carolina!'' Abby exclaimed.

''Why not?'' Abby's best friend, Yvonne Kirschner prodded, walking in unannounced. ''Tomorrow's Saturday.''

A weekend with Tad is what had gotten her into trouble in the first place, Abby thought darkly.

Sensing something out of the ordinary was up, Yvonne looked Tad over before returning her glance to Abby. ''Who's the hunk?'' she asked with a curious smile.

Unsure how to answer that, Abby looked at the forty-one-year-old Features editor for *Trend.* In her power suit and heels, her short red hair impeccably coiffed, Yvonne was not just the epitome of the New York City career woman, she was Abby's role model and mentor in the publishing world. The person Abby most frequently turned to for advice. But what could she say to Yvonne about this? Yvonne was—and always would be—married to her career. Yvonne would never have eloped on a whim the way Abby had.

Tad stepped forward. He stretched out his hand. ''Hi. I'm Tad McFarlane. Abby's husband.''

Yvonne did a double take.

''We got married in Paris at the end of April,'' Tad continued.

Yvonne's glance cut to Abby's left hand, lingering

on the jade-and-gold ring she'd been wearing since her trip abroad. She looked back at Tad, who was wearing a plain gold wedding band. "You got married for the first and only time in your life and you didn't mention it?" Yvonne asked, aghast.

Abby lifted her hands. "Everyone was so upset about the magazine, the financial problems we've been having, that I…" Abby was blushing furiously.

"I still think I would have mentioned it," Yvonne retorted.

Not if you were getting an annulment, you wouldn't, Abby thought. "Look, don't tell anyone else," Abby insisted quickly, wanting her embarrassment to end here and now.

"Okay," Yvonne agreed, like the devout friend she was. "But, uh…" Yvonne's glance returned to Tad, then focused on the sparks flying between Tad and Abby. "Maybe you should go ahead and go. It won't do any good to sit here wondering—"

"Good point," Abby interrupted, not about to let Tad know she—and everyone else at the magazine she had lovingly labored over for the past year and a half—was currently in jeopardy of losing her job, thanks to a recent takeover of the parent company by a huge conglomerate. "I do need a vacation," Abby said bluntly, vaulting to her feet. Even more urgently she needed to get Tad out of there. She snatched up the airline tickets he'd left on her desk, then grabbed his arm and her briefcase simultaneously. "Let's get out of here."

"Don't be a stranger," Yvonne called to Tad as Abby hurried him down the hall.

Tad glanced at Abby. "Don't worry," he promised softly, letting her know he wasn't giving up on them no matter how difficult she proved to be. "I don't intend to be."

"WELL, WHAT DO YOU think?" Tad asked Abby early the next afternoon after they'd completed the whirlwind tour of the brick building that housed the *Blossom Weekly News*.

"About what—western North Carolina?" Which was incredibly beautiful and heavily wooded. "Or Blossom?" Which was a charming little town of around ten thousand people in the Great Smoky Mountains, about sixty miles from the Tennessee border.

"About the newspaper," Tad said, gesturing around them.

Abby had the feeling he was talking about a lot more than that; he was talking about the prospects for renewing their marriage. Stubbornly she focused only on what she was prepared to discuss at that moment—the business he had just purchased. "It's a fine building. Well constructed. I'm not sure I like the bullpen atmosphere. I sort of like working in individual offices myself—find it easier to concentrate."

He picked up a copy of the newspaper. "What about this?"

Abby searched for something nice to say. "It's, um, compact."

"And poorly written and designed and limited in scope," Tad agreed.

Almost hopelessly so. "And yet you bought it," Abby observed, thinking Tad was more an enigma to her than ever.

"Precisely because it does need so much work," Tad confirmed. He gazed around them happily, taking in the four desks that had been scrunched together in the big uncarpeted room. "Can't you see the potential here, Abby?"

What she saw made her think he was nuts. A journalist of Tad's caliber and renown would never be happy here in the long haul. But he was going to have to figure that out for himself, Abby told herself firmly. It was not up to her to educate him.

"There are no computers," Abby remarked absently as beads of perspiration sprang up along her neck and chest. Was it hot in here, she wondered as she tugged at the jewel collar of her cotton sweater, or was it just her imagination?

"That's easily fixed," Tad assured her with youthful enthusiasm. He picked up a paperweight and tossed it from hand to hand. "I'll have some in by next week."

Abby continued to pace the office restlessly, noticing that her knees felt a little wobbly, too. Why, she didn't know.

Nonplussed by her sudden wooziness, she rubbed at the back of her neck. "And there's only one section of the paper," she continued wearily.

Tad grinned confidently as he placed the paperweight on a desk and looked around. "I'm planning to expand. In fact, I'm looking for a Lifestyle editor for the new Lifestyle section as we speak."

Abby moved away from Tad. She drew a deep breath to see if that would help. "I'll let you know if I think of anyone," she said dryly.

Tad paused, his eyes on her face. "Actually I already had someone in mind."

Thinking maybe she'd feel better if she sat down, Abby eased herself onto the corner of the desk. "Really." She crossed her legs at the knee. "Who?"

Tad smiled. "You."

"Very funny, Tad," Abby drawled, trying hard not to let him know just how woozy she was feeling.

She'd been trying to ignore it, but the truth was she'd been feeling funny, sort of weak-kneed and dizzy, ever since he picked her up at her apartment in New York City to take her to the airport for the flight to North Carolina.

"You think I'm kidding?" Tad asked in a low sexy tone.

Abby's heart skipped a beat as she looked up into his eyes. *Saved by the bell,* she thought as the phone rang on the desk behind her. His eyes still on hers, Tad reached around her waist to answer it. "*Blossom Weekly News.* Yeah. Just a minute, Yvonne." Tad handed the phone to Abby. "It's for you."

Knowing something had to have happened for Yvonne to call her here, Abby pressed the receiver to her ear. "What's up?" she asked.

"You picked the wrong time to go out of town, kiddo," Yvonne told her in a discouraged voice.

Anxiety hit Abby like a Mack truck. Aware her hands were suddenly trembling, too, Abby gulped. "What do you mean?" she asked with trepidation.

Yvonne continued grimly, "*Trend* has just been purchased by The Hindemythe Group in Great Britain. They're moving the magazine overseas, pronto."

"What about us?" Abby asked Yvonne as her heart began to pound. "And the rest of the staff?"

"We've all been fired."

"WHAT IS IT?" Tad asked as soon as Abby thanked Yvonne for the information, told her they'd talk soon and hung up.

Abby wet her lips and tried to make sense of her increasingly fuzzy view of Tad's handsome face. Sweat was gathering between her breasts and there was a roaring in her ears. What was wrong with her? Was it the altitude? The fact Blossom, North Carolina, was five thousand feet above sea level? Or was it just being around Tad, knowing he wanted to continue their hasty marriage, that left her feeling so dizzy and disoriented? Whatever was causing it, Abby decided firmly, she had to get a grip.

"I just lost my job, as did everyone else at *Trend,*" Abby told Tad calmly.

"I'm sorry." Tad took her hands in his. He rubbed his thumbs across the insides of her wrists. "But maybe it's not such a bad thing, after all."

Abby blinked, stunned Tad did not see the development as the calamity it was. Her career was the one thing—the only thing—she had counted on through thick and thin. She'd put her heart and soul into her job at *Trend.*

"If it gives us a chance to be together," he soothed, wrapping a comforting arm about her shoulders, "maybe it's even a good thing."

His analysis was so hopelessly optimistic, so far off the mark, Abby didn't know whether to laugh or cry. She only knew, with the room taking on an increasingly precarious tilt, and her whole world crashing down around her, that she couldn't hold it together any longer.

She stopped trying to fight it, pitched forward into Tad's waiting arms and let the swirling dizziness overwhelm her.

Chapter Two

"What'd you say to make her faint?" Doc Harlan said as Tad carried his new bride into the doctor's office just down the street from the newspaper.

"What makes you think it was something I said?" Tad asked as he eased Abby onto the examining table. "It could have been something I did. Or something someone else said."

Doc grinned as he listened for her heartbeat and checked her pulse. "Always gotta see all the angles, don't you, son?"

Tad tried not to show his fear. It had scared the life out of him when Abby had collapsed in his arms. "That's the way I've been trained—the way all journalists are trained."

Fortunately he'd had Doc nearby. The sixty-year-old physician had taken care of the people in Blossom for the past thirty years. His kind eyes and comforting smile were as well-known to residents as the plaid sport shirts, khaki trousers and suede loafers he wore beneath his starched white lab coat. Tad searched Doc's face anxiously, taking solace in the fact Doc was such a capable family physician. "Is Abby going to be all right?'' Tad asked as Abby began to moan and come around.

"Yes, but I'd like to know why she fainted. Does this happen often?''

Tad shrugged as he turned his attention back to Abby's pale oval face. She hadn't fainted in Paris. Or when they got married in Memphis.

"Not that I know,'' Tad said. "But we've only been married a little over three weeks.''

Doc nodded, accepting that information as he broke open an ammonia capsule. "Did she just have a shock?''

Tad nodded, recalling the precipitous phone call from her friend Yvonne. "She just found out she lost her job.''

Doc gave Tad a compassionate look. He waved the capsule beneath Abby's nose. "That's probably it, then, but just to be safe, I'd better examine her.''

Catching a whiff of the ammonia, Abby coughed. Her golden-brown eyes fluttered open. Bewildered to find herself lying prone on an examining table, she looked at Tad, then Doc, then Tad again. Embarrassed color highlighted her delicately sculpted cheekbones, and the tip of her tongue snaked out to wet her soft pink lips. "What…?'' She tried to raise herself slightly, abruptly lost all color and lay back down again.

"You fainted,'' Tad told her, taking her hand.

Remembering, Abby groaned.

"I caught you,'' Tad continued.

Abby moaned louder and covered her face with both hands.

Doc grinned. "That'd be my reaction, too, if I was married to him.'' Doc angled a thumb at Tad.

Abby's eyes widened. She peered at Tad through her splayed fingers as if to say, *You told him?*

Tad shrugged. If it were up to him, he'd be shouting it to the world.

"Since you were in no shape to do so, I had to give him permission to treat you," Tad said to Abby. To Doc, "She's not really used to being my wife yet."

"So I gather," Doc said.

His nurse came in, patient gown in hand.

Hand on his shoulder, Doc ushered Tad toward the door. "There's a good selection of magazines in the waiting room. Make yourself comfortable."

"But—" Tad protested.

"I'll call you when I know something," Doc promised.

"IT CAN'T BE," Abby whispered hoarsely, tears glimmering in her eyes as she sat on the examining table, still in her pale blue patient gown.

"Honey, it is," Doc said gently.

Silence filled the small room as Abby tried to absorb all he'd just told her.

"I'll get your husband." Doc patted her knee. "The two of you can talk, then if you have any questions, you can ask me together."

"What is it?" Tad asked seconds later as he rushed into the room, looking worried.

Abby drew a deep breath and shot him an accusing look. This was all his fault! "I'm pregnant."

Tad stared at her, evidencing much the same gut reaction she'd already had. "That can't be."

Which was, as it turned out, exactly what she'd said.

"We used—"

"Protection, I know," Abby said grimly. "But as

Doc says, every kind of protection fails sometime. We just happened to hit one of those sometimes.''

"In Paris." Tad swiftly pinpointed the time and place.

"Or our wedding night in Memphis," Abby supposed, remembering how jubilant and uninhibited their lovemaking had been just after they'd eloped. "Either way, I'm due approximately eight months from now."

"A baby," Tad repeated in a low stunned voice as he sat down beside her and took her hand. Slowly his deep blue eyes filled with joy. "We're going to have a baby."

"Looks like," Abby said, still feeling as though she'd just had the wind knocked out of her.

She had always sworn she would never get pregnant until the man and the moment were right, until she could provide her child with the kind of loving stable home her oft-married-and-divorced parents had never given her.

Yet here she was. Trying to annul her marriage to Tad at the same time she discovered she was carrying his child. Could it get any worse?

"This changes things," Tad said firmly.

"Yes," Abby agreed, "it does." It made them much more complicated.

Tad smiled at her. "Looks like we have a lot to talk about."

"Yes, I'd say so." Such as, what were they going to do? She wanted this baby—Tad's baby—so much. But she was afraid, too, that in the end neither she nor Tad would be able to do right by their child and give him or her the peaceful loving two-parent home every child deserved. She did not want to hurt her child the way she'd been hurt when her parents had split.

"Do you need any help getting dressed?"

Just the thought of him helping her take off the examination gown and put on her clothes made her skin burn. Abby drew an unsteady breath. "I can handle it." She met his eyes. "I'm feeling fine now. Honest."

"All right." Tad rose reluctantly. "I'll be waiting for you in the reception area."

Abby nodded.

"And, Abby?" Tad came back to cup her shoulders warmly and kiss her brow. "This is good news."

"READY TO GO?" Tad rushed to his feet as a pink-cheeked Abby came out into the waiting room, several samples of prenatal vitamins and a prescription in hand.

As ready as I'll ever be, Abby thought, nodding.

"Good." Tad flashed a sexy grin that brought his dimples into prominence. "'Cause I've got a surprise for you."

Abby dug in her heels as they moved through the clinic doors and headed toward his Jeep. "I'm not sure I can take any more surprises."

"You'll like this one. I promise." Tad helped her into the passenger seat, climbed in himself, then drove across the center of the small town to a shady residential street of older Victorian homes. He parked at the curb in the center of the block in front of a house with a Sold sign in front of it. With a feeling of dread, Abby looked over and saw plenty of room, crumbling gray-white paint, windows smeared with years of grime, shrubs badly in need of a good trimming and a yard overgrown with weeds.

"Don't tell me…" Abby began, with a sinking feeling of dread.

"I bought it along with the newspaper," Tad announced proudly. He was already out of the car and sprinting around to her side. "You're going to love it."

Somehow Abby doubted that.

"It's the perfect place for rearing kids. Once it's fixed up of course."

Abby looked at the sagging steps leading up to the front porch. "It would take years."

Tad remained undaunted. He braced his hands on his hips and looked around with satisfaction. "Not with someone like you running the show."

Abby was the first to admit she had a lot of talent. She could spot an idea that would excite readers and compel them to buy a magazine in an instant. But this? Just the thought of tackling it made her feel overwhelmed. "Tad, I'm an editor, not—"

"A home-and-garden editor." Tad unlocked the door and opened it wide.

"I've never personally supervised the renovation of a home. I just okay the ideas behind different projects and oversee the articles written about such endeavors."

Wordlessly Tad picked Abby up in his arms and carried her across the threshold. He closed the door behind them, strode over to the ugliest olive green Naugahyde sofa Abby had ever seen in her life. He set her down gently and then sat beside her. "Our life together is going to be full of firsts, Abby," he told her gently, taking both her hands in his. "The first marriage, first child, first home, first newspaper, first lifestyle section…"

His enthusiasm made her want to grin. Holding on to the grim reality of the situation with effort, Abby replied, "Back to that again?"

Tad lifted her hand to his lips. He kissed it soundly, then laid it against his face. "I need you, Abby," he told her softly. "Together we can make all our dreams come true."

Abby wanted to believe that; she couldn't. Her life thus far had taught her to take nothing for granted, to depend only on what she knew to be a concrete basis for her life.

She rose and moved away from him. "My dream has always been to climb to the top of my profession," she reminded Tad.

Together they walked through the downstairs, viewing a large imposing entryway, living room, den, dining room and kitchen. All of which looked as if they'd been decorated by a color-blind two-year-old and furnished at a swap meet.

"You can still climb to the top of your profession if you work with me," Tad pointed out as they went up the stairs and toured the four bedrooms and two full baths. "It'll just be in a different format."

The third floor was an attic, and it was as filled with junk as the rest of the house. Feeling she'd seen enough, Abby turned and headed back down the stairs.

"Magazines and newspapers are very different. Just as your career dreams are very different from my career dreams, Tad."

"I'll concede that." Tad followed close on her heels. "But fate has taken a turn we didn't anticipate and can't change." Tad cupped her shoulders and turned her to face him. "And until you do find another job at a magazine, why not work here with me?"

Her skin warming to his touch, Abby sighed.

"It could take months to find another position on par with what you had at *Trend*," he went on.

"I know that!" The fact she'd been fired still rankled.

"You're going to need to be busy in the meantime. You're going to need to be someplace good for the baby. And I want you nearby so I can take care of you and the baby both."

It didn't take a genius to see where this was heading. Abby crossed her arms and stepped back, away from him. "You're talking about continuing our marriage?" she said, angling her chin at him.

He studied her with a fiery determination that set her pulse to racing. "Yes."

Despair swept her. "Tad..." As utterly romantic, as optimistic, as Tad's proposal was, she did not want to prolong the agony of defeat, and she had already conceded defeat in her marriage to Tad. He, however, had other ideas.

"Our baby deserves to be born legitimately, to two parents who love him. Our baby deserves the very best start we can give him." Tad drew her into his arms and held her against him. "I know this is unexpected—" he soothed.

Tears burned Abby's eyes. "You've got that right!"

"—but it's not that far off course, either," Tad said gently. "You already know I love you and you love me."

That Abby could not dispute. It was what came after the love that worried her. How many times had she seen her parents fall madly and passionately in love, marry, only to divorce mere months later?

Abby flattened her hands on Tad's chest and pushed

away from him. "It takes a lot more than a whopping jolt of love at first sight to make a marriage work, Tad." She paced in the opposite direction.

"But love is the basis on which all good marriages are built," Tad reminded her. Again he crossed to her and took her in his arms. He threaded his hand through her hair. "I told you in Paris that I wanted you to share everything with me, including my dreams."

Abby recalled that night. It had been oh, so romantic. She'd been enthralled. The problem was his proposal wasn't *practical*.

"Having a baby is one of my dreams. And yours," Tad stated persuasively.

"But not now," Abby protested in heartfelt agony. "Not when everything is so messed up." Not when she didn't even have a job!

"It doesn't have to be messed up." Tad gently kneaded the tense muscles in her back. "Stay here with me. Help me fix up this house and breathe new life into the newspaper. Wait out the birth of our baby with me by your side."

Abby reluctantly admitted she did not want to go through pregnancy alone. Plus, Tad was the father. He deserved to participate in the event as much as she did. And aside from the fact they wanted very different things out of life—he a chance to revive a small-town newspaper and a home in the mountains of North Carolina, she a career as a magazine editor in a big city— they did get along very well. Any child would be lucky to have him for a father.

"You understand I can't—won't—give up looking for work in my field in the meantime?" Abby said bluntly, wanting no more misunderstandings between them on this score.

Tad nodded.

"Because after the baby is born," Abby continued, "I intend to go right back to work." Work was the sustaining force in her life. It had seen her through a lot of good times and bad. It was the one thing in her life she had always known she could count on. Yes, getting fired was a setback, but it hadn't been her fault, and with time she knew she would bounce back stronger than ever.

"What about after the baby is born? Are you proposing we split up?"

"From a practical standpoint, we'll probably have to, if we get jobs in different states. But that doesn't mean we couldn't both participate actively in our child's life. Commute. Have him or her spend time with both of us. I'd be more than amenable to working things out on that score. I'd just want to know…I'd want you to promise me that when that time comes—"

"If it comes," Tad interrupted.

"—that we'll part gracefully and both do whatever it takes to work things out on a practical level."

Tad's kneading hands stilled. "All right," he said eventually, "as long as you're here with me in Blossom when the baby is born and agree to share every moment of our baby's development and birth with me, then I promise I'll be supportive of your efforts to get back into the magazine business, no matter what that entails. But in return," he said in a low intense voice, "you have to do a favor for me."

Abby's heart skipped a beat as she lifted her gaze to his. At that moment she felt she could drown in his sexy blue eyes. "That favor being…?" she asked on a halting breath.

"I don't want anyone in Blossom to know our marriage is being held together only by the baby,'' Tad warned her. ''People talk, especially when the subjects involved give them something to talk about.'' Compassion gilded the handsome features of his face. ''I wouldn't want anything hurtful coming back to haunt our child later on.''

''Like the fact his parents were about to divorce and had to stay married,'' Abby guessed. She recalled the gossip she'd endured as a kid about her own parents and their oft-changing love lives. There was no getting around it. It had hurt.

''Right.'' Tad kissed the inside of her wrist. ''Let's just let it be known we eloped in Memphis after spending the weekend in Paris. We'll tell people the truth— that we're both delighted to be having a baby, and for the moment, anyway, you're going to be helping me out with the newspaper, with the intention of one day going back to magazine work.''

Abby couldn't fault Tad's thinking; it seemed he had covered everything. ''That sounds fair.''

''Good.'' The set of his broad shoulders relaxed.

''In return for my cooperation, however, I'd like to ask yours.''

His expression sparked with masculine interest. ''On what?''

''The sleeping arrangements.''

Tad's dimpled grin broadened and his eyes twinkled sexily. ''As I recall, we never seemed to get much sleep.''

''Exactly my point,'' Abby said, flushing, reminding herself it was the unbridled passion flowing between them that was responsible for all their miscommunication and had gotten them into this mess. They needed to be a lot more circumspect in the future, and there was no way they could do that if they were making love to each other like there was no tomorrow. "I don't think we should be sharing a bed. We should be talking instead. Besides," she hurried on, aware how ridiculous she sounded, but not about to back down now that she'd laid out the rules, "I'm pregnant. I need my sleep."

He lifted a dissenting brow. "You also need to be loved."

Abby pushed the memories of their ardent love-making from her mind. It was rushing headlong into bed with Tad that had gotten her into this situation in the first place. She swallowed and tried not to think about his lips on her skin. "Things are complicated enough as it is without bringing sex back into the mix, Tad," she told him sternly.

He studied her, but the passionate argument, the insistence on having his own way in this that she expected, never came.

"You want us to concentrate on getting to know each other, instead," he guessed, stepping back and mulling over the idea.

Abby nodded and folded her arms. She didn't know why—the day was quite warm—but she suddenly felt chilled. And oddly bereft. "I think it'd be a good idea, since we're going to be rearing a child together, don't you?"

His expression impassive, Tad continued studying her. Finally he let out a long slow breath and allowed, "I have to admit there's a lot I want to learn about you."

"Same here."

"And a lot more you should know about me," he concluded just as the phone rang. With a last backward look at her, he went to answer it. He listened intently, then frowned, promising, "I'll be right there."

"Trouble?" Abby asked as soon as he hung up.

Tad nodded. "It's my aunt Sadie."

"Is Aunt Sadie one of the reasons you moved back?" Abby asked as, minutes later, they climbed back into Tad's Jeep.

"She's my only living relative, and—"

"She's ill?"

"Not exactly."

Abby waited as Tad started the engine and pulled the Jeep away from the curb. "What do you mean, not exactly?"

"That was one of her neighbors who called. Said she's been worried about Aunt Sadie ever since she retired last year. That she'd been acting a little strange."

Abby frowned. This did not sound good. "You think she's getting senile?"

Tad shook his head. "She's always been sharp as a tack."

Abby heard the reservation in his voice and knew there was some sort of problem, even if he wasn't coming right out and telling her so.

As they turned onto the next street, loud music filtered out to greet them. Wordlessly Tad pulled up in front of a small tidy brick house with tons of gingerbread trim.

In tandem they turned their gazes in the direction of the commotion. Abby blinked and did a double take. "Oh, my heavens," she said.

Chapter Three

"Let me guess—Aunt Sadie," Abby murmured as the two of them approached the spry-looking woman in full flapper regalia, doing the Charleston on her front porch while her bassett hound lay prone beside her, watching.

"One and the same," Tad confirmed with a grin.

"Come on up and join me!" Aunt Sadie beckoned them with a wave, then went back to kicking up her heels and crossing her hands over her knees.

Before Abby could guess Tad's intent, he had taken her by the hand and swirled her around to face him. The next thing she knew they were both kicking up their heels to the lively beat of the music for which the dance had been named. While Sadie threw back her head and laughed, the three of them danced round and round in the warm May air, till finally the music on the old Victrola stopped.

"Whew!" Sadie put a hand to her perspiring forehead, adjusting the vivid blue band that encircled her head, and peeked out beneath the thick silvery bangs of her wedge-cut hair. Sadie turned sparkling eyes on them. "That'll get the old blood pumping!"

"And then some," Tad concurred, laughing.

Taking Abby's hand, he led her to a seat on one of the white wicker chairs on the front porch. She sank into the cushions gratefully while Sadie moved to a table to pour three glasses of icy lemonade.

Tad reached down to pet Buster, then also took a seat. "Did you forget your doctor's appointment this afternoon?" Tad asked his aunt.

"No, not at all," Sadie said breathlessly, as she settled opposite him on the porch swing. "I just had more important things to do."

Abby wondered what could've been more important than an appointment with Doc Harlan, the town's only physician.

"Dancing," Tad guessed, no expression readily identifiable on his face, though Abby sensed inwardly he was a little piqued about the blown-off appointment.

"Cheering up Buster," Sadie corrected. She pointed to her bassett hound, who was still lying on the porch, his head resting between his paws. "He's been very depressed," Sadie continued.

Tad looked at Buster, then turned back to Sadie. "How can you tell?"

Sadie sighed, exasperated. "That face!"

Tad laughed and shook his head. "Aunt Sadie, Buster always has that mournful look."

"True, but usually he doesn't just lie there like that all day long, and that's all he does these days," Sadie complained, fanning herself.

"Have you taken him to the vet?" Tad put his lemonade aside, then hunkered down in front of Buster and scratched him behind the ears.

"Yes." Sadie sniffed indignantly. "They can't find a thing."

"Then maybe he's just tired," Tad suggested, straightening. "He probably hasn't been sleeping much, either, if *you're* not sleeping nights."

Sadie sighed and scraped her teeth across her lower lip. "I hadn't thought of that."

"Which is why, as you recall, you have an appointment with Doc Harlan—" Tad consulted his watch "—twenty minutes ago."

Abby noted Sadie looked less than eager. "I think I should let someone else go," Sadie said. "Someone who's really sick."

"Oh, no." Tad strode toward his aunt. "You're not getting out of it that easily. So c'mon." He held out a hand and assisted his aunt out of the swing. "Let's go."

"Oh, all right, just let me freshen up," Sadie grumbled. She slipped into the house.

Abby turned to Tad. "You're taking her to her appointment?"

Tad nodded. He looked at Abby, his eyes filled with concern. "It's the only way to make sure she'll show up."

Sadie sailed through the door. Abby was amused to see that Sadie was still in her flapper outfit. "Now you listen to me, Tad McFarlane," Sadie scolded as she led the way down the steps to Tad's Jeep. "This is the very last doctor's appointment I am letting you make on my behalf. There is absolutely no way I am going to let you or anyone else turn me into a hypochondriac just because I retired from teaching last year."

Tad held the door for his aunt. "Aunt Sadie, no one is calling you a hypochondriac," he said wearily.

"Might as well." Sadie snorted, incensed, as she

accepted Tad's help getting up in the Jeep. "Insomnia! Whoever heard of going to the doctor for that?"

As it turned out, Tad was disappointed to hear, there wasn't a whole lot Doc Harlan could do for Sadie.

"I don't want to put you on sleeping pills if we can avoid it," Doc told Sadie. "I'd rather you increase your activity during the days and cut out all naps no matter how drowsy you get. See if that doesn't get you back on a normal sleep pattern. Meantime you can try some of these."

He gave her a list of things to do that included, among other things, sleeping in a dark quiet room and drinking a glass of warm milk before she retired. "You might also buy some eye shades down at the pharmacy," Doc said. "They don't work for everyone, but they might work for you."

While Abby walked down to the pharmacy with Sadie to get them, Tad stayed behind to talk to Doc. "She really is okay?" he asked anxiously.

Doc nodded and gave Tad a comforting smile. "Fit as a fiddle as far as I can tell." Doc made a final notation on Sadie's chart, then handed it to his receptionist/nurse for filing. "It may be she just has something on her mind."

That much Tad had guessed, too. "Any idea what?" If it wasn't an illness or the possibility of one keeping Sadie awake nights, then what was?

Doc shook his head. He looked equally baffled. "You're a lot closer to her—you'll need to figure out what. But my guess is your aunt probably just needs to stay busier during the day. I gather she hasn't been all that active since she returned from her last cruise in February.''

"That's true." Tad shook hands with the gray-haired physician. "Thanks, Doc."

"Anytime." Doc winked. "Take care of your new bride now, you hear?"

If she'll let me. Thus far, Abby had one foot—no, make that half her body—out the door.

He went to join Sadie and Abby, who were just leaving the pharmacy. Together, they climbed back into the Jeep.

"I want the two of you to stay for dinner," Sadie told them firmly. "Abby and I have a lot to catch up on."

When they returned to Sadie's, Buster was still lying on the porch. His expression remained mournful and his tail barely lifted as he followed them inside.

"Poor thing," Sadie murmured compassionately. "I don't think he likes me being home all day."

Buster didn't? Or Sadie? "So this blue mood of Buster's has just happened since you retired," Tad said as Sadie led the way into the homey confines of her peach-colored kitchen.

Sadie brought out a mesh bag of baking potatoes and carried them to the sink. She thought about Tad's question as she rummaged around for aprons for herself and Abby. "Actually it didn't start right away. At first he was happy to have me home."

"When did he begin acting so listless?" Tad asked as Abby began scrubbing the three potatoes Sadie had picked out.

Sadie returned to the refrigerator and pulled out an armful of salad fixings. "It didn't happen overnight.

It was more of a gradual thing, since last…oh, March.''

Tad watched her bring out several pots and a large cast-iron skillet. ''Is it possible he's picking up on your mood?''

Sadie paused, caught off guard. Her glance lifted to Tad's. ''You think he knows I've been a little blue?''

Tad shrugged and exchanged concerned looks with Abby over Sadie's head. ''Well, Buster's been with you nigh on twelve years now, Aunt Sadie,'' he said gently. ''He has to know you better than practically anyone. If he thinks you're unhappy…'' Tad bent his knees and scrunched down so they were at eye level. ''Are you unhappy?''

Sadie straightened her slender shoulders and folded her arms. Her chin took on a militant tilt. ''Well, as much as I absolutely loathe to admit it, yes, I am.''

Abby looked sympathetic, too. She wrapped an arm around Sadie's shoulders and said, ''Your retirement not all it was cracked up to be?''

Sadie nodded miserably. Moving away from both Tad and Abby, she threw up both hands and said in exasperation and disappointment, ''It bothers me to admit it, but I'm no good at this!'' She shook her head. ''All those years I saved and scrimped, only to find out I got tired of traveling after just three overseas trips, and I'm no good at hobbies. And now that I'm home again the days are too long and I'm lonely here, rambling around this house on my own. I've tried volunteer work, but with everyone in these parts looking after their own, there's not a lot to do. The bottom line is, I no longer feel useful. And that makes me feel crabby and just plain bored and I hate feeling this way!'' she stated vehemently.

Buster perked up, hearing the passion in his mistress's voice. The droopy-eyed hound looked from Tad to Sadie to Abby and then back again, then sank back down, looking more mournful than ever.

"Then we're going to have to fix that," Tad told his aunt firmly.

"How?" Sadie returned glumly. She clearly saw no solution.

"By making use of your talents," Tad told her, moving forward to wrap his arm about Sadie's shoulders just the way Abby had. "I'm expanding the newspaper. I'm going to need someone else to help proofread all the copy, and I can't think of anyone who'd be better at it than you, Aunt Sadie."

Tad caught Abby's confused look and explained, "Aunt Sadie taught high-school English lit for thirty-nine years."

Abby smiled, impressed. "Wow. You did have a long career."

"And a very distinguished one," Tad added.

"You're sure I wouldn't be in the way?" Sadie asked, her blue eyes narrowing in concern.

Tad shook his head. "The only problem is limited budget. Until I can increase revenues at the newspaper, I'm not going to be able to pay you much more than minimum wage."

The diminutive Sadie waved off his concern. "Don't worry about that." She stood on tiptoe to kiss his cheek. "It'll be a pleasure just to be active again."

THAT SETTLED, the three of them quickly set out to make dinner in earnest. "So, Abby, tell me a little about yourself," Sadie said as she slid floured chicken into the frying pan while Tad and Abby worked together on the salad. "How did you end up working as a home-and-garden editor for *Trend* magazine?" Sadie asked as she moved the sizzling pieces of chicken around with a long-handled fork.

"I majored in English when I was in college," Abby replied. Still standing shoulder to shoulder with Tad, Abby lined up the carrots on the cutting board and began to julienne them. "Between my sophomore and junior year I got a job as a summer intern for a home-decorating magazine. Which was probably the last place I ever expected to be working, since neither of my parents were really into decorating. My mother's a fashion photographer and my father's a documentary-film producer. They divorced when I was a baby and agreed to split custody, so I shuttled back and forth between the two. Anyway, they moved around a lot and went wherever the work was." Abby smiled. "And they both really loved their work—still do. So we lived in hotels and rented houses and little efficiency apartments, none of which were decorated in anything but hotel chic."

Finished cleaning the lettuce, Tad paused to regard Abby affectionately. "Sounds like a challenging life," he said.

Reminding Abby that although they might be husband and wife and expecting a baby together, they still knew very little about each other. If they were going to coparent a child successfully, Abby knew that would have to change.

"It was." Abby paused, remembering what it was like, going to a new school nearly every semester. "Anyway, I'd always been fascinated by the little touches that made a house a home, so working as a gofer for renowned interior designers was really exciting. When I went back to college in the fall, I added interior design and gardening courses to my course load. And when I graduated, I got hired at a magazine in the home-and-garden department." Abby tried but could not discount the respect she saw in Tad's eyes.

"Did you always work for *Trend?*" Sadie asked as Abby checked the potatoes and found them fork-tender.

"Oh, no." Abby grabbed a couple of pot holders and carried the steaming pan over to the sink. With Tad's help, she poured the potatoes into the colander to drain. "I worked for half-a-dozen magazines before landing there. But it was at *Trend* that I really found my niche and was given the responsibility to lead a department on my own. Only now I've been fired." Abby set the empty pan aside.

"Oh, dear." Sadie clucked sympathetically as she got out the electric mixer and handed it to Abby.

"Everyone else was, too. Hostile takeover."

"Well, you'll land on your feet," Sadie soothed.

"Actually she's going to help me at the newspa-per," Tad told his aunt as Abby began to mash the potatoes, "by creating a Lifestyle section for the pa-per."

"Oh, my. That sounds exciting."

It was a challenging proposition. One Abby looked forward to tackling. "And Tad's going to give me free rein," Abby said, tongue in cheek, as she measured milk, butter, salt and pepper into the mixing bowl.

Tad's eyes glimmered with humor, too, as he gave her a look reminding her exactly who was editor-in-chief of the new and improved *Blossom Weekly News.* "Oh, I am, am I?"

Abby nodded, grinning and continuing in a light but

completely serious manner. "'Cause he knows that's the only way I'll take the position." *Even temporarily.* She was used to calling her own shots. She was going to continue to call her own shots. Temporarily still married or not.

"See that, Buster? Those are sparks in their eyes. All newlyweds should have them," Sadie murmured.

"So what do your parents think of Tad?" Sadie asked Abby as they sat down at the table minutes later.

As they began to add generous portions of southern fried chicken to their plates, Abby looked at Tad uncomfortably before answering his aunt. "Um, they haven't met him yet. They're both rather inaccessible at the moment. Mother's in Europe compiling photos for a book on reigning royal families. Father's in Tibet, beginning work on a new documentary."

"But they do know you're married," Sadie questioned as she added gravy to her mashed potatoes.

Abby nodded, doing her best to keep her expression neutral. "I dropped them both a line."

"And they were happy about your marriage?"

Not exactly, Abby thought, as she ladled succotash onto her plate. "After five divorces, Mother no longer feels marriage per se is a valid institution. Father just thinks I should have waited till I was a little older, say fifty or sixty, before taking such a big step. He's been divorced six times." Abby's lips curved wryly as Tad passed her the bowl of tossed green salad. "Both have vowed never to marry again, and frankly I think that's wise. The ability to stay married just isn't in their genes." Each time her parents had gotten hitched, they'd thought they were marrying The One. Each time they'd come out of the failed union more disillusioned than ever.

Sadie looked at Tad. "Goodness!" she exclaimed. "You're lucky you talked Abby into matrimony at all."

"You don't have to tell me," Tad drawled, looking at Abby in a way that made her think he intended to stay married to her come what may.

Sadie turned back to Abby. "What do they think about the baby?" she prodded.

Abby flushed uncomfortably. She watched Tad break open a fluffy golden biscuit. "I haven't had a chance to tell them yet."

Sadie gently patted the back of Abby's hand. "You should tell them as soon as possible, dear. I'm sure they'll both be very excited."

About being grandparents? Not bloody likely, Abby thought. Nevertheless, she promised, "I'll write them tonight." As far as the rest went, she and Tad might have made a child together, but there was so much she still did not know about him. Like how he'd chosen his career.

It was time she'd found out. "How did you end up covering the international beat?" she asked Tad casually as they began to eat. "You never said."

Tad's shoulders tensed. "I moved around a lot as a kid, too."

A tinge of almost unbearable sadness and compassion entered Sadie's eyes. "Especially after Houston and—"

Tad cut his aunt off with a look that warned her to say no more. A curious silence fell. Tension still flowing between Tad and Sadie, Tad turned back to Abby and continued explaining matter-of-factly, "That was when my dad started taking on international assignments. He was a geologist. He worked for an oil company.''

What didn't Tad want her to know? Abby wondered. Until now she hadn't been aware of any deliberate secrets between them. But this clearly was one. ''Where all did you live?'' Abby asked casually, determined to find out more.

''All over the Middle East, Alaska, Central and South America. We were never in any one place for more than four or five months.''

''That sounds rough.'' And a lot like her own childhood, Abby thought.

''It was. But it was good for me, too,'' Tad said, smiling reminiscently. ''It made me more adaptable. And it's what first fostered my intense interest in the news.''

Sadie shook her head in silent admiration. ''I never saw a child insist on reading so many different newspapers every day!''

Tad shrugged off the compliment. ''That's how I caught up with all the news on the places I'd been and acclimated myself to whatever city or country I was in. I read the newspapers.''

''So you knew when you entered college that you wanted to be a reporter,'' Abby guessed, admiring his single-minded ambition, so like her own.

Tad nodded as his dazzling blue eyes met and held hers. ''Once I got my first job, I was a natural for the international beat.''

''And he's been traveling nonstop ever since,'' Sadie recounted proudly. ''Which is why I'm so glad he's settling down here. Sad and difficult as it was, it's high time he got over it,'' Sadie said firmly. ''And moved on with his life.''

High time Tad got over what? Abby wondered, putting clues to his past unhappiness together, an unhappiness she'd heretofore known nothing about. What had happened to Tad and his family in Houston?

"Anyone else want coffee?" Tad asked. Abruptly leaving the table, he headed for the kitchen. "Sadie, why don't you help me in here for a minute?" Tad commanded from the adjacent room.

Her curiosity mounting, Abby started to rise.

Her expression concerned with something a lot more important than coffee, Sadie shook her head and lay her hand across Abby's wrist. "No, dear, you stay. I'll take care of this."

Sadie exited the room.

Abby looked down at Buster, who was reclining next to the sideboard. Face on paws, he looked as mournful as ever. "They're hiding something from me, aren't they?" Abby murmured. It was up to her to find out what.

Unfortunately Tad was not going to make her fact-finding mission easy.

As soon as they got back to the white-elephant house where she and Tad would be living as long as they were in Blossom, Tad carried in her suitcase.

"You must be tired," he said.

Not too tired to ask a few questions.

"Tad?" Abby followed him upstairs to the master bedroom, not sure where to begin, just knowing she was going to, come hell or high water.

"Hm?" He set her suitcase down on the narrow double bed and turned to face her.

"What happened in Houston? What are you not over yet?"

Chapter Four

"Look, Abby," Tad said tiredly, the reflection of a thousand sleepless nights in his eyes, "the time my family spent in Houston was not a happy time for us. Beyond that, I don't care to discuss it." A muscle clenching in his jaw, he brushed by her brusquely. "So if you've got everything you need for tonight..."

Everything except a few moments of intimacy with you. How were they ever going to really get to know each other, Abby wondered in mounting frustration, if he kept pushing her away? Didn't he realize it was situations just like this that would doom their marriage for even the short time they planned to stay together? "That's it?" she asked, propping her hands on her slender hips and mocking his abrupt tone to a T. "That's all you're going to tell me?"

"Like I said." Tad turned around to face her and pushed the words through clenched teeth. He gave her the once-over, making no effort at all to hide his impatience with her. "I don't want to talk about it."

"Maybe you should."

Tad closed the distance between them, not stopping until they stood toe-to-toe. Tilting his head down at her, he gave her a smile edged with a weariness that seemed to come straight from his soul. "So now what? You want to be my shrink, is that it?"

Abby tried not to think how much she liked the tantalizing scent of his aftershave. "I want to understand you," she said quietly but emphatically.

He shrugged and slid his hands into his back pockets. His eyes connected with hers and held for a breath-stealing moment. "You do understand me."

"Not enough."

Grinning devilishly, Tad wrapped his arms around her and urged her close with the flat of his hand, until their bodies fit together with the smooth familiarity of a lock and key. She could feel his arousal and remembered without wanting to what a demanding and yet fantastically giving lover he was. With an unrepentant grin, he whispered playfully in her ear, "Oh, I think you know enough."

Abby burned everywhere they touched. Her breasts were tingling. Her thighs were fluid, her knees weak. Abby pulled away from the evidence of his virility. "Oh, no. You are not going to distract me that way." No matter how long it had been since they'd made love.

Tad slid his palm from her shoulder to her wrist, eliciting even more tingles of awareness. He smiled at her wickedly. "How would you like to be distracted, then?"

"Not—" the fluttering in her tummy slipped a little lower "—the way you're thinking."

Tad sighed regretfully and made no effort to hide his disappointment. "Then we both lose out, don't we?"

Heat started low in her body and welled up through her chest, neck and into her face. He wanted to lose himself in lovemaking, forget the things that should be discussed, things keeping them apart. When he knew—had to know—that it was their hasty foray into bed, before they had learned all they should have learned about each other, that had gotten them into this situation in the first place.

"You're infuriating," Abby said, still angry he wouldn't confide in her. Whether he wanted to admit it or not, Tad was shutting her out of the most intimate revealing details of his life, letting her get only so close. And Abby wanted no part of that kind of man.

Tad studied the resolve in her eyes, showing her in an instant he was as frustrated by their situation as she was. Finally he shrugged and stepped away. "Yeah, well, as much as I'd like to stand here chatting with you about things I have no intention of ever sharing with you—or anyone else for that matter—I've got things to do."

"Like what?" Abby demanded.

"Like the editorial meeting I've set up for first thing tomorrow morning," he announced glibly as he headed out into the hall, his strides long and confident.

Abby let out an exasperated breath. Tad turned. Their glances meshed.

Since they'd known each other, they'd covered the range of emotions. Now, for the first time, it seemed to Abby that a wall had gone up between them, one he wasn't about to let her scale, now or ever.

"Get some sleep, Abby," Tad advised, his expression gentling slightly. "You and the baby both need it." He disappeared from view, continuing on down the stairs.

What she needed more, Abby thought moodily, was the straight scoop from Tad. Sadie had hinted that whatever was haunting Tad was something he'd been running from for many years.

Common sense told Abby Tad needed to explore his feelings on whatever had happened in the past. Maybe, with time, and a lot more trust on his part, she'd be able to help him do that.

She dug out paper and pen from her suitcase. She'd promised Sadie she would write to her parents about the baby tonight, so she might as well get started on that, difficult as it was going to be.

"EVERYONE, I'D LIKE YOU to meet my wife, Abby. She's going to be the editor of the paper's new Life-style section and will feature our own house renovation as her first series," Tad began the next morning, as all six people—himself included—gathered around the conference table for the first official meeting of the entire newspaper staff.

"Most of you already know my aunt, Sadie Mc-Farlane," Tad continued, after Abby had greeted everyone. "She's going to be doing all our proofreading."

Sadie smiled and said hello to everyone, too.

"Raymond Burke is going to run our printing press. He's just moved here from Charlotte."

Everyone sent the older man with the amiable grin and salt-and-pepper buzz cut a smile and soft hello.

Tad nodded at a slim young woman in denim overalls and an appliquéd T-shirt. She had short curly red hair and dangling blue-and-white earrings shaped like a Tarheel footprint. "Cindy just graduated from Chapel Hill," Tad told the group. "She's going to be in charge of the classifieds and head up a major drive for new advertisers."

Tad gestured at a preppy blond kid not much older than Cindy. "And last but not least, I'd like to introduce Sonny to everyone. He's our roving reporter and photographer rolled into one. He's the lone old hand among us, since he's worked here off and on since high school. He just graduated from North Carolina State."

"It's nice to meet all of you," Abby said.

Cindy grinned enthusiastically. "We're glad to meet you, too. Ever since Tad took over a couple of weeks ago, he's been hoping you'd agree to work on the newspaper with us."

Yet he'd only just now mentioned it to her, Abby thought.

"We didn't know the two of you were married until the day before yesterday when he called to let us know you were coming back with him," Sonny chimed in.

Abby knew exactly why Tad hadn't said anything about the two of them being married. He hadn't known if they were even going to give their whirlwind relationship another chance.

Sensing some explanation was required of them, Abby said, "It all happened rather suddenly."

"As did the news we got yesterday," Tad said, glad to change the subject and grinning like a proud papa to be. Giving her no chance to stop him, he went on, "If you haven't already heard, Abby fainted while we were looking around here." His smile widened all the more as he announced happily, "Doc confirmed she's expecting."

Abby felt herself flush as congratulations were offered all around. "When is the baby due?" Cindy asked.

"January twenty-ninth, give or take."

"Meanwhile," Tad said, rolling up his sleeves, "we all have a lot of work to do if we want to make the *Blossom Weekly News* into the acclaimed regional newspaper I envision it as being."

"Speaking of the next edition, have you seen this?" Frowning, Sonny gave a handwritten note to Tad. "What do you think about this letter to the editor? It was under the door when I came in this morning."

"'Dear Editor,'" Tad read aloud to the group, "'I hope now that we've got a world-famous reporter running the paper here in Blossom that we'll finally get some decent investigative reporting done, because there are some real crooks operating in this town who need to be put out of business and fast!'" Tad stopped reading abruptly.

"Who are the crooks?" Abby asked, intrigued.

Tad frowned. "It doesn't say. The note's not signed, either." He looked up at the group. "Any idea who the writer is talking about?"

Everyone shrugged. No one ventured a guess.

Tad turned to his aunt. "Aunt Sadie, you've lived here for the past forty-some years. Do you have any idea who the writer might be talking about?"

Sadie colored slightly. "I've heard stories, of course, about this and that. Everyone has. But I make it a policy not to speak ill of people without proof. So you'll just have to smoke them out."

If anyone knew how to do that, Abby thought admiringly, Tad did.

"FIND OUT ANY MORE about the identity of the town crooks?" Abby asked Tad later that evening as the two of them sat down to their first official dinner in their new home.

His eyes gleamed in a way that let her know he was up to something. "I'm working on it. Meanwhile, you can say it if you want to," Tad told Abby frankly as he spread a napkin on his lap and passed the peas.

"Say what?" Trying not to notice how cozy it felt to be there with Tad that way, or think it could be that way for them forever if she wanted it to be, Abby ladled take-out mashed potatoes, cranberry sauce and rotisserie chicken on her plate.

Tad gave her a cocky grin that belied the hurt in his words. "You didn't like my idea about using the renovation of our white elephant of a home as the centerpiece of a series on home remodeling." Tad added some coleslaw to his plate.

Circumventing her mixed emotions about the way he'd pretty much announced his idea as a done deal during the staff meeting, Abby shrugged. She knew she shouldn't be annoyed. In the end this was going to be his home, not theirs. She was only staying there temporarily.

Keeping her expression carefully neutral, Abby dug into their hot almost-as-good-as-home-cooked meal. "Living room one week, dining room the next. Who wouldn't want to see what we do to jazz up the master bedroom?" And the narrow double bed that Tad had not slept in the night before. But that had been her choice, she reminded herself sternly. He'd only been following her lead.

"Plus," Abby forced herself to continue enthusiastically, "it will be great for the baby if we can get your house completely fixed up before he or she is born."

Tad continued to study her. If he'd noticed the way

she'd referred to the house as his, not theirs, he didn't show it.

"You're right. It will be good for the baby," he said calmly. "Which is why I don't understand why you're so ambivalent about the project." Tad's deep blue eyes searched hers. "As the new Lifestyle editor and the parent here with all the decorating expertise, it's going to be your show from start to finish."

He was acting as if they were going to be a real family, at least until their baby was born. Struggling to retain her equilibrium, Abby pushed back her chair and headed for the refrigerator. She rummaged around for the strawberry jam. "You were very generous, giving me free rein in the decorating. I mean, who knows?" Moving the three gallons of milk around, Abby finally found the jam and pulled it out. "My taste could turn out to be horrendous, to say the least."

Just the way their living together before the baby was born, as a sort-of-married couple, could also be a mistake. For Abby, the lines between reality and fantasy and wishful thinking were already becoming blurred. Was the same thing happening to him? she wondered as Tad got up and lounged against the opposite counter.

One corner of his mouth lifted at her prediction of doom in the decorating department. "I don't think so," Tad retorted dryly as he watched her peel the protective plastic seal away from the jam jar and toss it into the trash. "So what gives, Abby?" he asked bluntly, folding his arms. "What is it about this setup you don't like?" He hesitated only a moment before he asked, "Are you ticked off because I told everyone we were expecting a baby?" He reached out and plucked the jam from her hands.

Abby gave him a deadpan look, then turned away from him stiffly and sat back down at the table. "I would have waited a bit, if it had been left up to me."

"Okay." Tad opened the jam for her and sat down, too. "Next time I'll ask," he promised as he handed her the jam. "And together we'll decide on the timing." Beneath the small cozy table, their knees touched. At the contact little lightning bolts of warmth surged through her. Abby tensed beneath the onslaught; she did not want to feel desire for him.

"Now what?" Tad asked, watching the play of emotions across her face.

Abby swallowed and concentrated on her meal. "Nothing."

"It's not nothing when your cheeks get pink like that."

She'd thought the two of them could be just friends. But she was beginning to see this was going to be much harder than she'd thought. Every time she was around him, she was reminded how good it had been between them. And then she started wanting him and yearning to be close to him all over again. And she knew what a trap that was. If she let herself rely on him too much, it would hurt all that much more the next time he refused to confide in her or insisted on living out his dreams, not hers.

Abby's temper flashed as he continued to study her. She did not want him seeing into her heart and mind. "Stop being so solicitous!" she snapped. She felt like he was humoring her, and she did not want to be humored, any more than she wanted to be pampered just because she was pregnant.

Tad's face broke into a grin. "Oh, I get it. This is

one of those moods, isn't it, that comes with the fluctuations of hormones?''

Abby fumed. She was definitely not moody! And she was definitely not the follow-him-anywhere wife he wanted her to be. She gave him a dark look, aware she would've rather died at that point than ask him for any favors. "I would not go there if I were you," she warned as she pushed her empty plate away.

"Fine." Tad's eyes took on an amorous sheen as he stood and carried both their plates to the sink. "What would you like to do tonight?"

What a loaded question, Abby thought on an unaccountably wistful sigh.

If she wasn't pregnant…

If they hadn't rushed into marriage…

But she was, and they had, Abby realized uncomfortably. And there was no denying that if she felt his lips on her skin again, there was no telling what would happen.

Assuring herself her caution was for the best, Abby kept her distance and regarded him cheerfully. "Since you brought home dinner for us, I'll do the dishes. Then I plan to go back to work." Knowing how much work she had to do to get the Lifestyle section launched in the time frame she'd set for herself, she'd spent most of the afternoon setting up a temporary home office for herself in her bedroom upstairs where she could work as much as she wanted, undisturbed.

"You don't have to do the dishes alone," he told her pleasantly.

"It's okay," Abby said, bracing her hands on either side of her and staking out her territory by the sink. "I don't mind."

His expression inscrutable, Tad crossed his arms

again and continued to study her. "You're sure about that?"

Abby nodded, never more aware of the agreement they'd made not to bring sex back into the mix. Given the way things were, the fact that their marriage was not going to continue after the birth of their baby, she did not want to fall for him any more than she already had. "Positive," she told him.

He returned her smile with one of his own. "Okay then," he said as he grabbed a pocket-size notepad and pen and slid them into his shirt pocket.

Watching him head for the door, Abby asked, "Where are you going?" She wondered even as she spoke why it mattered so much to her. Or why she should feel so lonely without him.

"Back down to the newspaper to grab a camera, then over to the Rotary Club meeting, the softball games at the Little League fields and then maybe the local tavern." Tad came back just long enough to give her a brief kiss on the brow and a hug goodbye. Turning, he headed straight back to the exit and said over his shoulder, "We have a helluva lot of news to gather if we're going to put out our first edition of the *Blossom Weekly* by Saturday."

So it was back to business as usual.

Why was she not surprised?

TAD STOPPED SHORT at the bedroom door. "Sonny's gonna be here any minute to photograph the Before pictures of the house and you're not—"

"—dressed," Abby grumbled, as she rummaged madly through her closet. "I know," she said, uncomfortably aware of the way her short and silky kimono-style robe clung to her suddenly too-plump breasts.

"What's the problem?" he asked sympathetically as she held up one garment after another to her and then promptly hung it back up.

The problem was, Abby thought as she sorted quickly through her collection of highly sophisticated summer business attire, in an effort to avoid prolonged contact with Tad, she'd been working out of the house the past four weeks. Challenged to build a new Carolina Life section of the paper with minimal resources and an even more minimal budget, she'd been on the telephone nonstop. That being the case, it had made sense to work at home, away from the often chaotic bullpen atmosphere of the *Blossom Weekly News*.

Thus far, she'd had a fair amount of success contacting the journalism departments of all North Carolina universities and recruiting freelancers to submit samples of their work. From there she'd doled out assignments to capable writers, their fees due upon acceptance of their articles.

The problem was, in deference to the warm and often muggy June weather, she'd been wearing shorts and T-shirts, and she hadn't realized until too late how her body had changed by the end of her second month.

"I'm just running a little late," Abby told him as she plucked out a sky blue suit that had always been a little large on her, stepped over a sliding stack of old editions of the *Blossom Weekly News* and headed for the adjacent bath.

Very much aware Tad was waiting on the other side of the closed bathroom door, Abby slipped off her robe and draped it over the rim of the old-fashioned claw-foot bathtub. With a slight prayer she stepped into the pale blue knee-length skirt. She tugged it up

over her hips and found—just as she'd feared—that
the zipper was a good inch away from closing.

Hoping against hope that the jacket would cover
what the skirt did not, Abby reached for the long tunic
jacket and slid her arms into the sleeves. Swiftly she
buttoned it up the front and found—to her delight—
the jacket would close. It was a little snug around her
hips and breasts, but otherwise okay.

Breathing a huge sigh of relief, Abby ran a brush
through her hair and stepped out of the bathroom. She
was shocked to see Tad shifting her clothes to the
other side of the master-bedroom closet and putting in
a bunch of his own.

"What are you doing?" she asked, trying not to
notice how good he looked in the dark green polo shirt
and jeans.

"Putting my clothes in here."

Abby blinked, not aware that anything in the current
platonic nature of their relationship had changed.
"Why," she asked drolly, "when you have so much
room in the other closet?"

"Because I don't want everyone in Blossom to
know we're sleeping in separate bedrooms," Tad told
her practically as he reached over to the other side of
the double bed where he should have been sleeping
had theirs been a normal marriage and rumpled the
covers there, too.

"Shouldn't you be making that bed, not mussing it
up? Since it's going to be photographed and all,"
Abby questioned him.

Tad inclined his head at the ringing doorbell. "No
time. Besides, this is a Before picture and we want it
to look as bad as possible so that the After one will
look even better," he told her. "What time is the de-

signer you selected to supervise this project supposed to get here?''

"Same time as Sonny." Abby glanced at her watch. "Right now." Abby lifted the hem of the bedspread. "Have you seen my beige pumps? Never mind." She knelt to get them and heard the first tiny rip of a skirt seam. "Here they are."

Better not bend down like that again, Abby thought just as the doorbell rang again.

Oblivious to the damage Abby had done to her skirt, Tad stepped around another huge stack of files, three unpacked suitcases and several boxes of her belongings that had been sent from the New York apartment she'd had to let go and headed for the door. "I'll get it."

Abby nodded. Praying her skirt would hold through the photo session, she said calmly, "I'll be right down."

"WHOA, THIS IS SOME MESS you got here," Sonny said as he extracted the camera from the case and looked around.

"Tell me about it," Tad agreed grimly as he led Sonny into a living room packed with an assortment of his and hers moving crates.

Call me a fool, Tad thought, but when he'd asked Abby to share his dream with him, he'd expected them to be together twenty-four hours a day. The reality was they rarely saw each other. Abby was always on the phone, out of the office, working at home or off on appointment, lining up freelancers and even a dietitian to do a cooking column. And while he appreciated the gusto with which she was doing her job, as her husband and the man who'd once made passionate love to her—and was dying to do so again—he felt very neglected.

Sonny snapped several pictures of the disorganized heaps of carpet, tile, wallpaper and paint samples that covered much of the spacious front hallway. "Abby really likes to get into her work, doesn't she?" he remarked.

"You got that right," Tad murmured, aware it was taking a real effort on his part not to feel completely disgruntled.

The truth was if he'd known how thoroughly Abby would throw herself into the job as Lifestyle editor, he never would have offered it to her. As it was, she worked until she crawled into bed, exhausted, and then slept for ten or sometimes even twelve hours straight, only to wake and start the same routine all over again. When they did talk, it was about business and little else.

And while part of him admired her dedication, another part was increasingly frustrated and ticked off. He wanted to kiss her and remind her what it was like to be really married to him, the way they'd been married that first glorious night, but he'd made a promise to allow them to get to know each other first. The only problem was she wasn't letting him get close to her. In fact, he felt more removed from her than ever.

Delicate feminine footsteps sounded on the stairs. Seconds later Abby swept into the room, looking more beautiful than ever. "Hey, Ab," Sonny said, "ready to get those pictures taken?"

"Sure." Abby grinned warmly. "Just make sure you're focusing on the rooms, not us."

"Easier said than done," Sonny said, looking down into his lens, "'cause the camera loves you."

That, Tad could believe. Just as he could imagine what Sonny was clearly so struck by. From her glowing tresses, sparkling eyes, graceful movements and luminous skin, there wasn't an inch of Abby that wasn't both gorgeous and compelling. It didn't matter what she wore or how she did her hair, whether she was in shorts and a T-shirt, with her hair drawn up in a bouncy ponytail on the back of her head, or—like now—wearing crisp tailored clothing and high-heeled pumps that showed off her spectacular legs. She was sexy as hell. So sexy, in fact, that he was in a constant state of arousal whenever he was around her. The knowledge she was carrying his child made it even more difficult to control himself.

Politically correct or not, he wanted to take her and make her his, again and again and again. And he was still thinking about it as Abby led a madly photographing Sonny through the entire first floor, then up the broad front staircase to the master bedroom and bath.

"Whoa. Is this a bedroom or an office?" Sonny asked, stepping around the piles of work, a half-dozen as-yet-unpacked boxes of Abby's stuff from New York and two open overflowing suitcases.

"Both," Abby said.

Sonny quirked an amazed brow. "Some honeymoon, huh?" he said, guessing—correctly—that not much besides work went on here.

Which was, Tad noted, exactly what Abby wanted him to think. That was not, however, the impression Tad wanted to leave. Nor was it a situation he wanted continued.

Knowing it was bound to tick off his wife, yet feeling bound to provoke things a little, anyway, since she'd already done the same, Tad laced a proprietorial arm about Abby's shoulders. Ignoring the way she stiffened almost imperceptibly at his touch, he tucked her close to his side.

Watch it, her simmering look said.

No, you watch, his look said right back.

Planting his other hand on the small of her back, he trapped her against him. "Hey, there's no rule that says you have to make love in a bed," he said, lowering his head to hers. Caressing her lips with his eyes, he continued softly, "Red-hot loving can happen anywhere." *Like Paris.* Wanting to remind Abby of that, lest she forget everything good that had happened between them before they'd quickly and foolishly jumped into marriage, Tad threw caution to the wind and kissed her soundly. At the touch of their lips, she melted in his arms, just the way he'd thought she would.

"Now that's a honeymoon." Sonny sighed enviously, snapping photos of that, too.

Ignoring the flash and whir of the camera, Tad gave in to the bittersweet pangs of desire and the urge to be close to her again. How long had it been, he wondered, shifting his hands to the soft skin of her upturned face, since he'd wanted anything even half as much as he wanted Abby? How long since he'd ached with pleasure and been more drawn to the present and the future than haunted by the past?

As Sonny came closer, still snapping photos manically, Abby groaned low in her throat and pushed against Tad's chest.

Reluctantly he broke off the kiss. Abby's eyes were liquid pools of fire, reminding him that she had not agreed to have another honeymoon with him here. Which was just too bad, Tad thought, on yet another whisper of regret. Because he wanted one and thought they should have one.

"Back to the tour," Abby ordered.

She could hold him—and the possibility of making love again—off for a while. But not, if that scorching kiss was any indication, forever, Tad knew.

"So how much of this stuff is going to stay and how much is going to be hauled to the junkyard?" Sonny asked as he wandered into the bedroom-turned-study across the hall and paused to take an up-close-and-personal-photograph of an ugly brown Naugahyde recliner.

"That's yet to be decided," Abby said, knowing that was one piece that was definitely going to have to go.

"But the chair'll go to the dump, right?" Sonny said.

If she had her way? "Absolutely," Abby said.

"Not on your life," Tad said. "This chair stays. It has history." It was not only where he'd been sleeping ever since he'd been back in Blossom, it was also his first ever furniture purchase. He'd had it all through his college days, and it had been in storage ever since. Now that he finally had a home, after all those years as a roving reporter, he wanted it with him; he wanted it in a place of honor. Abby, however, refused to understand that. To her it was just a piece of furniture that was hopelessly out-of-date.

"I'm thinking attic or garage," Abby said.

Tad smiled, as willing to wage war on this as she was. "I'm thinking main-floor living room," he countered.

"There isn't an interior designer in the world who'd agree to that," Abby replied hotly, "never mind consult for free and put her name to a room with that piece of history in it.''

Tad had the sense Abby wanted to pick a fight with him. More surprising, he wanted to pick one with her, too. He kept his eyes level on hers. "The chair stays," he said firmly.

Abby glared at him. "Not it if messes up my first big series for the new Lifestyle section, it doesn't."

"Hey," Sonny said, grinning, as he snapped a couple of photos of the two of them squaring off toe-to-toe. "A lovers' tiff. Great. Maybe we can put this in the paper, too!" he crowed victoriously.

"Like hell we will," Tad growled as the doorbell sounded again downstairs. "There are some things, kid, that stay private."

On that, Abby quite agreed. She didn't want any of her private life played out for the newspapers the way her famous parents' various highs and lows had been. Glad to be able to change the subject, she glanced at her watch. "That's probably the interior designer," Abby said.

"You finish showing Sonny around. I'll bring the designer up." Tad hurried off.

"He's a little testy about the chair, isn't he?" Sonny said as he walked into the room that would one day be their child's nursery and took photos of that, too.

"Tad's putting a lot of pressure on himself to make this paper a success," Abby explained. Worse, she had the feeling that this living-together business was not exactly how either of them had envisioned it.

When she'd agreed to stay, she'd expected them to live together but still go their own separate ways. And while that was true to a point—Tad had been busy covering various community events, introducing himself and his plans for the paper via editorials, and penning much of the routine news—he had also been reveling in his newfound status as brand-new husband and father to be in a way that surprised her. For on that score, Abby knew, much to her own discomfiture, he had the unabashed envy of many of the men in town.

Worse, newlywed jokes—like the one Sonny had just made about the lovers' tiff—had abounded wherever they went, and Tad did nothing to discourage them. Instead, to her mounting exasperation, he seemed to welcome the kidding around with an audacious smile and a twinkle in his eyes that left no doubt as to the libidinous nature of his thoughts. Or his joy over the baby they were expecting.

Abby felt a mounting joy and anticipation, too. It went without saying that the day she and Tad welcomed their baby into the world would be among the happiest in their lives. But the fishbowl atmosphere of the small town reminded her of the past and made her want to bury herself in her work all the more. There was safety there, in the acquisition, writing and editing of various articles. There was no safety in their relationship when she knew—because of the hurried way it had come about and because he would only let her get so close to him—that it was doomed to end.

Not that this stopped her from fantasizing about what might have been if only they'd shared the same dreams and aspirations, Abby mused while Sonny took photos of the attic. She often found herself wondering what it would take to get Tad to give up this pipe dream and go back to New York so she could find another job and resume her career as a magazine editor. With his experience and reputation, she knew Tad would have no trouble finding a job at a big-city news-paper. And if they were both living in the same area, they could stay together permanently, just as they'd originally planned.

But he wasn't willing to compromise, Abby reminded herself grimly. Instead, he expected her to give up everything to follow his dream. And that just wasn't fair. And there were other things that bugged her, too, she thought as she led Sonny back down-stairs. Like the way he was always pushing milk and vitamin supplements on her. And while he'd said he would give her free rein over the house decor, he hadn't told her that he wanted to keep every ragged piece of furniture and memorabilia he'd had in storage since his college days. A fact that made her job over-seeing the redecoration of their home all that much harder.

But maybe, Abby thought, as she strode toward the lovely thirty-something woman in red standing in the front hall chatting with Tad, Donna Delaney would be able to help.

Tad looked up at her, surprised. "You didn't tell me you'd hired Donna."

"Do you two know each other?" Abby said, amazed at the camaraderie between them.

Donna threw back her head and laughed. "Do we!"

Chapter Five

"We're old fishing buddies," Tad explained.

Donna nodded. "We met one year when Tad was on one of his solo summer visits to see his aunt Sadie."

"I used to spend a couple of weeks here with Sadie every summer no matter where my parents were living at the time," Tad said.

"And those visits became even more important after…" Donna caught Tad's look and the subtle but unmistakable wish she not confide more. An understanding that eluded Abby passed between them, then Donna shrugged and—to Abby's frustration—continued in a low friendly tone, "Well, anyway, we lost touch about ten years ago when Tad stopped coming around for those long visits with Sadie and my folks moved to Charlotte."

"And let's not forget your marriage," Tad said, grinning. Arms braced on either side of him, his ankles crossed in front of him, he relaxed against the banister. "Donna was just showing me pictures of her husband, Ron, and their three kids." He cast Donna an admiring almost envious glance that reminded Abby how much he wanted the baby she was carrying inside her. "You've got quite a crew there."

"Thanks." Donna beamed. "They really keep me hopping. You and Abby will have to come by sometime and meet them."

"Look forward to it," Tad said. He straightened and turned to Sonny. Suddenly both men were braced for action. "Ready to go out and get the pictures of the garage and that wilderness we call a backyard?"

Sonny nodded. The two men left, talking about what Tad proposed they shoot.

"You didn't tell me you knew Tad," Abby said as she began to walk Donna through the main floor. As she stepped over a stack of papers, she heard another little rip and felt her skirt seam widen another inch.

Donna acknowledged this was so with a glittering smile. "I wanted to get this job on my own merit if I got it. I didn't want anyone accusing me of pulling strings." She paused and gave Abby a woman-to-woman look. "I hope you don't mind."

"Not at all," Abby said, respecting the path Donna had taken even as jealousy stirred inside her at the thought of Tad with another woman, even way back when. Which meant what? she wondered, stunned by the unfamiliar emotion. That she was more possessive of Tad and the brief passionate affair they'd had than she knew?

Abby swallowed as her skirt slipped a little lower on her hips, thanks to the ever-widening rip in the seam. Discreetly Abby pressed a hand over the tear. "So were you as surprised as everyone else when Tad bought the *Blossom Weekly News?*" Abby asked Donna as she tried, through the fabric of her jacket, to keep the unraveling side seam of her skirt together.

"Not really." On the other side of Abby, Donna smiled as she removed a pen and pad from her briefcase and began to take notes. "Tad's always been the kind of guy who wants to try everything once. That's why I wasn't surprised when I heard he'd become a roving reporter years ago. The job suited him perfectly. He could see every part of the world, get clued in to what was happening there and then move on to the next adventure."

And then move on to the next adventure. Was that what she and the baby were? Abby wondered. The next adventure?

"Were you surprised to hear he was married?" Abby asked, praying her skirt would stay together long enough to get through this meeting. Like it or not, she was really going to have to get some maternity clothes.

"No." Donna's green eyes sparkled with an almost sisterly affection. "He was always a big hit with the babes. And he absolutely adored kids. Still does. But then, you probably know that from the amount of articles he's done on children and children's issues around the world."

Actually Abby hadn't known that. Which just went to show, she thought as she led the way upstairs to the second floor and felt her skirt slip another inch, how little she and Tad really knew about each other.

The next few minutes were taken over by talk about the house. To Abby's delight, Donna's view of what could and should be done matched hers to an enviable degree, and they were still bubbling over with plans when Tad and Sonny came back in looking equally satisfied with the way things were going.

Tad smiled at Donna. "So, we'll see you at the open house at seven o'clock, then?" he asked her.

"Absolutely," Donna said. "And I'll bring my portfolio, too."

Was she the only one who hadn't a clue what they were talking about? Abby wondered, confused. She shot a look at Tad, then turned to Sonny and Donna. "What open house?"

"You know, at the paper tonight," Sonny said. "We're all supposed to be there with bells and whistles on."

"No, I didn't know," Abby enunciated carefully.

"We've been talking about it all week at the staff meetings," Tad explained.

Most of which Abby had missed in her attempts to avoid spending too much time with her new husband. Nevertheless Tad could have told her about it, couldn't he? Unless he'd been trying to make a point by deliberately leaving her out.

"That's right," Sonny said thoughtfully as he put his cameras away. "You weren't there, were you?"

"No, I wasn't." Abby forced a smile and saved face as best she could. "But it sounds like a good idea."

"We thought it would help drum up advertising," Tad said as their eyes connected briefly.

Donna glanced at her watch. "I want to take a quick look at the backyard and then I've got to head over to the pool to get the kids before I swing on home." She dashed off.

Sonny said, "I've got all I need."

Seconds later both had exited and Abby and Tad were left alone. Tad held her glance. And suddenly saw just how steamed she was at having been left out of the loop. He grimaced unhappily. "I've done it now, haven't I?" he said.

Knowing she had to get her ripped skirt off before

it slid down her hips and fell off, Abby turned on her heel and headed for the stairs, her high heels making a sharp staccato on the polished wood floor.

"What, no comment?" he said, following.

Abby turned and shot him a sharp look over her shoulder, then raced up the stairs, her hips swaying provocatively beneath her skirt. "I don't know what you're talking about."

"I thought you knew," he told her grimly.

Abby gritted her teeth and stared around her morosely. The house that had seemed so full of possibilities only minutes earlier, now seemed like a metaphor for the confused state of her life. She kicked off her heels, stepped out of her ripped skirt, tossed it on the bed and folded her arms. "Obviously."

Outwardly Abby looked calm, but Tad knew her well enough to realize she was about to explode. He was sorry he was responsible for the stress. He wasn't sorry he had asked her to work with him on the newspaper. It was not only a good challenge for them both professionally, it was an activity that was guaranteed to give them much satisfaction and bring them much closer probably by the time the baby was born. But for the moment they had this calamity to work through.

Reluctantly he tore his eyes from the sight of her shapely, stocking-clad legs. He could still recall how they'd felt wrapped around his waist. He wanted to feel them there again.

"It's not as if you've missed anything," he told Abby calmly as hot excited color poured into her cheeks. "Nothing's happened yet. You can still be there—"

"How do you know?" Abby interrupted, her

golden-brown eyes flashing as she tore off her jacket, too.

They squared off in silence as Abby slipped back into the short kimono robe. "Can you be there?" Tad asked finally, reminded by the way she was standing, feet planted slightly apart, fists propped on her hips, that his wife never gave an inch without a major battle of wills. Luckily he liked a challenge. And if there was one thing Abby Kildaire McFarlane was, he thought admiringly, it was a challenge.

"Does it matter?" Abby glared at him, the pouting thrust of her lower lip letting him know she felt furious, humiliated and embarrassed by the oversight.

He cleared a place on the rumpled covers of the bed and sat down. "Don't be like that."

Abby didn't want to, but given what had just transpired, she was unable to help feeling hurt and a little left out. Plus, like it or not, there was the larger problem of what to wear. Business attire was called for. And she had just ripped the very last skirt she could fit into.

"The open house is in two hours," she reported grimly. Worse, the closest maternity store was a good forty-five-minute drive away. Not that this was all Tad's fault. She really should have taken the time to shop before this situation came up. But it was too late now for regrets.

Tad continued to look perplexed. "Do you want to skip it?" he asked. "Because if you do, I'll cover for you."

The fight went out of Abby as swiftly as it had come. Exhausted, she sat down next to Tad on the side of the bed. "No, I don't want to skip it," she said wearily. "But unless I suddenly find myself able to conjure up a dress out of a bed sheet, I really can't go. I don't have anything I can fit into except a pair of jogging shorts, and that would hardly do.''

"The suit you just had on was a knockout."

Wordlessly Abby handed him the skirt and pointed out the rip. "Why didn't you say so?" Tad folded her skirt neatly and handed it back to her. "I can solve this problem for you." It was one of the few things he could do.

"I don't know how," Abby retorted.

Tad winked. "I'll show you," he told her confidently. Five minutes later he revealed the "surprise" a little early. "Luckily Aunt Sadie had already finished the first dress," he told Abby. "She's bringing it over right away."

"She's really planning to sew a whole wardrobe for me?" Abby asked, amazed by the surprise Tad's aunt had been planning. Her own parents had never done anything for her themselves they could hire out.

Tad nodded. "This is her first grandnephew or niece. She's very excited. And she wanted to welcome you into the family."

Abby told herself it was the unexpected thoughtfulness of the gesture—not the idea of really becoming a part of his family and spending a lifetime with Tad here in Blossom—that had her head swimming and her heart beating triple time. "That's really nice," Abby said appreciatively. Incredibly nice.

"No doubt about it. Aunt Sadie is one fine lady." Tad slipped his fingers beneath Abby's chin, lifted her face and studied her eyes. His own eyes softened as he leaned forward and gently kissed her cheek. "And in case I haven't told you lately...so are you."

TWENTY MINUTES LATER Abby stood in front of the mirror. As Abby had anticipated, Aunt Sadie was an excellent seamstress. The only problem was, as far as maternity dresses went, Aunt Sadie was stuck firmly in another era. The bright pink dress was covered with fat white polka dots and featured a white Peter Pan collar, puffed sleeves that threatened to overwhelm the entire dress and a huge bow. Made to be worn right up until the day of delivery, the tea-length dress fell in voluminous folds that literally threatened to swallow Abby whole. She looked both fat and ridiculous. So ridiculous she didn't know how she was going to muster the courage to model the garment in her own home.

Tad shut the bedroom door behind him. He headed straight for her. As he neared her, he rolled his eyes. "It's hideous, isn't it?" he whispered bluntly.

Abby was unable to take her eyes off her reflection. "Oh, I wouldn't say that," she murmured, her humorous expression mirroring how they both felt. "If I were Lucy Ricardo or June Cleaver," she quipped, "this would have been a great dress."

Tad continued to regard her skeptically. "Look, you don't have to wear it. I'll just go down and talk to Aunt Sadie."

Abby thought about the hours of work that had gone into this and curled a hand around his biceps before he could depart. "No, Tad, don't," she said, her fingers warming to the solid feel of his flesh. "You'll hurt her feelings." And that was the last thing in the world Abby wanted.

"I know, but—"

"But nothing," Abby said firmly, already thinking of ways to accessorize the dress to make it a little more current. "She's your aunt. And she did this out of love for both of us." Abby smiled at him warmly. "I'll wear it."

"THERE'S SOMETHING your husband needs to understand and, quite frankly, doesn't," Joe Don Jerome told Abby at the open house. Dressed in an all-white summer suit, white boater-style hat, white shirt, white shoes and black bow tie, the only used- and new-car dealer in Blossom was as flamboyant in person as he was in his humorous television commercials. "It isn't good for business when he prints inflammatory letters to the editor like the one he ran last week."

"There are no crooks in Blossom," Nowell Haines, a buttoned-up banker in a three-piece suit continued, sweat glistening on his brow.

Cullen Marshall, who was known as much for his bad toupee as the insurance policies he sold, said smugly, "Your hubby never should've started that Troubleshooter hot line, either."

Nowell Haines nodded as he mopped his face with a handkerchief. "Businesses around here don't need to be investigated."

There Abby disagreed, as did the rest of the *Blossom Weekly* staff.

"Particularly when those same businesses supply a lot of his advertising revenue for this newspaper," Joe Don Jerome told Abby flatly.

"And, as the little woman in this situation," Cullen Marshall continued, "you undoubtedly have a lot of influence over that new hubby of yours." Well, that, Abby thought, was a matter of opinion. She couldn't think of a single thing she could dissuade Tad from doing if he really had his heart set on it.

"And now that you know how things are done by those in the know here…" Cullen began when Tad sauntered over to join the four of them. He wrapped an arm around Abby's waist and tugged her close. Everywhere they touched, Abby felt solid male muscle.

"Gentlemen." Tad nodded at Joe Don, Nowell and Cullen, then looked at Abby as though she was the only woman in the world. "What's going on, darlin'?"

Cullen Marshall adjusted his toupee, elbowed his way forward and cut in before Abby had a chance to answer. "We were just explaining to your wife here why it'd be smart of you not to stir up any more trouble, running unsigned letters to the editor in the town newspaper."

"'Cause if you do," his buddy Nowell Haines warned, "we might be forced to pull our advertising."

Tad smiled like a shark in a wading pool and studied the trio of businessmen skeptically. "Is that so?" he countered pleasantly, a warning to back off— now—underlying his low tone.

"You better believe it," Joe Don Jerome replied, stepping forward and flashing Tad a crocodile grin of his own. His eyes narrowed maliciously as he continued threatening Tad with grating Southern charm. "'Cause we know you put your life savings into this. And we'd all just hate to see you lose your shirt."

Tad remained unimpressed. "I wouldn't worry about it," he drawled.

"Do the right thing and you won't have anything to worry about," Cullen Marshall warned smoothly as the three businessmen moved off.

As soon as they did, Abby released a long breath.

She hadn't realized until the three businessmen left how tense they'd been making her.

Tad kissed her head just above her ear. "Are you okay?" he asked.

There was no doubt she felt a lot safer in his arms. Staying cozily within his protective grip, Abby turned to him. "You're the one who should be worried," she murmured, looking up into his handsome face.

"About the Three Stooges?"

As Abby watched them leave the building, a shiver ran through her. "They're angry, Tad."

"They are also most likely crooks. Otherwise they wouldn't be so worried."

Abby bit her lower lip. Aware she didn't know quite as much about Tad's financial situation as she'd like, she continued to regard him steadily. "Can they put you out of business?"

"Not unless I let them," Tad told her confidently as he led her toward the refreshment table and paused to pour them both some lemonade. "And I don't intend to let them."

"How much revenue do you get from the ads they place?" she asked quietly.

Tad helped himself to a flaky cheese puff from Audrey's Bakery and Café down the street. "In the past their ads have paid for nearly twenty percent of every issue." He handed Abby one, too.

"Ouch." Abby bit into the fragrant flaky appetizer.

"Yeah," Tad said, now helping himself to a stuffed mushroom cap. "But I don't want their dirty money. Besides, I had two new advertisers sign up this evening already."

"That's great." Abby sampled the quiche squares.

"And we'll have even more signing on when we get the Lifestyle section up and running."

The rest of the evening was a blur of introductions and question-and-answer sessions. By the time Tad and Abby picked up a pizza and salad and got home at ten-thirty, she was exhausted. Tad poured the milk while she brought out the plates. Both kicked off their shoes. They settled down on the sofa and dug in.

Tad playfully nudged her thigh with his. "Did I mention how pretty you looked tonight?"

Abby blushed and rolled her eyes. She'd done her best to accessorize the outfit, but even with her hair down and a white summer sweater over her shoulders, she was acutely aware she'd still looked like the heroine out of a fifties TV sitcom.

"I'm serious," Tad said gently as they clinked their milk glasses together in a silent toast. "Most women couldn't have managed to look thoroughly competent and professional in a dress like that, but somehow you did. Whenever you talked about your plans for the Lifestyle section, you just glowed."

"You looked and sounded pretty excited yourself," she said. In fact, it was impossible not to get excited about the prospects for the future when Tad spoke about his plans for the newspaper.

"It was really nice of you to wear that dress," he continued.

Abby shrugged. "No nicer than Sadie making it for me," she said as their eyes met.

"Speaking of Sadie—" Tad grinned "—she got a promotion tonight. She's going to be doing some writing for the newspaper, too. So she's not going to have time to sew any more dresses for you. I told her that was okay because I'm driving you to the closest maternity shop first thing tomorrow morning. And I'm going to do my husbandly duty and make sure you're outfitted properly from head to toe.''

Abby considered this while she munched on her pizza. ''And she wasn't hurt?''

''No, excited.'' Tad smiled. ''I also told her we needed some hand-sewn quilts and blankets and sheets for the baby's room. So she's going to talk to you and Donna about color schemes and get right on that.''

Abby shook her head in silent admiration. ''That was really nice of you,'' she said softly at last.

Tad put his plate aside and pulled her onto his lap so that her bottom was nestled snugly in the warm hard cradle of his thighs. ''Don't you know there isn't anything I wouldn't do for you?'' he said tenderly as he sifted his hands through her hair.

''Tad...'' Abby groaned as his sexy bedroom eyes met and held hers again.

''Abby...'' He mocked her lightly, then lowered his head and took her mouth in a searing kiss. Abby moaned. Tad deepened the kiss and wrapped his arms around her, the pressure of his hands on her back bringing her intimately close. A torrent of need swept through her, sending all her senses into an uproar. It felt so good to be wanted and touched again, Abby thought. Desire trembled inside her, making her insides go all warm and syrupy.

Tad made a low contented sound in the back of his throat. ''I'm ready to make love anytime.'' He brushed the hair from her nape. His warm breath caressed the skin of her neck, sending yet another shiver of desire coursing through her.

''All you have to do is let me know you've changed your mind, and we'll turn this into a real marriage.''

But was that true? Abby wondered without warning, a tidal wave of conflicting feelings surging through her. Whether she wanted to admit it or not, there was still so much she didn't know about Tad. Things that Sadie—and perhaps even his old friend Donna—knew. Like what had happened in Houston. If they wanted to have a chance of making things work for the long haul, the two of them had to get to know each other first and form a friendship that was so strong, so enduring, it would last the lifetime of their child. She knew Tad well enough now to realize that wouldn't happen if she let them be distracted by passionate sex.

"I'll just bet you are." She sighed wistfully, a part of her wishing she could still be as foolish and impetuous and driven by passion as they had been in Paris. But with a baby on the way—their baby—that was no longer possible. Like it or not, Abby told herself sternly, she had to be responsible. Her child's happiness—and hers and Tad's—depended on it.

"But?" Tad prodded as his black brows drew together.

Reluctantly Abby reminded herself they were only in this predicament because she'd rushed into bed with Tad. She was far too savvy to make the same mistake again. "But we have to get up very early tomorrow if we're going to go clothes shopping together before we head to the paper."

Tad tensed from head to toe. "So no go," he guessed, disappointed.

"No go," Abby confirmed, delivering a look meant to quell him into submission even as she wished she weren't so damn susceptible to his kisses.

He loosened his hold on her. While he accepted her decision, clearly he was not giving up. "You know where I'll be if you change your mind,'' he told her as he lightly, triumphantly kissed her forehead one last time.

Yes, Abby thought, sighing wistfully as her still-tingling body continued to telegraph its regret. That was the problem—she did.

where I'll be if you change your mind," he told her as he dully triumphantly linked her forehead one last time.

Yet, Abby thought, staring wistfully as her still-tingling body continued to struggle to resist. That was the problem—she did

Chapter Six

"You're not playing fair," Abby told Tad late the next morning as she cornered him in the supply room at the rear of the building.

Figuring this was one conversation the rest of the staff did not need to hear, Tad shut the door behind him and put down the package of yellow legal pads he'd been about to tear open. He took his time getting to her side. "What do you mean?"

Abby tossed her head imperiously. Color swept into her cheeks. She pursed her bow-shaped lips together. "Asking everyone how to sex up the copy during the staff meeting."

"I think the word I used was jazz," Tad corrected, amused and pleased to see he'd gotten under her skin just as he'd hoped. "Jazz things up."

"Then you went on to say sex sells."

Tad braced his shoulder against the wall and tilted his head down at her. "It does. Everything from toothpaste to cars to beer."

Abby rolled her eyes in exasperation. "I'm not arguing that."

"Furthermore," Tad continued, more aware than ever how pretty and pulled-together she looked with her golden-brown hair fastened by a stylish silver barrette at the nape of her slender neck, "no one else seemed to mind."

Abby folded her arms militantly and leaned back against the wall. "That's because they were full of ideas about features on the most romantic places to dine, what kind of mattresses were best and where to go on dates in the good old summertime."

Tad stepped close enough to inhale the intoxicating vanilla fragrance of her perfume. "Cindy's idea about starting a G-rated Personals column was a good one, don't you think?"

"Yes. I'm sure it'll cause quite a stir."

He looked into her eyes, deliberately holding her gaze, daring her to look away. "Then what's the problem?" He was tired of putting his desire for her on hold, and yet he didn't want to hurt her. He didn't want her thinking that the only reason he wanted them to stay married was the baby they were expecting, because it just wasn't true. He'd wanted her from the first moment he'd laid eyes on her and he still did. The question was, how could he make her believe it? Not just in her head but in her heart.

"Like you don't know exactly what I'm so fired up about."

His expression all innocence, Tad flattened his hands over his chest. "I don't." And it was true.

"Then I'll spell it out for you, my dear husband." Abby propped both her hands on her trim hips. "It was the way you've been looking at me all morning long!"

Ahhh. Now they were getting somewhere. He touched her face with his callused palm, cupping her chin in his hand, running his thumb across her lower lip. "Like I wanted to put my arms around you and kiss you again?"

"Yes!"

"Can't help that." Tad shrugged and dropped his hand. "It's the way I feel."

Abby glared at him, refusing to back down. "Tad, this was a staff meeting," she admonished with a weariness that went all the way to her soul.

"We're all one big family here. I thought I'd made that clear." Plus, everyone—except Abby, it seemed—knew he was head over heels in love with his wife and always would be, no matter how this hasty marriage of theirs turned out.

Abby turned away from him stubbornly. "Yes, you did."

"Then you also know that no one else seemed to mind if every once in a while there was a spark or two between us."

"A spark!" Abby echoed. "More like a bonfire!"

So, Tad thought, pleased he was getting to her. Maybe more than he'd realized.

"Did I tell you how much I like what you're wearing?" That morning, before they'd gone shopping, she'd asked to borrow one of his shirts and a tie. Curious to see what she was going to do, he'd opened up his closet and given her free rein. She'd selected a jade green twill dress shirt and a jade, black and amber necktie and later paired both with a pair of dressy black maternity slacks and leather flats.

Abby sighed and fiddled with the hem of his loose-fitting shirt. "You probably think I should be wearing one of those maternity blouses we purchased for me this morning."

Tad grinned and shook his head. That wasn't the

case at all. He loved the idea of her in his clothes. The buttoned-up look was damn sexy on her. He even liked the way she'd rolled up the cuffs twice to make the sleeves the proper length for her. "You look a lot better in that shirt and tie than I ever did," he said. And he understood Abby's reluctance to make the leap to total maternity wear just yet, when she was showing only a little bit. He curled a hand about her waist and guided her close. "You look…very sexy in a Katharine Hepburn sort of way," he said, kissing her cheek. "What's even sexier is this." He slid a hand beneath her shirt and caressed her tummy.

Abby sighed and melted against him. Tad gave in to a whim and touched her face with the back of his hand. It felt like hot silk beneath his flesh, softer than the petals on the bouquet of roses he'd bought for her their first night in Paris. He let his hand slide beneath her hair to the nape of her neck. He tilted her face up to his. The way she looked at him then—all soft and wanting and vulnerable—made his heart pound even harder. This was tough on her, too. Tough on both of them. He knew she needed him, even if she wouldn't yet let herself admit it.

"I meant what I said last night," he told her softly, guiding her closer still. "There isn't anything I wouldn't do for you." He knew damn well there would be hell to pay later, but right now he couldn't help himself. Abby was his wife, she was carrying their child, and he wanted her more than life itself. He lowered his lips to hers, slanted his mouth over hers and poured everything he felt, everything he wanted, into the slow leisurely caress.

Abby moaned, soft and low in her throat. Her hands came up to ineffectually push at his chest, then ended up wrapped around his neck. He felt the need pouring out of her, mingling with the desire and the tenderness that was so much a part of her, too. And knew no matter what happened, he would never get enough of her.

Abby hadn't meant this to happen. But then, she thought, as Tad kissed her with a thoroughness that shook her to her very soul, she never did. The yearning that swept through her was almost unbearable. Her breasts ached and burned for the nimble play of his fingers while lower still she longed to be as one. Moaning, she chalked up her wantonness to pregnancy hormones and surrendered to the need pouring through her. She stopped fighting him, fighting this, and let herself go. Threading her hands through his hair, she kissed him back passionately, wildly, until everywhere their bodies touched, liquid fire pooled.

And that was when it happened. When the door swung open behind them and an unsuspecting Sadie barged in.

"Whoops!" Sadie said, laughing and clapping an astonished hand to her face.

"Honeymooners," said Raymond, who was standing behind her and chuckling, too. He shook his head. "When we noticed the two of them had disappeared, we should've known."

"YOU CAN STOP blushing now," Sadie told Abby as they went over the layout for the next edition of the paper. "It was only a little kiss."

Using her computer mouse, Abby changed the positions of two of the articles. "There's no such thing as a little kiss from Tad," she grumbled. Each one knocked her socks off.

"So? I know we're at work, but no one here minds," Sadie was quick to reassure her. "In fact, we all kind of enjoy watching the sparks fly between the two of you." She looked at Abby closely. "The question is, why are you holding that nephew of mine at arm's length?" She held up a hand, silencing Abby's protest. "I'd have to be an idiot not to notice the yearning looks and touches and near kisses. Yet he doesn't seem to act on any of those very often."

"It's complicated" was all Abby could say.

"Not that complicated," Sadie replied firmly. She pulled up her chair so the two of them were sitting knee to knee and took Abby's hands in hers. "Listen to me, sweetheart. When I was your age, I thought just the way you're thinking. But now I know. True love comes along so rarely. Maybe once in a lifetime." Sadie sighed wistfully. "I've never had it, much to my regret. But if I had ever felt the magic that you and Tad are feeling," she said firmly, laying a hand across her heart, "I sure as heck wouldn't squander it."

Was that what she was doing? Abby wondered uncomfortably. Or was she merely being practical and saving them all from more hurt?

"Is it my imagination or are Sadie and Raymond attracted to each other?" Abby asked Tad that night as they sifted through the three proposed decors for the entryway and living room—the first rooms Donna was proposing they redo for the newspaper.

Tad picked up a swatch of wall-to-wall Berber carpet and compared it to a sketch of an Oriental rug over a hardwood floor that dominated another sketch. As he studied both thoughtfully, he said, "I think there's definitely something going on there. Raymond's been a widower for the last ten years, you know. He never had any kids, either, and he said something to me the other day about being really tired of the bachelor life.''

Abby dropped a swatch of drapery fabric meant to go with the Oriental rug. ''You think he was talking about getting something going with Sadie?''

Tad shrugged and sat back on the sofa. ''Wouldn't surprise me. Every time I turn around those two are making up some excuse to go talk to each other.''

Abby discarded a third sketch that favored a stark modern decor. She'd noticed Tad didn't like it much, either. ''Hmm.''

Tad studied her. ''What are you thinking?''

Probably the same thing you are. ''I hope Sadie finds some romance.''

Tad took Abby's hand in his. He turned it palm side up on his knee and absently stroked her open palm from fingertip to wrist. ''It'd be nice, wouldn't it,'' he mused aloud, a hopeful light coming into his eyes, ''if she didn't have to spend her golden years alone?''

''Very.'' Abby clasped Tad's hand in hers, squeezed. ''Although there's the age difference. Raymond is…what?''

Tad frowned. ''Nine years younger than she is.''

Abby sighed. ''Think that might be a problem?''

''I don't know.'' Tad's worried scowl deepened. ''But there's no use borrowing trouble since they don't have anything but a friendship at this point.'' He nodded at the trio of sketches in front of them. ''So what do you think? Should we go with the carpet and the oak furniture, the wood floors and Oriental rugs, or the stark ultramodern look?''

Abby hesitated. ''If you still want to keep your

lounge chair and use it to a build a reading corner in the living room—''

''I do,'' Tad said firmly.

''—then I suggest you recover your chair and go with the oak furniture and Berber carpet. But,'' Abby amended quickly, feeling a little guilty for taking such an active part in decisions that were mainly going to affect him, ''it really should be your decision since you're the one who's going to be living here for the long haul.''

Tad's face changed abruptly. ''Right.'' He let go of her hand and stood abruptly.

Guilt flooded her anew, adding to the confused welter of emotions deep inside her and the disturbing feeling that her life was spinning way out of control. Abby bit her lip. She hadn't meant to hurt him. Neither was she willing to lead him on. She pressed her lips together, able to feel a massive tension headache coming on. ''I didn't mean—''

''I know what you meant, Abby,'' Tad interrupted gruffly.

Abby swallowed and tried again. ''I just don't think we should lose sight of our agreement.'' She forced them both to deal with what she knew they'd both rather leave unsaid. ''We have to be practical here,'' she insisted firmly. *We have to protect ourselves from getting hurt.* And in this one instance her parents were right. Given the hasty impulsive way it had happened, her marriage didn't have a snowball's chance in hell of surviving. Odds were it would be over as soon as their baby was born, if not before.

''Of course. Why didn't I think of that?'' Tad grabbed his jacket and headed into the front hall.

Abby followed him. She was determined to get an

answer about the decorating details even if he was being difficult. "I have to tell Donna tomorrow if you want this done, photographed and in the paper two weeks from now."

"Then you decide," Tad told her as he grabbed his car keys. "It doesn't really matter to me, anyway. One decor is as good as any other. Just make sure my chair stays—and if it is recovered, it has to be recovered in brown!"

Her heart sinking at the thought of how she'd hurt him when all she'd been doing was trying to protect him, Abby watched him stride out the door. She leaned against the jamb, all too aware that it was late, nearly ten-thirty. "Where are you going now?" There wasn't much open in Blossom at that time of night, except one fast-food restaurant and the tavern.

Tad stopped and gave her a look. "Why should you care? As you've pointed out on more than one occasion, this marriage is only a temporary convenience."

His angry words hit her like a stab to the heart. She held out a beseeching hand. "Tad, please," she said. "I don't want to fight with you."

"I don't want to fight with you, either, which is exactly why I'm leaving."

Just like her parents had left each other and every spouse they'd had since, Abby thought, as feelings of hurt and disillusionment came back to haunt her anew.

"Don't wait up," Tad said indifferently over his shoulder as he climbed into his Jeep.

TAD DROVE AWAY from the white elephant and headed for the outskirts of town. He hadn't told Abby where he was going because he didn't *know* where he was going. He only knew he didn't want to be around people at this moment, and he didn't want to face what was, more and more, looking like the inevitable end to his marriage to Abby.

He knew she felt unstable due to their impulsive marriage, the loss of her job, their relocation to North Carolina and the baby. The truth was, Tad acknowledged to himself as he left the Blossom city limits and headed out into the countryside, he felt the same. His feelings for Abby were not going to change, but that did not mean he could make her love him the way she needed to love him to make their marriage last.

Tad sighed as he turned his Jeep onto yet another winding country road. He was just going to have to find a way to convince her they did belong together, after all, and he was going to have to do that by finding a happy medium and not moving too fast or too slow. The one thing they weren't going to do, he decided firmly as he eased his foot off the accelerator, was talk about it anymore. They had done that enough as it was, to unhappy result.

Tad slowed as he came upon a shiny red pickup truck pulled over to the side of the road. Ernest Lee Scruggs, the head mechanic over at Joe Don Jerome's car dealership was standing with his head under the hood.

Tad parked behind the disabled vehicle and got out. "Hey there, Ernest Lee," Tad said.

The mechanic nodded. "Hey there, yourself," he said grimly.

"That's a new truck, isn't it?" Tad asked.

"You better believe it." Ernest Lee wiped his grease-stained hands on a rag. "It's less than a month old. And it just up and quit on me. The durn thing is deader than a doornail."

Tad regarded the mechanic sympathetically. "Want me to call for a tow truck on my cell phone?"

Ernest Lee sighed and banged the hood down. "Might as well. Thanks, Tad."

Tad made the call. Figuring this was as good a chance as any to see what he could find out about Ernest Lee's boss and whatever sleazy deals Jerome and his two cohorts might be in, Tad leaned against the side of the truck and prepared to wait it out with Ernest Lee.

"I guess you heard I'm not too popular with your boss," Tad said.

Ernest Lee rolled his eyes. "Ain't that the truth."

"They want me to take out my Troubleshooter phone line down at the paper."

"Yeah. I heard."

"Any idea why Joe Don and his buddies would be so opposed to it?"

Ernest Lee continued looking at the side of the road. Was it his imagination, Tad wondered, or was Ernest Lee beginning to look a little tense?

"They probably just don't want you stirring up trouble."

"I wouldn't be creating trouble, Ernest Lee. Just reporting on trouble that already exists. There's a difference."

Ernest Lee was silent. Finally he said, "Joe Don has the only car dealership in town. He talks to Nowell down at the bank and Cullen over at the insurance place and makes sure people that might not otherwise qualify for loans or be able to get insurance get it. That's a good thing."

"If he's running an honest business, it's a good thing," Tad agreed as a pair of headlights appeared in the distance. "If he's not, that's something else again."

"There's my tow truck," Ernest Lee said.

The conversation was over. Tad had managed to get one thing out of Ernest Lee. The Three Stooges were—at the very least—bending the rules to help local residents buy cars. And while that might have been laudable in some cases, Tad had the feeling that there was more going on than just that. And whatever it was, was probably not only benefiting the Three Stooges, but also illegal or unethical as hell. As the only newsman in town, it was up to him to find out what that was. And damned if he wasn't going to do just that, Tad decided firmly, with or without Ernest Lee's help.

"IF IT WAS ME, I'd forget about Tad's lounge chair, relegate it to some unseen unimportant area of the house, like the attic or the garage, and go with the design scheme that includes the Oriental carpet," Yvonne told Abby over the long-distance line. "But I'm not a home-and-garden editor, who instinctively knows what readers want to see in their homes and yards at any given time. And I'm not the one who's going to be living there. So what gives, kiddo? Why do you really need my advice? And for the record, I don't for one minute buy the story that you need my help with the decor decision."

Abby let out a breath. "Okay, here it is. I feel guilty making a decision on the house since I'm not going to be living here permanently. And yet I know it's what I'm expected to do...on some wifely level." And she had no idea at all about how to be a good wife to Tad or anyone else. She only knew, from watching her parents' numerous marriages fall apart, that when the passion faded and people were left with the reality of a disintegrating relationship, it could get ugly. Ugly enough to destroy everything good and decent that had gone before. Baby or no baby, she did not want that to happen to her and Tad.

Yvonne paused. "Then you're going back to magazine work?"

Like there could be any doubt about that! "Yes," Abby said. "As soon as possible after the baby is born."

Another silence on Yvonne's part, though somewhat briefer. "Have you started looking for a job?"

Abby went to the freezer and got out a pint of Chunky Monkey ice cream. "No. But maybe it's time I got back to that." Maybe that would make her feel like her life was back under control, she thought as she searched in the silverware drawer for a spoon. "Do you know any headhunters?"

"Absolutely. One in particular, too."

Abby put down her ice cream long enough to grab a pen and paper. "Give me her name and number."

They talked a few minutes more, then Abby hung up the phone. Carton of Chunky Monkey in hand, she looked at the trio of designs one more time, realized she'd eaten half the ice cream in one sitting and reluctantly put it away, no decision made. Her stomach still growling hungrily—what was it about pregnancy and these eating binges? she wondered—she went upstairs to bed.

The truth was, she thought as she slipped into her nightgown, part of her very much wanted to see this marriage through. Part of her wanted to know if she could do what her parents had never managed—build something lasting and true in the marriage department.

And, had she and Tad not had a baby on the way, had they both still been living their career dreams and working in New York City, maybe she could have risked everything falling apart and them detesting each other in the end if the passion that tempted them now eventually fizzled.

But with their baby coming, their marriage continuing only because of her unexpected pregnancy, common sense dictated she take a much more practical approach. She and Tad had to stay friends; they had to build a lifelong relationship that would enable them to coparent their child effectively. Their baby's happiness depended on it.

So, Abby thought, tears slipping down her cheeks as she climbed into bed, she would have to put aside the remembered passion and nagging temptation and do what she knew to be best—continue to hold Tad at arm's length.

THE HOUSE WAS SILENT, the light in the master bedroom on when Tad finally got home at midnight. Wondering if he was the only one feeling bad about the tension between them earlier, he paused to look in on Abby. She was curled up in the double bed fast asleep. Not wanting to disturb her, he walked soundlessly across the floor to turn off the bedside lamp. And that was when he saw the tracks of tears on her face and knew she'd cried herself to sleep.

Wondering if it was due to the words they'd come close to exchanging earlier or something much deeper, Tad pulled up the cover, and switched off the light.

Maybe she thought he didn't care. Well, he'd fix that first thing tomorrow morning.

"I LIKE THE DECOR with the hardwood floors and Oriental rug for the living room," he told her over breakfast.

Abruptly Abby looked as though she might break into tears. But she didn't. "Good." She drained her milk and stood. "I'll call Donna from the office."

"Want to drive in together?" Tad asked.

Abby shook her head. "I think I'd rather walk." She grabbed her briefcase, headed for the door and slammed the door behind her. Touché, Tad thought. *I walked out on you last night. You walked out on me this morning.* Maybe, if he was really lucky, tonight neither of them would walk out on the other.

Unfortunately it did not look as if that was going to be the case when he got to the office. Abby was by turns stressed and surly. Midmorning she just got up and grabbed her briefcase. She stopped by his desk on the way out, waited until he got off the phone. "I'm going home."

Tad stood and reached into his pocket for his car keys. He handed them to her, feeling as though he could step on a land mine any second. "You feeling okay?" He studied her face. She seemed awfully flushed.

Abby's golden-brown eyes flashed. She shoved a hand through her hair. "Can't I be in a bad mood every once in a while?" she snapped.

Tad shrugged as activity in the office stopped and all eyes turned their way. "Well, sure you—"

"Good." Abby cut him off autocratically. "Because I am." She handed him back the car keys and said, "Thanks, but I'd rather walk." Then she waved to the rest of the staff. "Later, guys." As she strode toward the door, she tossed off a last parting shot with a wry smile and self-deprecating humor. "Maybe by tonight my hormones will settle back into the non-lethal range."

"If you ask me, that was more than hormones," Sadie said worriedly as soon as Abby had left.

"She's definitely not herself this morning," Cindy said.

Tell me about it, Tad thought. He'd been as nice as he could be all morning and still felt like he was dealing with a lioness on the prowl.

"Are you sure she's feeling okay?" Raymond asked.

No. Tad wasn't. More to the point, he realized uncomfortably, he didn't even know what to look for when it came to danger signs. He found himself in Doc Harlan's office ten minutes later.

Doc listened intently while Tad quickly brought him up to date. He knew if anyone would know what to do, it was Doc, who'd been married thirty-five years, had six kids and sixteen grandchildren and, according to local lore, handled every moment of it like a pro.

"Sounds like your first instincts were right," Doc conceded. He sat back in his chair and steepled his hands in front of him. "It probably is hormones causing Abby's mood swings. Or it could just be the fact that she's pregnant. Her body and indeed her whole life are both undergoing tremendous changes right now. We men think we understand, but I have a feeling we don't, since we aren't the ones carrying the little one around inside us. So I'm going to give you a few simple rules to follow that should help even things out a bit. Okay?"

"Okay," Tad said. At this point he was willing to

try anything. He didn't want Abby crying herself to sleep again or leaving the office in a huff.

Doc held up the index finger on his right hand. "Rule number one—agree with her about everything, no matter what."

Tad leaned forward in his chair. "But—"

"No buts," Doc said from the other side of the desk. "Just agree with her. You'll both be a lot happier. Rule number two—give her presents for no reason, frequently." Doc smiled encouragingly. "You'll be surprised how much that'll help her mood if she knows you're thinking of her. And last but not least, rule number three—and this is very important, Tad—you need to let her know you love her."

Tad knew he did love Abby. But if he told her that now, in her current peevish mood, she'd probably burst into tears. Either that or she'd explain to him that he really didn't love her.

"Because she needs to know you love her whether she's pregnant or not, young or old, fat or thin, tall or short, already married or just engaged. Once she does, once she feels that in her heart, my guess is she's gonna calm down pretty quickly." Doc stood. The advice-giving session over, he clapped him on the shoulder. "Think you can handle all that?"

Tad nodded. Agree with her, give her presents, tell her that he loved her. It sure sounded simple enough. "Thanks, Doc." Tad shook Doc's hand. "I really owe you for this one."

"DID DOC KNOW what to do?" a worried Sadie asked Tad the moment he walked back through the newspaper doors.

Tad nodded, distracted. "Yeah," he said thoughtfully, sitting down behind his computer. The more he thought about it, the more it made sense to him.

Abby was already a little ticked off at him because he'd kept trying, however subtly, to preempt their agreement and get her back into bed with him. That had seemed—to him—a logical and speedy way to get them feeling close again.

Judging by what Doc had told him about pregnant women needing lots of reassurance and husbandly understanding, that had probably been a mistake. Abby already felt pressured by the many changes in her life. She probably thought sex was all he wanted from her. And though Tad knew nothing could be further from the truth—he wanted Abby in his life, baby or no baby, sex or no sex—he resolved to stop putting the moves on her until she gave him a signal that she wanted them to resume the physical side of their relationship.

Doc was right. Maybe if Abby realized he loved her for herself and not just the shape of her body or the incredible passion between them, she'd begin to have trust in him, in them, and see they had the potential to make their marriage last a lifetime, after all.

Chapter Seven

Tad tried calling off and on the rest of the morning. Abby was either not there or not answering or talking on the phone and ignoring the call-waiting beep. Whatever the case, Tad had to check on her or go crazy. When lunch hour came, he delegated a breaking story about a potential salmonella outbreak at the Mighty Fine Restaurant to Sonny, then hopped in the Jeep and drove home.

The red, white and blue express-mail truck was just pulling away from the curb as he turned into the driveway. Abby was standing in the doorway. She looked pale and wan and had what appeared to be a receipt in her hands. In deference to the warm and sunny July day, she'd changed into an oversize navy blue T-shirt and matching running shorts that deftly disguised her pregnancy. Her feet were bare and her golden-brown hair had been caught in a bouncy ponytail on top of her head. Color flooding back into her cheeks, she waited while he approached.

"Everything okay?" Tad asked as he followed her into the house.

She shrugged her slender shoulders, her expression noncommittal. The pink spots in her cheeks deepened.

She swallowed hard and took a deep breath. "I could ask you the same thing." Their eyes met as she folded her arms beneath her breasts. "What are you doing home?"

"I left some papers here," Tad fibbed as he moved close enough to inhale the intoxicating vanilla fragrance of her perfume. He wasn't sure what he'd expected from her today. Recriminations for walking out on her the night before, not telling her where he was going or letting her know when he'd be back. At this point he'd even take the silent treatment. Instead, she seemed determined to let him know she couldn't care less what he did. And that left him feeling panicked.

Determined not to let her know that, however, Tad sauntered into the living room and stepped around his favorite recliner. Recalling his purported mission, he looked around for papers—any papers. "I tried to let you know I was coming home to pick them up—" he paused to retrieve a folder of papers from the coffee table he was half-afraid she knew he didn't need "—but the phone line was busy, I guess."

Abby put her express-mail receipt and several new copies of her résumé in her briefcase. "I've been on the phone all morning talking to a headhunter Yvonne recommended."

The news Abby was now actively pursuing a job hit Tad like a sucker punch to the gut. He was irritated with Abby, but remembering Doc's advice not to upset her, Tad lounged against the back of the sofa and pretended an amiable attitude he couldn't begin to feel. "Yeah?" He studied her with growing curiosity. "What'd she say?"

"She thinks she can get me something, but it'll probably take at least six months," Abby replied.

"Meanwhile, she wanted copies of my résumé ASAP, so I printed them out and sent them to her."

Again Tad feigned approval of her actions. She hadn't left yet, he reassured himself. He still had months to get her to change her mind. Tad spotted the ginger ale and saltine crackers on the coffee table. "You feeling okay?"

Abby tossed her head. "If you must know, no. At least I wasn't earlier." She pivoted on her heel and headed for the kitchen. "I'm starving now."

Now was not the time to be noticing how sexy her legs were or that she was not wearing a bra.

"Feeling better, then?" he asked gently.

"Yeah." Abby smiled. "Plus," she continued happily, "I think I've *finally* figured out why I've been so depressed and moody lately."

Tad had to admit he was very curious about why she'd cried herself to sleep the night before. Aware once again of the overpowering need to comfort her, he watched as she pulled a package of linguine off the shelf and put some water on the stove to boil.

"I'm listening," he said, all the compassion he felt for her reflected in his eyes.

"I think it has to do with the fact that I hadn't started my job search." Her golden-brown eyes serious, Abby moved away from him. "I told myself I'd delayed it because of the pregnancy, because I was so busy here, but I don't think that's why I hesitated at all," she confided as she bent down to get a skillet from the storage bin beneath the stove. As she straightened, she seemed to lose her balance. He moved forward and put out a hand to assist her. The feel of her soft hand in his was enough to make his heart pound, and he longed to kiss and hold her all the more.

Removing her hand from his, Abby turned to put the skillet on the stove. For a moment her eyes narrowed reflectively and her mood turned brooding again. Finally she shook her head, let out a soft self-deprecating sigh, then turned back to him. "I think I was just afraid that I wouldn't get another editing position on par with what I had. I know." She held up a hand before he could interrupt. "It's silly of me to even think that way, not to mention self-defeating, so I've decided to stop," she told him happily, looking up at him with new resolve, "and just have a more positive attitude."

No question, Tad wanted her to feel good about herself and her work. "That's smart," he told her, knowing even as he encouraged her to shoot for her dreams, too, that he still did not want her to leave. Could he help it if he wanted her in his life? he wondered guiltily. For now, forever?

"You're right, it is smart," Abby replied, squaring her shoulders. "Because the future is coming whether I want to think about it or not and I've got a baby to support."

"We both do," Tad reminded her. He only hoped one day soon she would see that this was also something they could do together.

"Right." Abby smiled, relieved to find he understood. "Anyway, I need my work to sustain me, always have, always will, so knowing I'm eventually going to pick up where I left off is a big morale booster." She strode past him and headed for the refrigerator.

What about the work we're doing here? Doesn't that count? Tad wanted to ask. He recalled Doc's advice, the fact Abby had already admittedly been sick once today, and knew he had no choice but to agree with her. "I'm sure it is."

Abby got out the makings for clam sauce. She put butter and garlic in a saucepan and turned the burner up to moderate heat. "In fact, I think if I'd just made finding a new job in my field my number-one priority from the beginning, I would've felt a lot better from the get go." Abby paused to add flour and then clam juice, blending the mixture with a wire whisk.

Tad had known their marriage ultimately might not work the moment he'd told Abby he'd purchased the newspaper and intended to move to North Carolina. But it still stung to see her acting as if they were already on the road to divorce when they still had a good six and a half months ahead of them before their baby was born to try to make things work.

The doorbell rang. Abby looked at Tad. "Are you expecting anyone?"

Tad didn't know if he was glad or sorry about the interruption. He only knew he didn't want to talk about her leaving anymore. "No. You?"

She shook her head. Tad went to get it, and a moment later Sonny and Tim Grau, the owner of the Mighty Fine Restaurant, came barreling in. Tad knew before one word was spoken what the visit was probably about.

"You can't do this to me," Tim shouted at Tad angrily, his face turning almost as red as his rust-colored hair. "Not after all the advertising dollars I gave your paper."

"Look, I'm sorry if you have a problem down there, but one thing has nothing to do with the other," Tad said. The scent of simmering clam sauce filled the air and a perplexed Abby came out to join them, wooden spoon still in hand.

"The hell it doesn't!" Tim countered as Abby walked over to Tad and stood next to him. "I just opened three weeks ago," Tim continued. "If you lead with a story on food poisoning, I'm finished."

"Not necessarily," Tad said.

"Oh, yeah?" His expression grim, Tim looked at Tad. "Would you want your pregnant wife eating there if you read in the *Blossom Weekly News* that six people got sick after eating the chicken special last Thursday?"

Tad understood why Tim was upset, but there was no way he was censoring the news to protect some people and expose others. The truth was the truth. The news was the news. And that was the way it was going to be.

"Six people did get sick, according to the health department," Tad said matter-of-factly.

"It wasn't my restaurant's fault! The poultry was tainted when I got it!"

"If the facts bear that out," Tad said, knowing full well that the investigation by the health department had not yet been completed, "then the article will say that."

Tim Grau glared at Tad. He looked mad enough to punch something. "You know, I heard from some of the other merchants in town that you were going to be unreasonable," he said, a muscle working in his jaw. "But pulling stuff like this is going to do you in, McFarlane. In fact, unless you adhere to the local creed and give more favorable coverage to those who place the bigger ads as a sort of professional courtesy, from one merchant to another, I'll bet you go out of business faster than I do.''

Tad was betting he wouldn't. ''I've never purposely held back on a story and I'm not going to start now,'' he told Tim as Abby slipped her hand in his and gave it a squeeze.

''Then you're going to be sorry.'' Tim Grau turned on his heel and left in a huff.

Sonny looked at Tad apologetically. ''I tried to stop him, but in a town this size, it wasn't hard to figure out where you were. Since he was headed over here, as the reporter covering the story, I figured I'd better come over here, too.''

''It's okay,'' Tad reassured Sonny.

''It certainly is.'' Abby smiled at him, too.

Relief flooded Sonny's youthful features. Once again he looked to Tad for advice. ''So what should I do about the story?''

''Write it. Talk to everyone who got sick, including Doc and the health department, and then put it on my desk. It's going in the next edition.''

''Are you sure that's wise?'' Abby asked after Sonny had left and she and Tad sat down to steaming plates of linguine with clam sauce.

Tad liked the idea of coming home to have lunch with his wife, even if it had been sort of a spur-of-the-moment deal. It was cozy and intimate, sitting here with her like this. So much so that he wanted to take her in his arms, cement their conciliatory words with a hug. He knew he couldn't, not without being tempted to do more, so he sat where he was.

''I purchased my own newspaper because I was disgusted by the increasing bias in the news and the pressure put on me by the brass to slant certain stories certain ways and forget others entirely. I'm going to give fair balanced reporting or none at all.''

''I admire the way you're sticking to your convictions,'' Abby said with a smile as she got up to get out dill pickles and chocolate syrup. While Tad watched in amazement, she added chocolate to her milk and pickles to the edge of her plate. ''That was one of the things I always hated about magazine work. We were so dependent on advertising.''

''Well, you won't have to do that at the *Blossom Weekly News,*'' Tad said as he dug into the delicious pasta. ''If there's a story of interest to our readers, we'll cover it, and we'll leave the editorializing to the editorial page.''

He held her gaze, amazed as she continued to down her food with all the gusto of a hungry linebacker. ''You're really going to eat that dill pickle with the linguine?''

''Disgusting, isn't it?'' Abby replied cheerfully as she ate one spear and then helped herself to another.

Tad remembered Doc's advice to agree with his pregnant wife at all costs. ''No, actually it looks pretty good.'' Tad pushed aside his revulsion and downed a couple of tart dill pickles, too.

''You're nuts, you know that, don't you?'' Abby said.

He had to be, Tad thought, to be living here with her, and not making love to her. But that was the agreement they had struck, he reminded himself, and until she believed he loved her just for herself and nothing else, that was the way it would have to be.

''THAT'S THE FOURTH present this week, isn't it?'' Donna said as the finishing touches were put on the living room in late July.

"Yes, it is," Abby said, bringing in the dozen red roses that had just been delivered from the local florist. Before that, there'd been a box of Godiva chocolates, a CD she'd been wanting and an array of scented hand soaps. The two weeks before that had been equally rife with gifts. Not a day went by, it seemed, that Tad didn't come in at night with her favorite food or beverage or even a newspaper or magazine he knew she liked to read. At first it had been nice to be the object of so much thoughtfulness. Now...well, now Abby didn't know what to think.

Sonny loaded film into his camera. "So what'd Tad do to land in the doghouse?" he asked.

It was possible he felt guilty about working so much. Since the brouhaha over the publication of the article on the salmonella outbreak at the Mighty Fine Restaurant, he had worked increasingly long hours, as had she.

"Nothing. He's not in the doghouse—at least not with me."

"Right." Sonny's lip curled with suppressed amusement as he got down on one knee to photograph the interior of the two rooms. "Maybe someone should tell him that."

Donna plumped the pillows on the long cream-colored tuxedo sofa just so while Abby adjusted the white plantation shutters to let in the maximum amount of light. The newly refinished wood floors gleamed beneath the beige-brown, cream and marine blue Oriental rug. Gleaming white trim and crown molding put the finishing touches on the handsome marine blue walls. And last but not least, Tad's recliner sat in a corner, in a place of honor, newly covered in a beige-brown jacquard that coordinated well with the two other overstuffed armchairs in the room.

"I know where Sonny is coming from." Donna chuckled as she straightened the bookcases and the streamlined laptop computer on the antique writing desk. "My husband, Ron, gives me gifts for only two reasons. A special occasion, like my birthday or our anniversary, or when he's trying to make up to me for something he's done." Donna paused to open a door of the armoire, to show the stereo and television set hidden within. "The size of the gift is usually directly proportionate to the degree of guilt he's feeling."

"Amen to that," Sonny said, directing both Donna and Abby into the next picture. "It didn't take me long to discover that the right pair of earrings or bottle of perfume can go an awfully long way toward making up."

Abby smiled for the camera. As they moved into the finished entryway to photograph that area, she wondered what was going on with Tad.

"DID YOU GET my flowers?" Tad asked, immediately seeking her out when he came in about ten o'clock that evening.

Aware work would begin on the formal dining room in the morning, Abby was in there standing on a chair when Tad strode in. In a vivid blue cotton sport shirt worn open at the throat, casual khaki slacks and loafers that had seen better days, he looked casual and at ease. His naturally curly black hair was agreeably rumpled, his jaw shadowed with evening beard and scented with aftershave. And there was a seductive smile tugging at his sensual lips.

"Yes, I got them."

Trying hard not to react to his presence or think how much she'd begun to miss his once-persistent passes, Abby turned her eyes from his handsome profile and continued taking down the threadbare flocked-velvet drapes that had come with the house. How long had it been since he'd kissed her, she wondered, or even wanted to kiss her? The answer was easy. It had been weeks. Meanwhile, her waist was thickening by the day.

Tad glanced around. "Where are they?"

"The kitchen."

He studied her. "You like red roses, don't you?"

Actually they were her favorite. Which, in Abby's estimation, made it all the worse. She stopped what she was doing and turned to face him. Figuring they might as well get it all out in the open, she told him, "You don't have to do this, you know."

Tad blinked in confusion. "Do what?"

Feeling depressed and disappointed, she let her arms fall to her sides. "Try and buy your way into my good graces."

Tad hooked his hands around her waist and helped her down from the chair. He kept his hands there even after her feet touched the floor. "I was trying to show you how much I appreciate you."

Abby shrugged and said nothing.

"Obviously you think there's another reason."

Abby extricated herself from his grip. "Look, let's not talk about this."

Tad caught her by the shoulders and ever so gently spun her around to face him. His eyes glimmered with barely suppressed frustration. "Too bad, 'cause I think we should."

"Have it your way," Abby muttered, as he motioned her to sit in the chair she'd just been standing on.

"So what's up?" Tad pulled up another chair, turned it around backward and sat, folding his arms over the top. "What's got you so upset?"

When she didn't answer, Tad prodded, "C'mon, Ab, just tell me."

"Why do you feel guilty?" Abby blurted out.

Tad nearly choked. "Excuse me?"

"You heard me," Abby retorted grimly. "All the gifts have to be for some reason, so what have you done?"

"Nothing!"

Abby had half expected he might react this way. "I knew this was a waste of time!" she said, bolting to her feet.

Tad followed. Started to speak, stopped, then thought for a long tense moment in which he seemed to change his mind and, in fact, change courses completely. "You're right of course," he said finally in a smooth cultured tone she didn't believe for a moment. He smiled and held out a hand. "I have been feeling guilty for not spending enough time with you. The gifts were just a way of showing you that I appreciate you. If they upset you in any way, I'm sorry."

He was much too agreeable, Abby decided. The Tad she knew and fell in love with, the Tad who reported the unvarnished truth come what may, would never have backed down so readily.

Which meant, of course, Abby thought, fuming all the more, he had to be feeling really guilty about something! It was up to her to find out what.

An idea began to form. And she knew it was a

doozie. Knowing he wasn't the only one who could change tacks rapidly, she smiled at Tad sweetly. "Have you eaten dinner?"

"Yeah." Tad regarded her with the caution one approached a skunk who was about to spray. "I grabbed something earlier when we were putting tomorrow's edition of the *News* to bed."

"Well, I'm famished. I was just going to have a snack. Want to join me?"

"Uh...sure."

Abby led the way into the kitchen. This was going to be the test. "A sandwich okay with you?" she asked, already knowing what his answer would be. Her back to him, she mouthed, *Whatever you're having.*

"Whatever you're having," Tad said.

Well, Abby thought, revenge very much on her mind, *you asked for it.* With Tad lounging against the counter watching her every move, she brought out pumpernickel bread, strawberry-flavored cream cheese, sardines, onions, green and black olives and chili sauce.

Abby saw him swallow and it was all she could do to repress a giggle. "This looks disgusting, I know, but you're going to love it, I promise," she said enthusiastically as she quickly put together a sandwich he would never ever forget. "Here you go." A scant minute later she motioned him to the table and put the plate in front of him.

Tad watched as she began to put the ingredients away. "Aren't you having any?"

"I changed my mind." Abby touched her middle. "Heartburn." *And you caused it, you scoundrel.* "But you go right ahead. I'll just sit with you and watch."

Tad looked at her and again seemed to really struggle with himself and whatever it was he was thinking.

"Well, maybe just a bite," Abby said, reaching over and cutting off a wedge of his sandwich. She popped it into her mouth. "Mm-mmm." Ignoring the hideous taste in her mouth, she sighed and laid a hand across her chest. "This is so-o-o good. Try it."

A smile on his face, Tad lifted the sandwich to his mouth. For a moment she thought he was going to chicken out, but finally he took a bite. Swallowed. Took a long long gulp of water.

"Now," Abby said cheerfully, as the nauseating mess made its way to his stomach, "look me straight in the eye, you scoundrel, and still tell me everything I do is wonderful. I dare you."

Very, very slowly, Tad set down the sandwich. He wiped his hands and his mouth with his napkin. And looked her straight in the eye. "What do you want from me?" he demanded, a muscle clenching in his jaw. Suddenly he seemed every bit as near his limit as she was.

Hot angry color swept into her cheeks. "How about a little honesty?" Abby snapped, pushing her chair back and vaulting to her feet.

"Fine. You want honesty!" he said in a voice that was so low it sent shivers down her spine. "I'll give you honesty. That was disgusting, but I tolerated it."

"That's what I thought." Abby stomped forward until they stood toe-to-toe. She tilted her head back and glared up at him. "Then why did you eat it? No. Don't answer. I think I know. Darn it all, you're humoring me, aren't you? *Aren't you!*"

Tad grimaced. He slid his hands into his back pockets. "Yes. I am. On doctor's orders."

"*What?*"

"Doc told me just to agree with you on everything."

"Oh, he did, did he?" Fuming, Abby began to pace. She hadn't been this angry since...well, since she didn't remember when.

Tad continued, his words as calm and deliberate as hers were furious and emotional. "He said your pregnancy would go a lot smoother for both of us if I humored you, and he should know. He has six kids and sixteen grandkids and a beautiful loving wife who still worships the ground he walks on after thirty-five years of marriage."

Abby sent Tad a withering glance. "The gifts?" she prodded coolly.

Tad drew a deep breath, then confessed, his jaw set. "He told me to do that, too. He said what you're doing for me—for us—carrying our baby is nothing to be taken lightly. He said I should make sure you knew that, and gifts are one of the easiest ways."

Abby raked both hands through her hair, not sure whether to laugh or cry, just knowing she felt like doing both. "Not to mention the fact that it would probably get you in my good graces."

"But it didn't," Tad said.

"One or two probably would have." If they'd been given of his own volition, Abby thought. "But a dozen?" Abby stared at Tad, shaking her head, as her eyes filled. Did he think she could be bought? Was that it? "That's overkill, don't you think?"

"Not really, no." Tad's expression gentled as he stepped even closer. He put his hands on her waist. "If it were up to me, I'd be giving you presents every day the rest of our lives," he said softly. "If it were up to me—as long as we're being honest—we'd still be making love and you'd be sleeping in my arms every night. If it were up to me…''

Letting the ardent thought hang in the air, he scooped her up in his arms and carried her toward the stairs.

"What are you doing?" Abby demanded.

Tad smiled down at her and kept moving. "It just occurred to me, it *is* up to me." He sailed through the door to her softly lit bedroom and lowered her gently to the bed.

"You mean it, don't you?" Abby asked breathlessly as he gazed at her with the passion she'd ached to know again. "You really want to make love to me."

"With all my heart and soul." Tad stroked her hair. The next thing Abby knew, his lips were on hers. He kissed her with the abandon they'd discovered in Paris, and she reveled in the hot insistent demand of his mouth over hers, the urgent thrust and parry of his tongue. He kissed her until they were lying on their sides, sprawled length to length in the middle of the double bed. Until she moaned and melted against him, her hands curling around his shoulders.

He drew back, the misty lights of desire and tenderness in his fathomless blue eyes as he scored his thumb across her lower lip. "What would ever make you think I didn't want you?"

Abby blushed. "My ever-expanding tummy, for one."

He smiled and slid lower, bent to kiss her tummy through the satin fabric of her pajamas, then touched and rubbed and stroked. "Your tummy is beautiful, and so is the rest of you."

Abby swallowed around the growing knot of emotion in her throat. "Tell me you missed me, Abby, as much as I've missed you," Tad whispered fervently as he shifted her onto her back and slid upward. Lying alongside her, he tucked one leg over hers. "Tell me you've missed this," he said.

He teased her tongue with the tip of his until her breath was as short and shallow as his. And though Abby's mind was still fighting him, fighting the surrender, her body had stopped long ago. Heaven help her, she wanted him to make love to her. She wanted to feel everything it was possible to feel. She did not want this moment to pass either of them by, because she knew, even if she didn't want to admit it, that it had never been like this for her. So intensely pleasurable and out of control. And it never would be again. For her, Tad was just it.

"Oh, Tad..." Abby whispered, already trembling from head to toe, and he hadn't even started to undress her yet!

As she whispered his name, Tad's eyes darkened with pleasure. Swiftly, still watching her face, he unbuttoned her pajama top.

"You know I desire you," Abby said, her voice filled with longing as Tad divested her of her pajama top and whisked off her bottoms, too. That had never been the problem between them. "But—"

"No conditions, Abby," Tad said as he impatiently tugged off his own clothes and, naked, joined her on the bed. She moaned as he circled her breast, then cupped the weight of it with his palm. "Not tonight and not ever again." He bent to pay homage with his lips and his tongue until her nipples were tight and achy. "Just love me," Tad said as he rolled her slightly onto her side, slid one arm beneath her hips and arched her lower body against him. "Just let yourself go and love me."

As he continued to kiss and touch and caress her, dizziness swept through her in waves. The hot melting feeling in her abdomen grew, and a need unlike any she'd ever known built within her. No one had ever loved her so fiercely, so possessively, Abby thought, as she returned his kisses passionately and her hips rose instinctively to meet him. No one had ever loved her in such a fundamental way.

Needing to touch him, too, she ran her palms across the smooth hard muscles of his back, across the hard muscles of his stomach and up across his chest, until she could feel his thundering heart. As she touched lower still, she marveled at the velvety hardness and the depth of his need, a need only she could ease.

As she looked into his eyes, the intensity and tenderness of his dark blue gaze held her mesmerized. When he looked at her that way, she felt beautiful, inside and out. And she knew he was right—they did need to love each other again, physically and in every other way.

The next thing she knew he had shifted her onto her back again and nudged her legs apart. She opened herself up to him as gently and irrevocably as a flower blooms in the spring. He caught her by the hips to steady her and then he kissed her. Again and again and again, commanding everything she had to give until she no longer knew where her body ended and his began, until she had never felt so much a woman nor been so aware of a man. She surged against him, loving the touch and taste and smell of him, loving the way their bodies automatically came in contact in all the right places as he satisfied one hunger and fed another.

Tad had always wanted a spirited woman. A woman who was strong but soft, feisty but giving, a woman who wouldn't be afraid to experience pleasure to the max. He knew she'd been hurt badly in the past. So had he, he thought as he trembled with the need to hold back his own release. That didn't mean they had to spend even one more day as husband and wife in name only. In six months they'd be having a child together. Starting now, they could really be a couple and have a life together, too.

Abby trembled from the fit of her body against his, from the pressure nudging her feminine cleft. His whole body was quaking as he stretched out on top of her, spread her knees and slipped between them. The soft V of her thighs cradled his hardness, and his sex throbbed against her surrendering softness. Again, he bent to kiss her, loving her an inch at a time, going deeper and deeper. She rocked against him, taking him inside her, closing tight. Sensations swept through him. He could barely control himself as she shuddered and writhed beneath him, her insides clenching around him, urging him on to release. He heard her moan and felt her tremble, and then it was just too much. Going deep, he followed her over the edge. And then they were both gone, floating, free, feeling a peace they hadn't felt in weeks.

AN HOUR LATER, as they lay wrapped in each other's arms, Tad shifted so that she was beneath him. Bracing his weight on either side of her, he said, ''Let's make a promise to look to each other for pleasure—at least until after the baby is born. I know, I know, you're worried us making love every night will complicate things.''

"It will," Abby told him sternly.

"But it'll also make things all the more bearable," Tad said, kissing her brow. "Admit it. You want me, too."

Abby sighed. "You know I do."

Tad grinned. Getting her to admit that was a major victory. "Then stop worrying about what's going to happen six months down the road," he told her gently. "We can't predict the future, Abby." Reaching for her hand, he turned it palm up and kissed the middle of it. "We can live in today."

The fight to keep him at arm's length faded as quickly and unexpectedly as it had come. "All right," Abby said. She touched a finger to his lips, compelling him to silence. "I'll do it on one condition." Her golden-brown eyes flashed an ardent warning.

Tad would have given her anything if it meant having her back in his life again. He grinned. "Fire away."

"No more fibbing to me, even if you think it's for my own good," she said as their ragged breaths meshed as one. "And no more gratuitous gifts. Okay?"

Relief flowed through Tad. These were conditions he could meet. He kissed her again, knowing, even if Abby didn't yet, that this was just the beginning. They would find a way to make this work over the long haul. He would see to it.

"Okay."

Chapter Eight

Two weeks later

"Why didn't you tell me?" Abby asked Tad after everyone but the two of them had gone home.

Tad looked up from the computer printout in front of him. Outside, a drenching rain continued. Knowing it was his job to protect his pregnant wife as much as possible from all of life's difficulties, yet knowing he owed her honest question an honest answer, he stood his pencil on end and met her eyes. "I didn't want you to worry." *And let's be honest, I didn't want anything to interfere with the immensely satisfying, immensely passionate turn our relationship has taken.*

Since Abby had surrendered to her feelings, they'd made love every night with as much passion, if not more, than they'd discovered in Paris, and selfish father to be and husband that he was, he didn't want anything putting a damper on their love affair. And who knew? Maybe, if things were good enough before the baby was born, she would decide to stay with him after the baby was born, Tad thought.

Abby's golden-brown eyes flashed and her chin took on a stubborn tilt as she continued taking him to task. "I should know when the newspaper is in trouble."

"We're doing okay," Tad defended himself.

Abby began to pace. Because she'd always preferred to wear skirts and dresses to work, she'd taken to wearing a variety of slimming above-the-knee maternity skirts with his shirts and ties. Tad knew he wasn't the only one who thought she looked as fetching as could be. In fact, now well into her fourth month of pregnancy, she was one sexy lady.

With a concerned glance out at the rain and another in his direction, Abby reminded him gravely, "Five of the major advertisers have pulled all their ads because of the final article on the salmonella outbreak at the Mighty Fine Restaurant. None of them have any plans to reinstate with us in the future."

Tad sighed, knowing, even if he'd been able to predict this calamity, he still wouldn't have done things any differently. "They may change their minds," he said evenly, "particularly if Tim Grau changes his mind and turns this unfortunate situation to his advantage."

Abby paced closer, her suede flats moving soundlessly across the polished wooden floor. "Did he get back to you on your offer to use the situation to further public awareness?"

Able to see they were going to be here for a while, Tad kicked back in his chair and propped his boot-clad feet on the corner of his desk. He folded his hands behind his head. "You want his exact words or the general idea?"

"That bad, hmm?"

Tad shrugged. "Tim doesn't want the general public to know that some of his help were chopping raw vegetables on the same cutting boards they used to cut up the raw chicken.''

Abby groaned and started to run her hands through her hair. Remembering belatedly she'd put it up with a barrette on the back of her head, she began to take it down. ''If only they'd all known to keep the two items separate and use a lot of hot soapy water on any surface the raw chicken touched,'' she lamented as she ran her fingers through her silky mane.

''My point exactly.'' Still enjoying the way the overhead lights hit her hair, making it sparkle with golden lights, Tad crossed one ankle over the other and steepled his fingers on his lap. ''The *Blossom Weekly News* could have made him and his staff out to be heroes for educating the public and reassured everyone at the same time that it wasn't going to happen again.''

''Instead—'' Abby stopped pacing and perched on the corner of his desk ''—Tim tried to bury the incident and now may go out of business as a result.''

Tad lifted his eyes to hers. ''While I can't fathom his shortsightedness, I do sympathize with him. I know what it's like to follow your dream.'' He knew what it was like to want something—someone—so much that nothing else mattered.

Abby raked her teeth across her lower lip. Her eyes lifted to his, held. ''Word on the street is that Tim has enough capital to keep going until Thanksgiving. That still gives him time to change his mind and take you up on your offer.''

Tad nodded. He could only hope Tim Grau came to his senses and did so.

''Meantime—'' Abby sighed deeply ''—we have our own problems to solve.'' She picked up the computer printout of figures from Tad's desk. She frowned as she studied the bottom line. "Like how we're going to replace the lost revenue."

Confronted by the aggravated longtime customers and the sudden loss of advertising revenue, he'd been thinking about that all day. "One way to go would be to cut back."

"But you don't want to do that," Abby guessed.

"No." Tad lowered his feet to the floor. He stood and now it was his turn to pace. "I want to expand the paper as rapidly as possible and try to pick up the slack with additional sales and subscribers."

Abby regarded him thoughtfully. "It might work."

Tad stared at the fast-running river of water moving along the curb to the storm drain. "Unfortunately for the two of us that's going to mean things are going to be tight." He turned away from the sight of the rain splattering the top of his Jeep and leaned against the glass. "I pay myself a percentage of the profits, and for the month of August, at any rate, there are none."

Abby smiled at him reassuringly. "I can live on a shoestring. Underwriting the costs of the white-elephant redecoration are another matter entirely, however. We've promised the readers a room every other week."

"And I'd like to up that to once a week," Tad said, thinking a move like that would boost readership more than ever. He rubbed his jaw. "The question is, where are we going to get the money?"

Abby's eyes lit up as she crossed to his side and stood on tiptoe to kiss his cheek. "Why don't you leave that to me?"

"IT'S ALL SET," Abby told Tad early the following afternoon as Sonny went out on assignment and Raymond went to the rear of the building to work on a minor printing-press problem that had just cropped up. "I got a list of craftsmen from Donna. They've all agreed to do the rest of the work on the house for free in exchange for in-depth interviews by me on how they work and learned their trades and so on. It's sort of a barter thing. We give them free publicity that will hopefully generate a lot more business for them, and they do a great job for us. Sonny is going to do the photo essays. So we're going to need a lot more space to fit all this in, because now we'll be focusing on donated materials, expertise and labor for every room."

Tad cast her an admiring glance. "Maybe we should make this a regular series even after we finish the white elephant," he suggested. "Perhaps even raffle off chances to have a kitchen face-lift or master-bedroom redecoration."

"Sounds good to me," Cindy said, setting a big paper bag on the counter.

Tad looked at the UNC grad. She'd just come from a run to Audrey's Bakery and Café down the street. "How are we doing with the classifieds?"

Cindy shrugged off her rain slicker, hung it on a hook by the door and returned to lift containers of milk, café lattes, a variety of sandwiches and freshly baked banana-nut muffins from the bag.

"I wanted to talk to you about that. I think we could do better if we lowered the cost of the ads by at least ten percent and started an aggressive campaign to get people to advertise using copy like this." As everyone picked up their snack orders, Cindy dashed to the ad counter. She returned swiftly, handing Tad and Abby two cartoon ads urging people to buy space in the newspaper.

"These are cute," Abby said.

"Definitely eye-catching," Tad agreed, as he took the top off his café latte. He sat back in his chair. "How big did you want to make the ads?"

Cindy regarded him hopefully. "Don't shoot me, but half a page at the beginning and end of each advertising section. I also thought we could put copies of the ads up on bulletin boards around town."

"Okay. Give it a try," Tad said with a smile, just as a rain-drenched Sadie burst through the door.

Tad had only to look at his aunt to know something was up. "What's happened?" He got immediately to his feet.

Sadie clapped a hand over her heart. "Buster ran away!"

"What?" Abby and Tad both rushed to the older woman's side.

Sadie removed her dripping rain hat and reported breathlessly, "I went home for lunch to walk him— you know how he hates to go out in the rain—and he wasn't there. I looked everywhere."

"Meaning what?" Abby asked.

"He went out his doggie door and dug a hole beneath the fence."

"Buster?" Tad asked, amazed. He had never known Aunt Sadie's mournful-looking bassett hound to do anything anywhere near that energetic or mischievous.

"I know." A red-faced Sadie threw up her hands. "I couldn't believe it, either." She began to tear up. "Tad, I don't know what I'm going to do…"

"Sit tight, Aunt Sadie." Tad enveloped his diminutive aunt in a hug. "He probably hasn't gone far. I'll find him."

"I'll help."

Tad looked at Abby. She knew exactly what he was going to say. "I'm pregnant, not water soluble. Besides, it'll do me good to get out of the office. You can drive and I'll look out the window."

"Bless you both," Sadie said, dabbing at her eyes.

"They'll find him, Sadie," Cindy said, patting her arm.

Tad and Abby grabbed their raincoats and took off. He carried the umbrella as they hurried out to the Jeep. Tad shook his head. "What a day to run away."

"The question is why," Abby said as she climbed into the passenger side. "Buster hates rain."

They found out soon enough—almost a mile away. Buster had a girlfriend. A cute little cocker spaniel. The two were cuddling beneath the front porch. They were also covered with mud and wet as could be. Abby and Tad groaned in unison as they contemplated how best to remove the lovesick canines.

"This ought to be fun," Abby said.

"Who lives here, anyway?" Tad asked.

"I don't know." Abby bit her lip. "We'd better ring the bell."

Unfortunately there was no answer at the door.

A neighbor, pulling into the driveway next door, stopped to roll down her car window. She cupped a hand around her mouth and shouted to be heard over the rain and her car.

"Problem?" the neighbor shouted, nodding at the two dogs, who looked very unwilling to come out from the bed they'd made under the front porch.

Tad nodded.

''Unfortunately Raymond's not home. He works at the paper during the day.''

''WELL, THE GOOD NEWS is,'' Tad told Aunt Sadie via cell phone from the front porch, ''we found Buster.'' Briefly he went on to explain. ''The bad news is I think it's going to take both you and Raymond to coax the dogs out from under there.''

Short minutes later Sadie and Raymond arrived. ''Belle's in heat,'' Raymond told Abby and Tad.

''Oh, dear,'' Abby murmured.

''And Buster can still be a papa,'' Sadie explained.

''Make that double dear,'' Abby—who'd never more acutely appreciated the miracle of life than she did since she'd been pregnant herself—teased. Wouldn't it be fun, she thought, if Belle and Buster had puppies?

''The question is, how did they find each other?'' Tad knelt down in the mud and helped pull a mud-caked Buster out. ''They weren't exactly living on the same block.''

Sadie and Raymond exchanged looks and colored deeply.

''Okay,'' Tad prodded, ''what am I missing here?''

''They've, uh, met before,'' Sadie told Tad and Abby reluctantly.

''We got them together,'' Raymond explained a little less self-consciously. ''Took them both to the park last week just before Belle went into heat.''

Sadie's color deepened even more. ''We just never thought they'd try to get together on their own!'' she exclaimed.

''A little romance going on here, hmm?'' Tad asked as he wrapped a drenched and muddy Buster in the towel Raymond provided and prepared to carry the mournful-looking bassett hound to his Jeep.

And not with just the lovesick pups, Abby thought as she studied the heightened color in both Sadie and Raymond's faces. She'd thought they were getting a little chummy at the newspaper! How nice for Tad's aunt. Maybe, Abby thought optimistically, Raymond would be the one for Sadie, and vice versa. "Well, the puppies—if there are any—will certainly be unique," she said cheerfully. "I wonder what they'll look like, given they'll be a bassett hound-cocker spaniel mix."

In unison everyone imagined it. And everyone groaned.

"I WAS GOING to ask you how things were going," Yvonne said from the doorway of the *Blossom Weekly News* an hour later. "But maybe this isn't the time."

Abby checked the impulse to hug her old friend and let a grin suffice, instead. She waved a hand down the length of her, then cast a look at her husband, who looked just as bad, if not worse. "We're a little muddy, huh?"

"And then some." Yvonne took off her trendy black silk raincoat and hung it up "What happened. Did you get caught in a mud slide?"

"My aunt's dog was lost. So we tracked him down..." Tad began.

"And then had to coax him in out of the rain and mud and give him a bath for Sadie," Abby explained.

"Which Buster absolutely did not appreciate," Tad continued.

"Finishing each other's sentences. I like that," Yvonne teased.

"What brings you to Blossom?" Abby asked, ignoring Yvonne's comment.

"I was en route home from a job interview in California and thought, what the heck, why not take a little detour and see how you were doing? That was, of course, before I knew it was raining here. Sheesh." Yvonne shook the dampness out of her coiffed flame red hair.

Abby smiled at her friend. "August is hurricane season around here. Even this far inland, we get some ferocious storms off the coast."

Tad looked at Yvonne and said, "Abby and I were about to close up here, go home and get cleaned up, then fix some dinner. Want to join us?"

"Actually," Yvonne said, "I'm looking for a place to spend the night first. Any recommendations?"

Abby looked at Tad and knew they were in sync. "Just one. With us," Abby said. "'Cause, girlfriend, I've really missed you."

Yvonne's eyes glittered warmly. "Ditto."

An hour later Abby had showered, put on a pair of maternity jeans and a long tunic top and gone down to the kitchen where Yvonne was seated, chatting away with a still-muddy Tad. He looked at Abby. "My turn?"

She nodded, aware of how easy and comfortable they'd become with each other, how very much a couple. It went a lot deeper than just finishing each other's sentences or making love. "Any thoughts on dinner?"

"Well—" Tad took a deep breath and looked out at the rain still coming down in sheets "—I don't think we should use the barbecue."

Abby rolled her eyes. "Very funny."

"You ladies decide," Tad said affably. "When I come back down, let me know what I can do."

As soon as he was out of earshot, Yvonne asked, "Can he cook?"

"You mean something besides beans and franks out of a can?" Abby said. "No. But he's great at pitching in with the dishes."

Yvonne studied her. "I can't believe you. You look so…"

"Pregnant?" Abby patted her belly.

"Domestic." Yvonne smiled.

"So how are the job interviews going?" Abby asked, changing the subject smoothly.

Yvonne made a face. "So-so. This was my third interview, but sad to say I don't think it's a good match. Plus, I'd much rather continue to live in New York than have to move across the country. So… onward and upward."

"How are you doing financially?"

Yvonne sighed and toyed with the glass of wine Tad had poured for her. "Not bad. The main thing is the lack of work. It's driving me a little batty." At age forty-two and with a history of being married to her career, Yvonne would be lost, Abby knew, without an office to go to every day.

"Have you been able to pick up any freelance assignments?" Abby asked.

Yvonne sighed. "Not enough to keep me busy more than a day or so every couple of weeks. It's a tight job market out there. I think there are far too many people like me who've been either downsized or merger-ed right out of a job they love."

"Then you've come to the right place," Tad said from the doorway. He'd changed into a clean pair of khaki pants and a loose knit shirt. His black hair was still wet and scented with shampoo, his closely shaven jaw with aftershave. He walked closer. "Because Abby and I have been talking about expanding the *Blossom Weekly News*."

"You're kidding, right?" Yvonne plastered a hand across her heart. "Me? Work at a small-town paper?"

Undaunted by Yvonne's not-in-this-lifetime look, Tad grinned. "That's what Abby said." He turned a chair around and straddled it. "Now she's almost busier than I am trying to turn the paper around." His expression sobered. "I'm familiar with your work." He ticked off several series Yvonne had helmed, surprising both Abby and Yvonne with the depth of his knowledge and admiration for her work. "We could use your expertise as a features editor. Think of it this way. It won't pay much, but it'll be an interesting whimsical addition to your résumé while you're waiting for the perfect job to come along."

Yvonne paused, intrigued by Tad's pitch despite herself. "I admit, after looking at how few feature articles there are in the samples of the paper Abby mailed me, that I'm tempted to show you how things should be done in that area. But alas, I have no place to stay."

Tad shrugged his broad shoulders and rested his chin on his fist. "We've got plenty of room."

"It would be nice, having my old friend around," Abby added persuasively.

"All right," Yvonne answered, no match for Abby and Tad's combined argument. She smiled, promising, "I'll hang around for a day or two and advise you— in exchange for the room and board and whatever token salary you can afford to pay. Just understand that if I get a decent job offer or another interview, I'll be out of here, pronto.''

RAIN WAS STILL POUNDING on the eaves when Abby and Tad retired to their bedroom later that evening. The sound was cozy and welcoming. Tad couldn't wait to climb into bed and snuggle with his wife.

As he stripped down to his boxers, Tad told Abby honestly, ''I invited Yvonne to stay with us, because I figured you might want the company of an old friend while you're making new friends.'' He climbed into bed beside her, switched off the light and rolled to face her. ''Was I wrong?''

''No.'' Abby turned toward him, and propped herself up on her elbow. ''You weren't wrong,'' she said softly, reaching out to caress the warm solidness of his chest. ''I've missed Yvonne and all my old friends at the magazine. But life here is exciting, too,'' she teased. ''I mean, who can beat crawling beneath a porch in the rain and mud to pull out two lovesick pups?''

Tad linked hands with her, then brought her hand to his mouth and pressed a kiss into her palm. ''That was pretty funny, wasn't it?''

Abby grinned, loving the coziness of the mattress beneath her and the hard male body cuddled next to hers. ''For the record, you looked really cute with a smudge of mud across the bridge of your nose.''

''Yeah, well,'' Tad teased right back, kissing her cheek as he curled his arms around her, ''you had some in your hair.''

''And you,'' Abby said, moving even closer, tenderly caressing the underside of his jaw, ''had some right here.''

Her fingers playing across his skin were more than he could bear. He tightened his arms around her and trapped her against him until she could feel the hard ridge of his arousal pressing her thighs. "You're very beautiful. You know that, don't you?" he said huskily, looking deep into her eyes.

Beneath the thin fabric of her lacy gown, her nipples had tightened into aching buds of arousal. "I feel beautiful when I'm with you," she confessed breathlessly, her heart filled with the wonder and the magic they'd found—and would always find—in their love-making.

His eyes held hers with the promise of limitless nights to come. And then he kissed her until her breath came in quick shallow spurts and he was taking off her gown, rubbing the tender crests with his thumbs and stroking her dewy softness, moving up, in. She surrendered against him helplessly, with a low urgent moan. "Tad..."

"I know." Tad smiled with thoroughly male satisfaction as she pulled off his boxers, rapaciously explored the hot hard length of him, then sat astride him and lovingly drew him inside. The gliding sensation of wet hot silk was more than he could bear. "Abby," he murmured between kisses. "What you're doing to me—"

He groaned again as she slipped free, replaced her body with the softness of her lips and the light gliding touch of her tongue.

He urged her up and over him. "Now," she whispered.

"Now," he said as her breasts brushed his chest.

He plunged inside her, kissing even as they touched and took. Together they learned anew what it was like to be with someone heart and soul. They learned what it was like to need. And take. And give. Until at last their control faltered and they soared higher than either of them ever thought they could go. When the inevitable climax came, they shuddered and clung, appreciating the moment for the wonderful precious tempestuous time it was.

Oh, Abby thought, as their pulses returned to normal and they continued to nestle together intimately, how she needed this, needed him. It might be foolish of her, but she had never felt so loved or cherished, and she didn't want it ever to end.

"I CAN'T BELIEVE it's still raining," Abby said, long moments later on a deeply contented sigh. She was lying on her side, her head on his chest, one leg thrown over his, her knee nestled between his thighs.

Tad wrapped his arms around her, aware if he moved to the left even two more inches they'd both end up sprawled ignominiously on the floor. Knowing he had never felt happier than he did at that moment, he kissed the top of Abby's head. "I can't believe the two of us can actually fit in this bed."

Abby giggled and Tad thought it was the most glorious sound.

Lifting her head, she nodded at his feet, which were hanging off the end of the bed by a good six inches. "It's made for midgets, isn't it?"

"Let's put it this way," Tad drawled, aware he'd had more backaches in the weeks they'd been sharing the bed than he had in his entire life. "It was definitely not designed for someone my size."

Her expression concerned, Abby started to get up. "I know I'm, uh, growing." She indicated the gentle slope of her belly. "So if you want me to get up and sleep downstairs on the sofa to give you more room—"

Tad pulled her back down. "Not on your life. You're sleeping with me, woman, right up to the very moment you run off to the hospital to deliver. So what if my feet hang off the end of the bed?"

Abby chuckled, knowing firsthand how much he liked to cuddle and kiss. She tucked her face into the curve between his shoulder and neck. The warmth of her breath caressed his bare skin. "I've already talked to Donna about incorporating a king-size bed in the redecoration of this room. Unfortunately it'll be another month before we get to it."

Wrapping her arms around him, Abby snuggled closer. Then she caressed his chest with long soothing strokes and finally gave him a leisurely kiss that sent fire sizzling through his veins. "So until then—" she paused and looked deeply into his eyes, letting him know in a glance the many ways she knew they could pass the time spent not sleeping "—we'll just have to grin and bear it."

"I think I can handle that," Tad murmured playfully. He drew her to him and set about making her his all over again. "That," he said, as he bent to kiss the enticing curves of her breasts, "and a whole lot more."

THE GROUP GATHERED around the conference table for the end-of-September staff meeting. These brainstorming sessions were a favorite of Tad's. Abby's, too.

Taking the opportunity to speak out, Cindy said with the ease of an old-timer, "And the reduced price of advertising and stepped-up promotion efforts have

tripled the number of ads we're running every week."
Tad knew she was doing a good job. The entire staff
was.

"Not to mention the fact that circulation has dou-
bled," Raymond said as he poured more coffee for
Sadie, seated to his left. "We're now printing twice
the number of papers and we still sometimes run out."

"Yes, but we've had a few complaints, too." Sadie
frowned as she lifted her coffee cup to her lips. "Some
readers feel there is too much hard news in the editions. And not enough on ice-cream socials."

"But people like reading the national and state
news, too," Sonny piped up, not afraid to make his
case, either. "In particular, we're getting a lot of com-
pliments on Tad's editorials.

"And it goes without saying Abby's home-and-
garden features—especially her series on the improvement of the white elephant—are a big hit."

"Even with all that, we're still struggling financially," Tad told the group. As much as he'd like to
give them all huge raises, it wasn't feasible yet. It was
a stretch to keep paying Yvonne's wages, and those
were but a fraction of what she would command in
the magazine world.

"But we're definitely in a lot better shape than last
month," Abby said cheerfully.

Tad grinned at the group. "Thanks in no small part
to all of you and the newest recruit." Tad gestured at
Yvonne.

Everyone nodded. "The personal profiles on local
businessmen are a big hit," Sadie acknowledged.

"Don't look at me," Yvonne said. "Sonny's the
one who's been writing them."

Sonny beamed under the praise. "Yvonne helped me shape the material."

"It's always a pleasure to work with talented professionals," Yvonne said.

Everyone grinned. "And now that we've given ourselves a much-deserved pat on the back for everything we've done right—and that's been a lot—we need to address the complaints we've had about the reduced local news," Tad said.

"I have an idea how to fix that," Abby said.

Tad looked at his wife. More and more they were becoming partners in every aspect of their life. To the point he hoped Abby would one day want to give up her search for another magazine job and stay on at the paper permanently. "I'm all for having a happy medium," Tad told Abby honestly, "but I don't want to go back to the gossipy self-congratulatory tone of the original weekly news." That would definitely be a step in the wrong direction.

"Why don't we start a new section of the paper called, say, About Town," Abby suggested. "It'll be for all social events. We'll invite people to submit any personal news and photos they'd like to share with their neighbors."

"That's a good way to get subscribers up," Raymond said.

Beside him, Sadie nodded, putting in her two bits. "People like to read about themselves and see their photos in the paper."

Sadie and Raymond exchanged looks again.

"Did I imagine that?" Abby asked after the staff meeting had concluded and everyone had gone home. She sat on the edge of Tad's desk, crossed her legs at the knee and rested her hand on the swell of her tummy. "Or were Sadie and Raymond looking pretty cozy?"

"They were pretty cozy. You want to know what else?" Tad hooked his hands around her waist and shifted her onto his lap.

Abby laced both her hands around his neck and nestled close. "What?"

"Sadie told me Buster is no longer depressed."

Abby smiled as she cast a look outside at the pretty September weather. "Neither is his owner." And neither was she. When she'd first come to Blossom, that day she'd learned she'd been let go from her magazine job, she'd worried that, still married or not, unexpectedly pregnant or not, gainfully employed or not, she would never truly be happy here. But all that was beginning to change. She could see having a future with Tad and their baby in Blossom. And she could imagine them being very much a part of each other's life in every way for the next twenty or more years while their child grew up, and that was a very comforting, very exciting thought.

"Aunt Sadie does look happy these days, doesn't she?"

"Very," Abby conceded, her thoughts turning all misty and romantic. "So does Raymond."

"Ready to go home?"

Abby made a low affirmative sound as she bent to kiss him. He helped her to her feet. As they left the building, she fell into step beside him and linked hands with him. "I have a surprise for you."

Tad unlocked the passenger side of the Jeep and helped her in. His blue eyes shone with excitement as he assisted her with her seat belt. "What kind of surprise?" he asked.

"You'll see," Abby promised mysteriously, glad Yvonne had agreed to cooperate with her on this.

Tad bugged her all the way home. "One hint."

Abby laughed and folded her arms. "No way."

"Please."

"Oh, all right." Abby rolled her eyes, her excitement building. "Since you put it that way. Yvonne is staying with Cindy tonight."

"She is," Tad replied slowly.

"Yep. Yvonne's going to tell her all about life in New York City. And they're doing the whole female-bonding thing—facials, manicures, hairstyling, the works."

Tad parked in the drive. Resting his arm on the seat behind her head, he said, "Meaning we have the whole house to ourselves."

"Mm-hmm." At least she hoped they did, Abby thought, if Donna had finished and gotten out of there.

"So the surprise is a candlelight dinner for two?" Tad asked after he circled around to help Abby out of the truck.

"Not exactly."

Tad opened the front door. "Then what?" he demanded as Abby shut the door behind them and took him by the hand.

"You'll see." She led him up the staircase.

Tad winked at her lasciviously. "I think I could get used to this."

"Hush."

"Don't tell me you actually unpacked all your stuff," he teased.

"Not exactly." She had, however, arranged for

most of her boxed possessions to be moved to the attic for storage. And that was a start.

"Then—" Tad came to a dead halt in the door to the master bedroom. For once, Abby thought, he was momentarily speechless.

Chapter Nine

"Do you like it?"

"Like it?" Tad echoed, stunned as he moved slowly into the master bedroom. The narrow double bed, mismatched furniture, stacks of books and papers and boxes that had been there since Abby had moved in had all been removed. The walls had been painted a soothing sage green, and a slightly darker sage carpet had been laid. The king-size sleigh bed was covered with a thick feather ticking for extra softness, there were plenty of pillows, and the bed ensemble was a masculine green, burgundy and white plaid. The matching mirrored dresser and cherry wardrobe allowed plenty of storage space for their clothes and possessions, while two deep upholstered chairs, end table and reading lamp provided a cozy sitting area.

Tad shook his head in open admiration. "It's magnificent."

Abby smiled and released an enormous sigh of relief. "I was hoping you'd think so." She'd spent an enormous amount of time secretly trying to please him with the decor.

Tad toured the bedroom, then kicked off his shoes and sat down on the edge of the bed. Grinning, he lay back on the pillows and folded his hands behind his head. "Now this is comfy," he said, sighing appreciably. "Except—" he turned on his side and frowned "—have you actually stretched out on this bed?"

Abby swallowed, wondering what in the world could be wrong. "Well, no…"

Tad shrugged. "Maybe it's just me, then."

Abby glided closer. "If there's something wrong with it, you need to tell me."

Tad studied her. "You try your side and tell me what you think," he said finally.

Abby kicked off her shoes, too. She backed onto the mattress and stretched out on the feather ticking. It felt like sinking into a huge down pillow. It was all she could do not to groan out loud in pure ecstasy. The enveloping softness was exactly the cure for the aches and pains of pregnancy, she thought, not to mention pure sensual comfort.

"Feel anything amiss?" Tad asked.

Abby turned toward him slightly and shook her head. "But you still do, don't you?" she observed, wondering what it could be. A flaw in the feather ticking, perhaps?

"Maybe it's just over here." Tad scooted toward the far edge on his side. "You lie here—" he pointed to the place where he'd been "—and tell me what you think."

He gallantly took her hand to assist her, and Abby scooted over to where he directed. "Now fold your hands behind your head," he said. He waited. "Do you feel it?"

Abby shook her head. Never had she been more aware of the brisk tantalizing fragrance of his after-shave. "I'm quite comfortable."

"Hmm." Tad's frown deepened. "Maybe if you close your eyes and concentrate."

"Okay." Abby closed her eyes.

"Now do you feel it?" Tad's voice was whisper soft.

All I feel, Abby thought, both amused and perplexed, *is a mounting desire for you.* But then, that was nothing new. Whenever she was with him like this, whenever they were in bed together, longing swept through her with disabling force. No matter how tired they were, no matter how uncertain their future, they couldn't seem to get through a night without reaching for each other at least once. And, Abby admitted silently to herself, she wanted it to stay that way. Physical passion might not last a lifetime, but while it was here, she intended to thoroughly enjoy every last nuance of it. And to that end, she thought, as she opened her eyes, reached up and took hold of Tad's tie... "The ticking is really comfortable," she murmured.

"As comfortable as this?" Tad asked softly, roguish amusement sparkling in his blue eyes as he feathered kisses down the side of her face. "'Cause when I lie here, Abby, knowing you've gone to all this trouble to make our marriage bed so very special, I've got to tell you. I feel—" he took her hand and lowered it to the most intimate part of him, then kissed her with a deep possessiveness that took her breath away "—quite a lot of this."

Abby had never in her life experienced such sweet invigorating kisses. Knowing he was her husband, knowing they were expecting a baby, added an extra sweetness to their love play. Still kissing him voraciously, she took off his tie, unbuttoned his shirt, unzipped his jeans. She'd never been the aggressor, but as she helped him shed his clothes and took him in hand, it seemed natural, right. Moving down his body, her hair slipping silkily over his skin, she adored him with lips and hands. Beneath the need to love him was the need to make him hers, in the same way he'd laid claim to her, body and soul, so many times.

She shifted herself higher, ready for a more intimate union. "Whoa there. You're getting ahead of me." He gasped, struggling for control. Gently he turned her onto her back. "Way ahead of me."

"Tad—"

"Let me love you," he said softly, already unbuttoning the front of her short stylish maternity dress. "Let me love you the way you were meant to be loved." His warm breath touched the soft vulnerable skin of her neck, then his lips followed. *Oh, Tad,* Abby thought tremulously as he began to kiss her again. *I love you. I love you so much.*

He deepened the kiss and pulled her close, divested her of her clothes and then loved her as only he could love her until her back arched off the bed and she was trembling, shuddering, begging for release. Bracing his weight fully on either side of her, he settled over her, the tip of his manhood pressing against her delicate folds.

Abby moved to receive him and he slowly, surely, surged upward, then inside her. Gently, gently, he rocked back and forth, until sensations hammered inside her and she strained against him, her body undulating, until she was sure she couldn't bear any more of this, until she was sure they had to find fulfillment. And it was then that he surged against her, wanting her and possessing her until every inch of her wanted every part of him.

Afterward they were, as always, loath to part. Replete and drowsy, Abby snuggled against him in blissful ecstasy.

"What are you thinking?" he asked, running his fingers through her hair.

Abby smiled and lovingly caressed the muscled hair-whorled skin on his chest. "That you are, without doubt, the sexiest most fun guy I've ever met." She propped her chin on her fist and looked up at him, her eyes sparkling. "You really had me going there for a minute, you know."

Tad grinned. "I know." He reached for her hand and pressed a kiss into the palm. "Couldn't resist. You looked so serious, and I wanted to make love to you so much."

Abby listened to the steady drumming of his heart and swept her hand down her body self-consciously. "Even with me beginning to give the term 'pear-shaped' new meaning?" she said playfully. Suddenly, as long as they were being honest, she needed to know. Was this all going to end?

Tad's eyes abruptly turned serious. "This is my baby you're carrying, Abby," he told her in an unmistakably ardent, unmistakably possessive voice. "A part of me and a part of you." He shifted lower and kissed her tummy lingeringly before returning to her lips. All the tenderness and passion he felt for her was in his eyes. "There's no greater turn-on than that."

Emotions soaring, he kissed her again. Still reveling at the happy way things were evolving, Abby kissed him back. And that was the last either of them said— or needed to say—for a very long time.

ON THE WAY to Abby's doctor appointment the next morning, Tad and Abby passed Joe Don Jerome's car dealership. Although the dealership did not open for business for another half an hour, at the side of the building there was most definitely a ruckus going on between Ernest Lee Scruggs, the chief mechanic, and Joe Don himself. Both were standing next to Ernest Lee's new pickup. Ernest Lee was gesturing angrily and pointing to the engine beneath the raised hood of his truck. "I wonder what that's about," Tad remarked as they paused at the traffic light.

"I don't know," Abby murmured as she watched Ernest Lee point out something in the engine. "He sure doesn't look happy." She glanced at Tad curiously. "Didn't you tell me he'd been having a lot of car trouble lately?"

"Mm-hmm. He's broken down a number of times, which is odd, because it's a brand-new truck, and he bought it from Joe Don."

The light changed. Abby turned and saw Ernest Lee stomp off in one direction and Joe Don another. "Well, whatever that was about, they don't appear to have resolved it."

"That's not surprising," Tad said firmly, "since Joe Don doesn't appear to be out for anyone but himself."

Abby cast a curious look at Tad. "Have you had any more complaints about Joe Don's dealership?"

"Nothing concrete," Tad admitted as he directed his attention to the road. "But every time you mention Joe Don's name to someone who's bought a car there—I don't know…" Tad frowned and shook his head. "It's like they want to tell you something and can't."

Abby reached over and squeezed Tad's thigh reassuringly. "Eventually someone will have to trust you enough to tell you what's going on."

"That may be. But it could take a long time. I've been here just a few months. People don't yet have all that much confidence I'm even going to stay. Whereas the Three Stooges have been here, firmly in control, for years."

"Just don't give up," Abby encouraged him seriously. "Sooner or later someone's bound to realize what a good guy you are and trust you enough to confide in you."

As they approached the doctor's office parking lot, Tad reached over and squeezed her hand. "Thanks for asking me to tag along," he said.

Abby was uncomfortably aware she hadn't asked Tad to go with her the first time she'd seen Dr. Ellison, the obstetrician Doc Harlan had recommended. "I'm sorry I didn't ask you the last time."

"That's okay. I know you're used to taking care of health concerns yourself, and that most women don't bring their husbands along for every visit. I'm just glad you asked me this time." Tad paused, looking down at her tummy, then back at her face. "So, I'm really going to hear our baby's heartbeat?"

Abby nodded. She wanted to share this with Tad and so much else. "Yep."

Tad shook his head. "Incredible," he said softly.

Abby's spirits rose even higher; she'd thought so, too. She started to undo her seat belt, then stopped, did a double take and gasped.

Tad's reaction was immediate. "What is it? Are you hurting? Is something wrong?"

Abby gasped again, barely able to believe. Suddenly her pregnancy was more real to her than ever. Face white, she turned to her husband and placed his hand squarely on her tummy. "Tad!" she whispered, stunned. "The baby just moved."

HIS HEART POUNDING, Tad sat with his hand on Abby's tummy. He waited. And waited. To no avail. Nothing.

Finally Abby sighed. She looked every bit as disappointed as he felt. "We're going to have to go in, or I'll be late for my appointment."

"Right." Tad got out of the Jeep.

"I'm sure the baby will kick again soon," Abby said as he helped her out. "I should have gotten your hand over here sooner. I was just so stunned."

Tad grinned down at her, looking every bit the proud papa. "That's the first time?"

Abby nodded. "A couple of times I thought maybe the baby might have kicked, just a little, but I wasn't sure. This time I was sure." She threw back her head and laughed. "It felt like I had a soccer player inside my tummy."

Tad grinned, enjoying the glorious autumn day as much as she was. They linked arms and headed for the building entrance. "So what do you think?" he asked. "Boy or girl?"

"I don't know." Abby snuggled into the warm protective curve of his arm. Tipping her head back, she glanced up at him. "Would it matter to you?"

Tad shook his head. "Just as long as the baby's healthy. That's all that matters."

Abby agreed. She waited while Tad held the door for her. "I used to hear people say that. I never knew what they meant. Now it…well, it makes sense."

"To me, too."

Tad may have missed out on the first kick, but he heard the baby's heartbeat loud and clear on the Doppler, a hand-held ultrasound device Dr. Ellison held against Abby's stomach to amplify the sound.

Ta-dum, ta-dum, ta-dum. The baby's heartbeat filled the examining room, the sound remarkably strong and steady. As their eyes met, Abby's filled with tears, and she thought, but couldn't be sure, she saw an answering sheen in Tad's. One thing was certain, she thought buoyantly. There was no disguising either's happiness.

"Well, everything seems to be in order," Dr. Ellison said after he'd palpated Abby's abdomen, discussed with her how she'd been feeling and checked the chart. "Your weight gain is right on target. Your blood pressure and urine check out fine. Call me if there are any problems. Otherwise, I'll see you again in a month."

The doctor slipped out of the room. Abby started to get up from the examining table. Then she felt it again. Rather than risk Tad losing out, she lifted her blouse with one hand, grabbed his hand with the other and pressed it to her stomach. Like the tapping of fingers on a tabletop, the rapid fluttering moved across the inside of her tummy. "That?" Tad said joyously. "That's it?"

The baby flutter-kicked again. "That's it," Abby said.

All the love he felt for her in his eyes, Tad bent down to kiss her lips. "Incredible," he whispered. "Just incredible."

"YOU TWO COULD BE an ad for happy parents," the receptionist said as she set up Abby's next appointment.

Abby knew it was true. The baby was bringing them together, closer and faster than she'd ever thought possible.

"I am pretty excited," Tad told Abby as they left the doctor's office and climbed into his Jeep.

"Me, too," Abby said. She rested her hand on her tummy and leaned her head against the seat back. "Now that I can feel the baby moving, it's beginning to seem so-o-o real."

Tad cast her a shy glance. "I know."

Abby watched him fit the key in the ignition. "At first it was…well, I knew I was pregnant, but I didn't feel any different. I didn't *feel* pregnant."

In no hurry to start the engine, Tad turned to her. "And now you do."

Abby nodded as a car pulled up beside them and a young couple got out. "Oh, yes," Abby told Tad softly. As she looked into his eyes, she knew he was going to make a great dad.

He caught her hand and kissed it. "I feel it, too."

Abby's heart soared at the revelation. "Probably not as much as me."

"Probably not, you're right." Tad cupped her face in his hands, caressed it gently. "But I absolutely feel something," he told her as he lowered his mouth to hers and kissed her with a tenderness that was so real, so potent, it was nearly enough to make her cry. He drew back slightly. "I feel love."

Abby gulped, aware she'd never felt such deep all-encompassing emotion or wanted anyone in her life so much. "I feel it, too," she admitted.

Tad regarded her with a thoroughly male satisfaction. And an intimate knowledge of her that was daunting. "This whole family thing is going to work out, Abby," he said firmly, accurately reading the fears that always seemed to lurk just beneath her outward confidence. "We're going to make it work," he promised, kissing her again.

Were they? Abby wished she could believe that even as she kissed Tad back with all her heart and soul. But inwardly she was not as sure that the love they felt for the baby they were expecting was enough to hold their marriage together over the long haul. Her parents had been head over heels in love plenty of times and yet never once had any of their marriages succeeded in the end, she remembered shakily.

Tad slowly lifted his mouth from hers. "This baby is a part of both of us and a testament to our love that no one will ever be able to take away," he said, reluctantly releasing her.

Abby nodded, steeling herself for the worst even as she hoped for the best. No matter what happened, she told herself sternly, she would never forget this time in her life. With the baby, with Tad. She just had to make the most of it while she could, for as long as she could.

Tad grinned and started the Jeep. "Now we just have to figure out a name."

Abby groaned, able to imagine what a task that would be, given the fact that she'd never known a couple who had managed it easily yet. "I've always been partial to Holly."

Tad made a face. "We are not naming our child after a shrub," he stated.

Abby settled more comfortably into her seat. "What would you pick, then?"

He paused, his expression turning very serious. "Corelle, after our first set of dishes."

Abby scowled at him playfully. She should have known he'd horse around. "Be serious."

Tad thought a moment. "Crystal, after our glasses?"

Abby rolled her eyes, then said with utmost gravity, "How about Robin, after the first bird we spotted in our yard?"

Tad's lips curved sexily. "Blossom, after the place where we live."

Abby chuckled. "On to the boys names. How about Lyon?"

Tad shook his head. "Too ferocious."

Good point. Abby studied his profile. "Okay, your turn."

"Boris."

Abby snorted. "Not unless he has a sister named Natasha."

Tad grinned again and at the next traffic stop darted her a look that was even sexier than the last. "I could work on a sister," he allowed.

Abby felt herself tingle from head to toe. "I'll bet you could," she drawled, enjoying the easy banter.

"Maybe we could even start practicing for the next big event now." Tad shot her an openly lascivious look. "I'm free after work. How about you?"

Abby shook her head with mock reproach. "You're incorrigible."

"What can I say?" Tad grinned. He parked in front of the closest storefront and pulled her close. "You inspire me."

"WHAT DO YOU THINK about getting a second car?" Tad asked as they passed Joe Don's dealership for the second time that morning.

"Now?" Abby asked, surprised.

Tad shrugged. "Well, we've been sharing one, and I know there've been times when it's been a pain."

Abby thought about the way the paper had been struggling, and now, with the baby on the way, Tad's finances were probably stretched to the limits, as were hers. "I don't mind walking to work or home. It's only five blocks."

Tad nodded thoughtfully. "True," he said, not looking as happy with her response as she would have expected.

"Besides—" Abby forced herself to be practical even though it was the last thing she felt like doing at the moment "—if I go back to New York to work at a magazine there, I won't need it."

The moment the words were out Abby could have shot herself. Hadn't they more or less agreed they'd just take it one day at a time until after the baby was born? But to his credit, Tad's expression remained unreadable. "True," he said again.

Abby gulped, wished she could erase her faux pas and rushed on, "It wouldn't be cost-effective to buy one only to have to dump it several months later. And financially it's such a big purchase, and we're still strapped for obvious reasons and—"

"You wouldn't mind me looking into it, anyway, would you?" Tad interrupted.

Because he was already in the process of making a U-turn, Abby couldn't see into his eyes. "What are you up to?"

"You'll see. Just play along." Tad turned the Jeep into a parking space in front of Audrey's Bakery and Café.

It was ten-thirty, and Ernest Lee Scruggs was sitting

at a table in the back, the classified ads and a notepad and pen in front of him. He was wearing his mechanic's uniform from Joe Don Jerome's dealership. Neither light blue shirt nor pants had a speck of grease or grime on them. His hands, too, were clean. Which could only mean one thing, Abby thought. He hadn't put in any work thus far today.

"Hey, Ernest Lee." Tad waved at the mechanic. He ordered two muffins, two juices and one coffee for him and led the way to Ernest Lee's table. "Mind if we talk to you a minute?" Tad said affably. Not waiting for a response, he pulled up a chair and sat down, then pulled up one for Abby, who, like Ernest Lee, was looking a little reluctant. "We've got a couple of questions," Tad continued. "See, Abby and I were just talking about buying a second car. The only problem is we can't afford a brand-new one. I'm a little leery of buying a used one 'cause there's no warranty. And if I pick it out on my own, it's almost a certainty we'll get stuck with a lemon. Not good, when you've got a wife with a baby on the way. So, I was thinking maybe you'd agree—for a fee of course—to take a look under the hood of any car I might want to buy."

Ernest Lee shrugged, looking perfectly willing to help. "Sure," he said.

Tad's brows knit together in a concerned manner. "Joe Don wouldn't mind you advising me on any car he's trying to sell off his lot?"

An angry look came into Ernest Lee's eyes. "You can get a better deal from one of the dealers in Asheville or Charlotte."

"Yeah, I know." Tad sighed. He leaned forward urgently. "The problem is financing. Things are a little tight for Abby and me right now." Tad reached over and patted Abby on the knee. "And since Joe Don has been known to help people who need a helping hand—"

Getting the drift of where this was all going, Abby interjected, "Not to mention it'd be a good way to mend fences with him." Abby looked at Ernest Lee with something akin to an apologetic glance. "You might have heard that Joe Don's been a little put out with us," she said.

Ernest Lee sighed. "Yeah, I know he pulled all his advertising from the paper in the summer."

"So you'll help us?" Tad pressed.

"Look, I—" Ernest Lee suddenly turned very red in the face, stared out the window, then turned back to them. "I'd like to help you folks out. Honestly I would." He crumpled his empty paper coffee cup in his hand. "But I wouldn't buy a used car here in Blossom."

"How about a new car or truck, then?" Tad said. "After all, you just bought one here."

"Yeah, and it's been nothing but trouble," Ernest Lee said darkly. He stood, pushing his chair back with a screech.

"Can't you do something?" Tad stood, too. "I mean, there's a lemon law in this state...."

Ernest Lee blew out a frustrated breath. "The dealer would have to agree the vehicle is a lemon."

"And Joe Don doesn't?"

Ernest Lee wheeled away from the two of them abruptly. "I've got to go."

"If I said something to upset you..." Tad rushed to apologize.

"It's not you," Ernest Lee said. He stalked out without a backward glance.

Audrey, who'd heard everything, came out from behind the counter. Proprietor of one of the most popular places in town, she knew just about everything that was going on. "He's upset because that new pickup he got isn't worth a plug nickel and Joe Don won't let him turn it back for another," she said.

"Why not?" Abby asked. After all, Ernest Lee worked for Joe Don. That ought to count for something.

Audrey shrugged. "'Cause I guess Joe Don doesn't agree it's a lemon. Heaven knows everyone who has the poor judgment to get a car there ends up having trouble with it," she said as she began to wipe down a few of the tables.

"Then why do they go there?" Abby asked.

Audrey sighed. "Because you can't beat the interest rates, the insurance and sticker price anywhere else in the state."

TAD DID HIS BEST to keep his feelings to himself, but the knowledge that Abby still wanted a magazine editor's job in New York bugged him repeatedly throughout the day. Part of him believed the life they were building together in Blossom ought to be enough, while another knew exactly what she yearned for, because there was a part of him that missed trotting around the globe for whatever story was currently breaking. There'd been an elusiveness to that kind of life that was appealing, if only because it'd been so darned easy to leave his problems behind him and forget all about them.

That was hard to do in Blossom, where everywhere he turned he was reminded of his yearning for Abby and the baby they were expecting. Where everywhere he turned he was reminded that, no matter how much he wanted her to stay with him, no matter how much he wanted to be what she needed and wanted, his best, just like back in Houston, might not be good enough. In fact, his best might be damn near disastrous.

Fortunately the work of getting out the next issue of the *Blossom Weekly News* kept them both busy from the time they hit the newspaper office until the time they returned, exhausted, to their half-redecorated home and fell into bed.

Still thinking how he might be able to make Abby love him as much as she loved the baby they were expecting, Tad fell asleep. Only to awake short hours later when Abby sat bolt upright in bed.

"Omigod!" she gasped, moaning and groaning and writhing sinuously as she attempted to extricate herself from the comforting warmth of him and the soothing feather ticking.

"What is it?" Tad cried as Abby flung the covers off her and stumbled, still moaning, from the bed.

"Don't touch me!" she shouted back as he followed her, the expression in her eyes as wild and confused as the state of her hair. "Omigod, omigod, omigod!" Abby's breath came out in a shuddering hiss as she did a strange one-legged dance around the bedroom in the moonlight.

"Are you hurt?" Tad bolted toward her. There was only one time in his life he'd ever felt anywhere near as helpless, he remembered, panicking, and that he did not want to think about.

Abby lowered her hands toward the floor, then lifted them toward the ceiling. "No, I'm dancing, you idiot," she pushed the words through her teeth.

Dancing. In the middle of the night. What she was doing looked more like an ancient tribal ritual to him.

Recalling Doc Harlan's advice to indulge his pregnant wife at all costs, Tad figured, what the heck. If she wouldn't tell him what she was doing or why, he'd just do it, too. Moaning and groaning in tandem to her wild sounds, he danced around with her in mirror image, stomping one leg on the floor repeatedly, writhing and moaning all the while.

Abby finally settled down, then she laughed until she cried, and he still had no idea what was going on as she sank onto the floor in a heap. He sank down beside her. "You want to tell me what's up with you?" he asked as she wiped away the tears of laughter flowing down her cheeks.

"I had a muscle cramp," she explained, when she could breathe again. "In my calf. It woke me up, and between you and the feather ticking and the covers, I was so tangled up I couldn't get out of bed. By the time I did, my calf muscle had practically rolled into a circle and the pain was excruciating. The only way to make it stop hurting is to straighten out the muscle, and the only way I've ever been able to do that is to put weight on it. The only trouble is, the process of putting weight on the calf muscle is excruciating, too, and until the cramp stops you can't really stand on that leg."

"Oh."

Abby peered at him curiously. "Don't tell me you've never had a cramp!" she said.

"Never." Tad shrugged. "Sorry."

Abby grinned and resumed rubbing her calf. "You really thought I was dancing?"

Tad grasped her leg and took over the rubbing for her. "Babe, I didn't know what to think," he drawled.

Tears of hilarity streamed down her face anew. When Abby could finally breathe again, she said, "That was so funny when you started dancing, too. You looked like some jungle tribesman, doing a dance around a fire."

Tad shrugged, tacitly admitting that was the look he'd been aiming for. "Imitation is the sincerest form of flattery, didn't you know?"

Abby rolled her eyes. "You're incorrigible."

"So you've said."

Silence fell between them, comfortable and affectionate. "Well," Tad said finally, "I'm awake. Wide awake."

"Me, too." Abby sighed, wondering just how long it was going to take them to get back to sleep.

Tad tucked her hand in his, lifted it to his lips, and kissed it gently. "Want to go downstairs and get some milk?"

Abby ignored the tingles. "I'll get it," she said. After all, he'd done so much for her.

Tad shook his head. "Stay right here. I'll bring it up." He returned with a tray of two glasses of milk and two pieces of chocolate cake Aunt Sadie had made for them.

Abby sighed. "We shouldn't be eating something that rich this time of night."

He waggled his eyebrows at her. "We shouldn't be doing a lot of things. That never stopped us before."

Abby laughed softly. Tad was so much fun. If he ever left her, she would miss him terribly. "That's true," she said ruefully as bittersweet melancholy overcame her.

"Hey now, you don't have to worry about your weight," Tad chided gallantly, misinterpreting the reason behind her swiftly shifting emotions. "You're right on track. The doctor said so. Besides, that dance you just did worked off a lot of calories. And I know a way to work off a few more."

"I know you do, sailor. But first things first..." Right now she had a mean craving for chocolate cake.

They sat back against the pillows and munched on their cake. "It's amazing, isn't it," Tad said, "how much our lives have changed since last April?"

Abby nodded. She sipped her milk and looked into his eyes. "To tell you the truth, as much as I wanted to have a child someday, I never really saw myself as a wife or a mom."

Tad's glance softened. "I never saw myself as a dad, either."

"But we're doing it, aren't we?" Abby beamed. "Becoming parents."

Tad nodded.

They fell into a thoughtful silence once more.

"It wasn't that I didn't want a home and family of my own," Abby said at last. "I did. I just thought it would never happen."

Again Tad nodded, understanding completely. "I know what you mean. Until you and I eloped I never even came close to marrying anyone."

"I know in the beginning it was just fireworks that brought us together. We really didn't know all that much about each other in Paris." And in some respects, Abby thought, knowing Tad still hadn't told her anything at all about his life in Houston, they still didn't.

"Now it's different," Tad said. "Now we're..."

"Friends," Abby finished.

"Great friends," Tad amended.

They forked up the last of their cake. "Do you think it's just the baby and the newspaper making us so close?" Abby asked.

"What do you mean?" Tad put his plate aside.

Abby shrugged. "We're sort of like two survivors of a shipwreck on a desert island," she said, suddenly feeling brave enough to face at least a few of her fears and voice them. "And that, in turn, sort of makes me wonder," she continued, carefully gauging his reaction. "When things return to normal, meaning the paper gets on solid ground and the baby is born and we get used to being parents and all that." Abby swallowed hard and forced herself to keep meeting his eyes and go on. "When things settle down again, do you think we'll feel less close or grow apart?" The way her parents always had in their various marriages.

"No. I don't. What we're building here is going to last a lifetime, Abby. And whatever happens we'll always be connected through our child." He turned off the light, helped her lie back against the pillows and then did the same. As had become their custom every night, they cuddled together in the darkness.

"Tad?" Abby asked eventually.

"Hmm?"

"One more thing." She smiled against his chest, loving his warmth and his strength. "I'm glad it's your baby I'm having."

"Me, too, Abby." Tad sighed contentedly and held her close. "Me, too."

Chapter Ten

"This is probably going to be the best tag sale we'll see for the rest of the year," Donna told Abby as they toured the barn full of antiques, secondhand furniture and all manner of knickknacks, decorator items and recreational gear.

Abby paused in front of a section of baby items. Each day she and Tad thought they couldn't possibly get any more excited about the birth of their baby. And each day they were proved wrong. "I'd love to buy a crib or a changing table, but Sadie made me promise to wait until after the baby shower."

"Well, we can go ahead and get the nursery carpet in and the stenciled border up." Donna paused before a gorgeous writing desk, checked the tag. "What do you think?"

Abby checked the tag. "I think it's way over budget."

"You're probably right." Donna moved on to the selection of paintings. "So how is Tad doing as a prospective papa?"

"Pretty good actually."

Donna smiled and shook her head. "I remember Ron's reaction to my first pregnancy. He had it all," she said, laughing. "Morning sickness, backaches, cravings, sleepless nights. Doc Harlan called it the most advanced case of the couvade syndrome he'd ever seen. Fortunately, by the time I had my second baby, Ron had relaxed enough to take it all in stride."

Abby paused in front of a his-and-hers bicycle set with a toddler seat strapped to the back of the man's bike. Abby immediately thought about sunny summer days, what it would be like to get on bikes with Tad and the baby and go for a ride around the neighborhood. "Tad hasn't evidenced anything like that," Abby said as she lifted the tag and saw the bikes were within her budget if she stretched.

"He probably will before all is said and done." Donna frowned as the cell phone she carried with her began to ring. "If you'll excuse me..." She walked a short distance away while Abby continued to look at the bikes. A minute later Donna returned, looking harried. "My youngest was just hurt at soccer practice. I've got to go. About the lamps and linen chest we picked out for the baby's room..."

"I'll make a bid on them and arrange for delivery."

"Thanks. See you later." Donna hurried off.

Abby went to find the cashier. Before the afternoon was out, she had purchased everything, including the bikes, which she'd had loaded into the back of the Jeep. Figuring she'd surprise Tad, she took them home and set them up in the middle of the living room, then decorated them with big red bows. She got out a stack of articles that still needed to be edited, then sat down to work on them and wait for her husband to show up.

He came home around dinnertime. "Abby?" he called as he walked through the door.

"In here," Abby called back.

Tad strode in, a smile on his face. His joy promptly faded as he took in the bikes, complete with baby seat. "What the hell is this?" he barked.

Abby blinked. He'd never berated her over anything she'd purchased before. She couldn't believe he was doing it now. It was so unlike him. She moved slowly to her feet. Head high, she said, "It's a present from me to you and the baby."

His face whitened. He stepped closer, unfairly using his height to force her to lean back to look up at him. "You should have asked," he said in a low disgruntled tone.

Abby swallowed and willed her heart not to pound. She didn't know what was going on here, but clearly something was. "That would have ruined the surprise."

Tad grimaced. "You're going to have to take them back."

"What?"

The muscles in his chest and shoulders flexed as he folded his arms. "We don't need bikes, Abby."

"Says who?" Abby loved to ride. Though she hadn't had much of a chance for years. But now that she lived in a small town, instead of the city, well, why the heck not?

"They'd just sit in the garage," Tad continued.

"So don't ride yours," Abby sputtered, no longer caring they were headed for an argument.

"Look," Tad growled as his eyes zeroed in on her, "I don't want them. Okay?" Giving her no chance to reply, he spun on his heel and stalked out of the house.

"DONNA WAS TELLING ME about husbands who have sympathetic symptoms, but this was ridiculous,"

Abby told Aunt Sadie tearfully half an hour later as she poured out her heart to Tad's aunt. "I mean, I've heard of mood swings, but…"

Unable to continue, Abby stared at the floor in front of her, where Buster lay on the floor next to a very pregnant Belle. His facial expression looked as mournful as ever, but the way the two dogs were cuddled said they were happy as could be.

"It wasn't a mood swing, dear," Sadie said, casting a glance into the kitchen where Raymond worked preparing dinner.

"Then what was it?" Abby asked, looking at the mingled concern and caution in Sadie's eyes and once again feeling like the odd man out.

"I can't—" Sadie stopped. Her eyes misted. "You're going to have to ask Tad," she said in a strangled tone.

Unfortunately Tad was not likely to tell her anything. And that hurt. She'd thought—hoped—they were becoming as close as she'd always thought a husband and wife should be. She leaned forward earnestly, determined to find out all she could from Sadie. "I did ask him, Sadie, but all he would say is that he doesn't want us to have bikes. He didn't tell me why it was such a sore subject. He just issued this edict and stomped out of the house like the biggest male chauvinist on earth. And you know Tad, Sadie. That's not like him. It's not like him at all!"

Sadie nodded. She didn't approve of her beloved nephew's behavior, but it didn't surprise her, either. "I agree. It sounds as if Tad was unreasonable and overemotional today."

"But?" Abby prodded, sensing there was more.

Sadie pressed her lips together stubbornly. "You still need to talk to him."

Nixing Sadie's offer of dinner, Abby went to the newspaper office. Everyone but Tad had left. He was sitting behind his computer working on the Web site he was creating for the newspaper. "I'm not good company tonight, Abby," he warned, his eyes focused firmly on the computer screen.

"Thanks to you, honeybunch," Abby drawled with provoking sweetness, "neither am I." Determined to clear the air between them once and for all, Abby moved a stack of papers and sat on the edge of his desk, facing him, so he had no choice but to hear her out. "I don't know what I did that was so wrong, but you had no right to treat me that way."

"I know," Tad said, guilt flashing across the features of his handsome face as he saved his material and switched off the computer with a decisive snap.

"I talked to Sadie—"

"Damn it." Tad vaulted from his desk chair and began to pace. "I told her I didn't want you to know about Houston."

Abby drew a breath and plunged on recklessly, "Sadie didn't tell me anything about Houston. But I sure wish someone would."

A silence fell that made Abby's heart thud all the harder. She continued to look at her husband steadily, knowing no matter how difficult it was, these things needed to be said, and said now. "If we're going to bring up a child together, Tad," she told him quietly, "we need to know these things about each other." *And we need to know them because we're married— so very married, in fact—that we may very well elect to stay married even after our baby's born. That is, if we can clear up some of these miscommunication problems before our son or daughter gets here.*

For a second Tad stood very still. With a sigh he turned to her. "I had a brother, Billy, who was two years younger than me." Tad swallowed hard and, a distant expression on his face, began to pace again. He paused to stare out the window at the swiftly descending darkness. "When we were kids we used to do everything together." A muscle working in his jaw, Tad turned back to her and said in a low rusty-sounding tone, "My parents always told me to look after him, and I did—" he jerked in a breath "—'cause I was the oldest. But I wasn't that great at it." Sorrow tinged his eyes. For a second Abby thought he wouldn't—couldn't—go on.

"I used to be impatient," Tad continued self-deprecatingly, "because he couldn't quite keep up with me." Another shadow passed over his eyes. He put his hand up and rubbed at them wearily.

"One day, when I was ten and Billy was eight, we got on our bikes and headed for the empty lot that we used as a baseball field." Tad swallowed and forced himself to continue. "It was just two blocks over on typical suburban streets. We'd ridden there plenty of times. It was no big deal."

Tad blinked rapidly as tears rose in his eyes and his chest tightened to the point he could barely breathe. "I wanted to take the lead so I rode on ahead. I knew better," Tad whispered hoarsely as he shoved his hands through his hair. He wished he could forever shut out the memory of that awful time, even as remembered images flashed in his head. "I should have made him go first," he said on a tortured breath, "kept a closer eye on him, but I didn't." God help him, he hadn't done so. He shrugged. "One minute I'm pedaling along as fast as I can go, Billy behind me, struggling to keep up as usual. The next thing I hear is the sound of a car turning the corner and a loud screech, then a smash." Tad felt the blood drain from his face. His stomach churned and his knees went weak. "I turned in time to see Billy get knocked off his bike." Tad shook his head. He balled his fists as angry anguished tears streamed down his face. "He never made a sound," Tad said, able to see it every bit as clearly now as he had then. "There was just that instant, his eyes frozen in terror, and then *wham*, he hit the pavement." Tad jerked in a deep breath as more tears streamed from his eyes and nose. "That was in the days before helmets, of course."

Ashamed that after all this time, that even now, he couldn't talk about the accident and hold it together, he wheeled away from Abby. His back to her, he wiped the tears away. Then he sighed and finished numbly, "The head injuries were massive. He died before they could get him to the hospital. And it was all my fault."

He turned to find Abby crying, too. Big gulping silent tears. "Oh, God. Tad…" she said brokenly.

Feeling like a robot, Tad said, "I haven't been on a bike since."

"I'm sorry," Abby whispered. She swept into his arms and held him tight. "So sorry. I didn't know." She sobbed against his chest.

Tad held her close, aware that they were both crying and it felt good. He hadn't cried about Billy since the funeral. "I'm sorry, too," he said hoarsely at length, rubbing the tension from her back with long strokes of his palms. "I shouldn't have overreacted." Tad paused, drew back. "But when I walked in and saw those bikes—" *not to mention the baby seat* "—it was just more than I could deal with."

Abby touched a finger to his lips, silencing him. Compassion lit her golden-brown eyes. "You don't have to say anything more," she told him softly, her very presence, the depth and breadth of her understanding, soothing him like nothing and no one ever had.

"Maybe it's time I talked about it to someone," Tad acknowledged quietly.

"You never have," Abby guessed.

"No." Tad handed Abby a tissue, too. "Donna knew Billy had been hit by a car and killed. I think everyone around here did. But I don't think anyone knew I was with him at the time. Aunt Sadie was pretty good at keeping the details to herself. It was her way of protecting me. Later, when I was older, and she wanted me to talk about it with her—" and she had tried to get him to do so many times, Tad remembered "—I wouldn't."

"What about your parents?" Abby asked curiously as she perched on a nearby desk. "Did you talk about it with them?"

Tad shook his head. "Aside from going over the details of what had happened, no." He met Abby's eyes, remembering the utter lack of joy that had encompassed the rest of the years during which he'd grown up. "You have to understand my family life was shattered by Billy's death. It was never the same again."

He moved to sit next to her. "Did your parents divorce?" Abby asked.

"No." Tad remembered wishing they had. "They

stayed married after the tragedy," he reported glumly as he turned toward Abby and she turned toward him. "But their relationship had a hollowness to it that was felt by everyone inside and outside the family."

Abby reached over and linked hands with him. "It must have been hard," she said compassionately.

"It was. Which is why, I think, my dad started taking field assignments that had us living in a lot of foreign countries and moving every few months. Anything to forget."

"Only forgetting was impossible," Abby murmured.

"Right." Tad studied their linked hands. "In some respects I think my parents might have been better off if they'd divorced, instead of staying yoked together by promises they'd made to each other but were, in the end, unable to keep."

Abby moved off the desk and came around to stand between his legs. "You weren't to blame for the disintegration of their marriage, Tad." She put her arms around him and tilted her face up to his. "Just like I wasn't to blame for the disintegration of my parents' marriage."

Tad wished he could believe that. He released the breath he'd been holding. "All I know is that I never want to feel like that again. Like my actions—deliberate or otherwise—robbed someone I love of the life they were meant to have or should have had."

Abby paused. "Is that the way your parents felt?"

Tad shrugged and forced himself to be ruthlessly honest. "I think my parents resented me for not being able to protect Billy. I know I blame myself." *And always will.* "I was faster than he was, older, more experienced. If it had been me bringing up the rear, I could have gotten myself out of the way. Him, too, probably.''

Tears flooded Abby's eyes as they both thought about what a profound impact all this had had on his life. "You don't know that," she protested.

"Yeah, I do," Tad said sadly, briefly closing his eyes. He pointed to his heart. "In here I do." He paused, still struggling with his emotions. With effort he pulled himself together. "Anyway, seeing the bikes in the living room brought it all back." The muscles in his jaw tensed.

Abby stepped away slightly and looked up at him. "I'll get rid of them tomorrow," she promised.

Tad touched a hand to her hair, burying his fingers in the silky softness. "I'd appreciate it." He drew a long breath and looked deep into her eyes. "I can't go back there, Abby."

"I understand." Abby caught his hand and kissed it.

A thoughtful silence fell between them.

"Sadie really understands how you feel about all this, doesn't she?" Abby asked finally. "I mean, even if you haven't discussed it."

"Yeah. She knows me pretty well." As Tad thought about his aunt, his mouth crooked up in an affection-laced smile. "That's one of the reasons I wanted to come back to Blossom to finally settle down—so I could be near Aunt Sadie. We're all the family each of us has now. Aside from you and me and the baby," Tad amended hastily. "I wanted to build something real and lasting. I wanted to build the kind of life my parents and I might have had together if only we'd dealt with Billy's death and the subsequent emotional fallout at the time. Because I know now that nothing is ever gained by putting off the inevitable or the painful."

"I agree." Abby thought of her parents' many divorces, and the long-drawn-out falling-apart period that preceded each one. She sighed and linked hands with Tad again. "When it comes to something like that," she agreed firmly, "procrastinating only makes it all the harder."

"EVERYTHING OKAY with you and Tad?" Sadie asked Abby at work the next day.

Abby nodded and confided to Sadie with relief, "We had a serious talk last night." She leaned forward to kiss Tad's aunt on the cheek, wordlessly thanking her for what she'd done to bring the two of them together. "I understand everything now."

"Good." Sadie smiled and gave Abby a brief motherly hug in return. "He's needed to talk to someone for a long time. I'm glad it was you."

Before either could say anything else, the front door opened and Tim Grau, the owner of the Mighty Fine Restaurant walked in. Though he'd cleaned up the kitchen and managed once again to get an A rating from the health department, his business had been struggling since the salmonella outbreak in the summer. "Can I help you?" Cindy asked from behind the advertising counter.

"I'd like to talk to Tad."

Tad came out of his glassed-in office just behind the bullpen. He shook Tim's hand as if no ill words had ever passed between them. "What's up?"

Tim's cheeks reddened slightly as he met Tad's eyes. "You know that idea you had last summer about me going the community-service route, instead of trying to sweep the scandal under the rug? Well, if the offer's still open, I'm ready to try it now. It's either that or close up shop altogether. So I'll host free classes on safe food preparation at the restaurant if you all will write it up in the newspaper.''

Tad grinned. "The next issue soon enough for you?" he drawled.

While the two men went into Tad's office to work out a publicity schedule for the event, Abby went back to work editing the article on fall tree planting. She was almost finished when a phone call came in for her. Listening, she could barely contain her excitement. "No, tomorrow afternoon will be fine. Yes, thanks.'' She hung up the phone.

"Tomorrow will be fine for what?'' Tad asked. He'd just shown Tim Grau out and was heading back to his office.

Abby drew a deep breath. "That was the headhunter I hired. *Chicago Living* magazine wants to interview me for a job as the Home Decorating editor. I've got an appointment set up for tomorrow afternoon. They're leaving an airline ticket for me at the Asheville airport.''

The mixed emotions Abby half expected Tad to manifest never came. "Wow, that's great,'' Tad said, as the other staff looked on in confusion.

Yes, it was great, considering how long and hard she'd worked to make a career for herself in the magazine-publishing world, so why wasn't she feeling a lot more excited? Abby wondered.

Aware of all eyes on her, she forced a smile and went on to reassure Tad brightly, "It's okay for me to fly, by the way. I asked Dr. Ellison, and he said it was okay through the seventh month. And since I'm only six and a half months along…'' Abby shrugged.

Tad nodded and everyone else went back to work. ''Are you going to spend the night?'' he asked.

''Yes. They've arranged for a hotel.'' And maybe that was a good thing, Abby thought. Maybe that would give her time to think.

Tad touched her shoulder and kissed her cheek. His eyes were filled with kindness and understanding. ''I wish you the best of luck,'' he said, really seeming to mean it.

''Thanks,'' Abby said softly. She pushed away an unexpected twinge of hurt. Tad was only being supportive and following the agreement they'd established at the outset of this pregnancy, Abby told herself firmly. He was not—as everyone else around her erroneously seemed to think—practically shoving her out the door.

''SO HOW'D IT GO?'' Tad asked as he met Abby at the gate upon her return from Chicago two days later.

Abby made no effort to hide her disappointment. ''Not well. I knew the minute they saw me and realized I was pregnant that I wasn't going to get the job.''

''They didn't know you were pregnant before you went?''

''The headhunter neglected to mention it,'' Abby said dryly. ''She said it shouldn't have made any difference to them if they were really interested in my work. And she's right. But you and I both know how things sometimes work in the real world. Some employers think pregnant women are not to be counted on.''

''I'm sorry.'' Tad enveloped her in a comforting

hug. He pressed a kiss into her hair. "I know you've been wanting to get back into magazine editing."

"Yes, well—" Abby shrugged "—it's probably for the best, anyway. Looking at the way the magazine was structured, I don't think I would have been a good fit for that job in any case." She just wished she hadn't had to go all the way to Chicago and spend a night alone in a hotel room, away from Tad, especially if their time together really was—as it appeared—drawing to an end.

Tad helped her collect her suitcase at the baggage claim, then walked her out to the parking lot. "How do you feel? Was the traveling hard on you?"

"Not at all." Abby waited for him to unlock the Jeep. "I feel fine, really. Physically I'm in great shape."

It was how she felt emotionally that was the problem. She was relieved and depressed simultaneously. Tad and the baby were beginning to mean so much more to her than her career. Knowing that her career was the one thing that had always sustained her, through good and bad times, she couldn't help feeling that letting go of that ambition was almost an invitation to disaster.

And she continued to feel that way all that evening and into the next day. So much so that it was a relief when Tad surprised her by nixing dinner with her to go hang out at the local tavern for a bit and watch the Duke versus UNC football game on the big-screen TV.

Maybe, Abby thought pensively, a little irked to be ditched for a night out with the guys, another night apart was exactly what she and Tad needed.

"WELL, DON'T YOU LOOK like you just lost your best friend," Doc Harlan said to Tad as he made room for him at the table where he was sitting.

"I second that!" Sonny remarked as he walked by, a plate of nachos in one hand, a beer in the other. "After the way you carried on while she was out of town, acting lonesome as all get-out," Sonny teased, "I thought you'd be home with Abby tonight, cuddling like crazy."

If only he could have been, Tad thought, as he reached for a handful of peanuts and began to shell them one by one. "Sadie's got that surprise for her tonight, remember?"

"Oh, yeah. Cindy whispered something about it before she left the office." Still chuckling, Sonny headed on over to the table where the just-out-of-college kids were sitting. "Enjoy your freedom!" Sonny called over his shoulder. "You sure won't get much of it after your baby's born."

"That what has you feeling so blue?" Doc asked. He called the waiter over and ordered a plate of buffalo wings and a pitcher of beer. "The impending lack of freedom?"

Tad shook his head. He explained about the job interview, concluding miserably, "To be perfectly honest, I feel like I cost Abby the Chicago job. If it weren't for the pregnancy, which as you have probably figured out by now wasn't exactly planned..." Tad trailed off as a frosty pitcher of beer was put on the table. He poured a glass for Doc and himself.

Just then, UNC scored the first touchdown of the evening. Doc—a UNC med-school grad himself—signaled a thumbs-up, then waited for the backslapping and high fives to subside before responding to Tad. "Has Abby been complaining about being pregnant?"

"No." Tad studied the bottom of his glass.

Doc broke open a peanut shell and shook two nuts out into the palm of his hand. "Does she seem at all unhappy about it?"

"Well, no," Tad said as he, too, reached for a peanut and broke it open.

"Because she's always seemed really happy about it to me," Doc concurred.

"She *is* very happy about the baby," Tad said quietly. "We both are." *Deliriously so.*

Doc paused, clearly wanting to understand, as their family physician and a friend. "Then...?"

Tad drew a breath. Damn it all, he hated feeling guilty. He'd lived a certain way all his adult life because he'd never wanted to be responsible for anyone's unhappiness and loss again, and yet here he was, up to his neck in soul-deep regret! He scowled. "It's just that, career-wise, for Abby, the timing couldn't be worse," he grumbled.

"Let me tell you something, son," Doc said as he refilled their glasses with beer. "My first two kids were born while I was in medical school."

"That must've been rough."

Doc grinned and nodded. "It was. I was working ungodly hours at the time. We were five hundred miles from either set of grandparents. And half the time, because I was at the hospital so much, my wife had to be mother and father both to our babies. But we learned something important from all that, Tad, something I've never hesitated to share with my patients and my own kids, as well. Babies don't always come along at the best time, but once they do come along, you realize it is the best time."

Doc gave Tad a moment to think about that, then

slapped him on the back and continued compassion-ately, "This is all going to work out for the best, Tad. You'll see. Once that baby is here, Abby's not going to want to be anyplace but right here in Blossom with you."

Tad hoped like heck that was so.

He didn't know what he would do if Abby did move on and they ended up commuting and splitting custody of their child, as previously agreed.

"WELL, WHAT DO YOU think?" Sadie asked after they'd said goodbye to the last guest and Abby had returned to the living room to admire Sadie's gift to her, Tad and the baby. "Did I or did I not pull off the biggest surprise thus far in your pregnancy?"

Aside from the actual conception? And the fact that every day she was falling more and more in love with her husband?

"You did great, Sadie." Abby hugged her. Return-ing home from work that evening, sans Tad, Abby had walked into the house to a chorus of "Surprise!" and more gifts and good wishes than she could have imag-ined. In fact, hours later, she was still reeling from the enormity of it all. Not to mention the timing. Sadie had told her the shower wouldn't be till well after Christmas, just to throw her off.

"I was completely bowled over both by the party and your gift to us," Abby told Sadie gratefully. She leaned forward to give the diminutive older woman a hug. "The cradle is just...well, it's incredible."

Sadie smiled and hugged her back. "It's a family heirloom. I always thought I'd be using it for my own children, but it didn't turn out that way, largely be-cause I kept waiting for everything to be perfect, and that kind of guarantee—the guarantee I wanted and needed at that time—never came." Sadie paused to pick up some plates while Abby did the same.

"Consequently the chance to have a baby of my own passed me by. Although I did have children in my life, lots of them, in my teaching and in my nephews—Tad and his brother, Billy."

"And now you have Raymond," Abby said gently, knowing from having seen them together how much the two were beginning to mean to each other.

"Yes, I do. And I love him with all my heart."

"Are you going to marry him?"

Sadie released a shaky breath. "To be perfectly honest, I don't know. If it wasn't for the nine-year age difference, I probably would."

Abby carried another stack of plates into the kitchen. "You're not going to let *that* stop you!"

Sadie smiled. "From loving him, no. From the possibility that he might have to spend a lot of his best years nursing me through the vagaries of old age, probably, yes."

"Oh, Sadie—"

Sadie raised a quelling finger, then, as the two of them began to load the dishwasher, said, "Now don't you feel sorry for me, Abby Kildaire McFarlane. Raymond and I have lots of good times ahead of us, not to mention a soon-to-arrive litter of the most unusual puppies."

Abby thought about Buster and Belle. The two dogs had become as close as their masters. Abby grinned. "I'll bet those puppies are going to be cute as can be."

"I bet they will, too." Clearly torn between speaking her mind and not interfering, Sadie finally said, "I know you're feeling uncertain. Your marriage to Tad and the baby happened awfully fast. But that doesn't mean you should value either any less.''

"Value what any less?'' Tad asked, coming in through the back door. He'd walked home in the brisk November air. His cheeks were flushed, his hair wind-blown. As he shrugged out of his jacket and came close enough to give Abby a kiss, he smelled wintry and sexy and wonderful.

"You.'' Abby grinned, enjoying the feel of the possessive arm he'd wrapped around her, and snuggled against him. "And the baby.''

"I was lecturing,'' Sadie confessed with a twinkle in her eye. "One of the results of being a teacher for so long, I'm afraid. I feel duty bound to point out the meaning of all manner of things.''

Abby took Tad by the hand. "Come on. I want to show you what our friends and neighbors gave us.''

Later, after Sadie had left and Yvonne retired to her own room, Tad insisted he lock up while an exhausted Abby went on to bed. He found her in the bedroom, clad in her nightgown, pacing and rubbing her lower back. "Problem?''

"Just the normal aches and pains of pregnancy. My back aches after I've been sitting for long periods of time,'' she explained.

"Maybe a back rub would help,'' Tad suggested.

Willing to do just about anything to ease the discomfort, Abby lay on her side on the bed while Tad went to get her favorite skin lotion. "So what was Sadie really lecturing you on?'' he asked as he kneaded the tension from her muscles with hands as warm and soothing as a hot bath.

Abby closed her eyes, loving the feel of his hands

on her skin. It was one of many things that she would really miss if they ever parted. "She thinks I've got one foot out the door of this marriage," Abby reported reluctantly.

Tad stopped what he was doing momentarily, then resumed his kneading with slow heavenly strokes. "Do you?"

Abby tried not to wince at the lack of emotion in his voice. "I can't help but feel skittish, Tad," she confided honestly. Aware the ache in her back was gone—to be replaced by one in her heart—she broke free and rolled to face Tad. He looked as if he felt as confused as she did about everything and yet wanted to understand. "After seeing my mother marry and divorce five times, my father marry and divorce six, I feel like I know all the warning signs of a marriage in distress and little else," Abby told him softly. "I don't want our baby to suffer through even one marital breakup."

Tad nodded. "Can't disagree with you there."

"On the other hand—" Abby sighed regretfully "—I don't know anything about the normal happy all-American family you see on TV, either."

Tad rolled her away from him once again. "We're doing fine, Abby." His hands worked magic as they kneaded down her spine. "Between the two of us we'll figure it all out."

Abby didn't know if it was hormones or what, but suddenly she was near tears as he began working his fingers across her shoulders and down her right arm. "There's so much more to it than that."

"I know," he said as he returned to her lower back and continued to work out the kinks.

Abby barely suppressed a groan of contentment.

"Tad…" she said as a wave of longing swept through her. Her limbs felt heavy and weak.

"Hmm?" Tad sounded totally absorbed in his work as he made his way down her legs.

"That's not my back."

"Oh." Tad's hands moved upward. "So it isn't," he said mischievously.

Abby smiled and arched against the playful wandering of his hand. "That's not my back, either."

Giving up on the massage altogether, Tad rolled her onto her back. He looked down at her with such intensity she caught her breath. The next thing she knew their mouths were locked in a searing kiss and he was stretched out on the bed beside her. "I forgot to tell you something," he murmured as he divested her of her gown and dizziness swept through her in waves.

"What?" Abby gasped.

He drew all of her against all of him. He kissed her cheek, her nose, her temple, then buried his face in her hair. "When I smell that perfume of yours, I get sidetracked very easily."

Abby kissed his throat. Her fingers slid through the silky mat of hair on his chest, then lower, to the waistband of his low-slung pajama pants. "I'm not wearing any perfume."

Tad smiled. "My point exactly."

One kiss turned into twenty as they touched and tempted and teased, putting everything they had, everything they wanted, into their caresses. Until all that mattered to either of them was the desire sweeping through them both in powerful waves, and he was straining against her, letting her know he wanted her as wildly as she wanted him. And she wanted him that way, all fire and passion, nothing secret, nothing from their pasts, nothing from their future, standing between them.

His kisses were just as sweet, just as filled with longing. As their ragged breaths meshed, Tad taught her what it was to love, not just with hearts and souls, but through touch. He taught her she was just as insatiable as he, that it was better to let their passion build and build. He skimmed her body with his fingers, filling his hands with her soft hot flesh. Then threaded his hands through her hair, pushing it away from her ear, and kissed and caressed his way down her neck. She knew he wanted her just as she wanted him, and she also knew, as he drew back to look at her, his blue eyes alight with unbearably tender protectiveness, that, before they went any farther, he had something to ask.

"Just out of curiosity, Ab—" his voice was rough, filled with the longing for more and the equally important need to know "—are we going to have to stop making love at some point?"

"Soon, yes," Abby said breathlessly as Tad kissed the taut aching crowns of her breasts and the graceful slope of her tummy. "We won't be able to have intercourse. But for right now, for at least the next two weeks," she said as he slid upward, "we can, um…"

"Do this?" Tad guessed as he sat against the headboard, took her with him and lifted her ever so gently, ever so carefully, onto his lap. As she faced him, he delicately, intimately caressed the inside of her thighs. Letting her know, despite the swollen curve of her belly, she was just as desirable—if not more desirable—to him than ever.

"Mm-hmm," Abby confirmed as she shifted and made them one. "We can absolutely do this," she said, knowing he was definitely the sexiest man she had ever met.

"Then we better make the most of it," Tad said hoarsely, kissing her and cupping her breasts until she shuddered in response and her nipples beaded against his palms, "don't you think?"

"Oh, yes," Abby returned lovingly. Overcome with need and yearning, overcome by the tenderness he displayed, she took up the rhythm he started, merging their bodies as intimately and irrevocably as they'd begun to merge their lives. Afterward Tad cuddled her close. "I love you, Abby," he whispered in her ear.

Abby's eyes filled to overflowing. Maybe it was her pregnancy—the surge of hormones flowing through her—but she'd never felt so wanted, nor at the same time more vulnerable, as she did tonight. "I love you, too," she whispered back, holding him close. *So much.*

The problem was, love had never really been the issue for them. They'd both easily confessed to falling in love with each other in Paris. That was why they'd gotten married immediately upon returning to the States.

The problem was, she knew—through bitter life experience—love alone, no matter how passionate or exciting, wasn't always enough to hold a marriage together over the long haul.

There were times when love wasn't nearly enough. She only hoped, desperately so, that this wouldn't turn out to be one of those times.

Chapter Eleven

Abby stood at Tad's elbow, watching anxiously, as he tried to insert a large pinecone into the small end of a rough-barked horn of plenty. "That's the wrong end to be stuffing, isn't it?"

Tad took the pinecone, inserted it in the other end, then added an unshelled walnut and bunch of grapes into the smaller opening of the Thanksgiving centerpiece.

Arms folded, head cocked to one side, he studied his "masterpiece" with a comic expression. "I think I know my cornucopias."

Abby snorted and went to lower the volume of the football game on TV. "That's what you said about the turkey," she reminded him, returning to his side.

Tad shrugged. "So I got the neck and the...well, you know, mixed up."

Abby rolled her eyes. "I'll say!"

"It all turned out all right in the end."

Yes, Abby thought, it had. In fact, this was the best holiday she'd had in ages. Tad wrapped an arm around her shoulders and teased, "Whoever would've thought you'd be standing around in our kitchen, wearing an apron and holding a meat thermometer.''

Until she'd met Tad, she'd been a career woman all the way. "Just don't tell anyone, okay?" she murmured, disgruntled, glad Yvonne—who'd gone home to be with her own family for the holiday—wasn't around to see this.

Tad appeared to consider it. "I could be bribed." He gave her the look that made her blood heat.

Abby blushed as she thought about the many ways they had made love. "Really."

"Really," he said softly.

"What's going on out here in the kitchen?" Sadie poked her head in.

"Exactly what you'd think," Tad said, making Abby's blush deepen. He picked up the turkey baster, put it in Abby's hand and pointed it in the direction of his chest. "I'm being held hostage."

"Absolutely true," Abby agreed. "I'm not letting him out of here until the centerpiece is just right."

"You're having a good time?" Sadie beamed, pleased.

"Oh, yes," Abby said as Tad pulled her close. "How are the puppies doing?"

"Great. They're just starting to wake up. We thought you might want to come and see them."

They all trooped into the mudroom behind the garage and peered into the quilt-lined whelping box Raymond had built for her. Buster was curled in the corner, carefully keeping watch. Belle was lying on her side, all six of her puppies cuddled up against her.

As they woke up, they squirmed and began to nurse, making little mewling sounds.

"They are so cute," Abby said.

"They've got the best of both parents," Tad agreed.

A mixture of brown, black, white and buff-colored short fluffy hair covered their compact little bodies. Their faces were tiny and appealing, their ears long and drooping.

Raymond had loaded the box into the rear of his pickup and brought the crew to Tad and Abby's for the day. Sadie was dizzy with delight, watching the new pups. "I don't think she's going to let you take the puppies back home with you," Abby teased.

Tad nodded. "You, Belle, and the pups might just have to move in with Sadie and Buster," he told Raymond, "so Aunt Sadie can keep an eye on them, too."

"Actually," Sadie said shyly as she and Raymond linked hands, "we've sort of addressed that issue."

Raymond grinned. "I asked Sadie to marry me last night."

Sadie held up her left hand, which sported a brand-new diamond ring. "And I said yes."

"Congratulations." Abby embraced them both in turn, and Tad followed suit.

"Have you set a date?" Tad asked, looking as happy as could be for his aunt.

"New Year's Day," Sadie said.

"WHAT ARE WE GOING to give Raymond and Sadie for a wedding gift?" Abby asked Tad one lazy Sunday afternoon a couple of weeks later as they sat in the family room, making wreaths out of pine boughs and red velvet ribbons.

Tad shrugged. "I don't know. A triple leash?"

Abby gave him a look. "Very funny," she told him in the soft playful voice he loved. "And we already got them one when the puppies were born."

Tad paused to give it some serious thought. "How about tickets to the Charlotte Symphony and an overnight stay in a hotel there?" He looked at Abby for her reaction, knowing it was important they get this right, and that it be from the two of them. "They both like classical music."

Abby smiled, as relieved as he was to have that problem solved. "That's an excellent idea."

"Now all we have to decide is a name for the baby."

Instead of the groan Tad was expecting, Abby smiled a secret little smile. She put aside her wreath and came over to sit next to him. "I've been thinking about that. I have an idea."

She was serious, Tad realized. "Go ahead." They'd already discussed—and rejected at least once—every name, male and female, in the baby-name book they'd bought.

"I think the name of our first child should have sentimental value."

First child. Tad liked the sound of that. Nothing would please him more than making more babies with Abby.

Abby took his hands in hers. "I was thinking of your brother. I'd like to name him William if the baby's a boy, and Wilhelmina if it's a girl. Will if it's a boy. Billie if it's a girl."

Not so long ago he would have reacted vehemently to such a proposal, Tad knew. But now he seemed to have made peace with the past, more than he could ever have imagined doing. And he had Abby to thank. "I'd like that," he said softly, looking deep into her eyes. "Very much."

Abby breathed a sigh of relief. "Good," she said, smiling. "Me, too."

They were silent a few minutes more. It was a good feeling, just sitting there together that way.

"So...any word from Yvonne?" Tad asked. She'd come back briefly after Thanksgiving, helped out a little more at the newspaper, then left again.

Abby shook her head. "Her interview with *Personalities!* magazine was on Friday. She was going to spend the weekend with friends in New York and then head back here on Monday or Tuesday."

The phone rang. Abby got up to answer it. "Well," she said, after greeting the caller affectionately, "speak of the devil." As Tad listened, ebullient congratulations followed. "Of course we understand!" Abby exclaimed. "No. Don't worry about it. I'll take care of everything. All right. Good luck to you—keep me posted. Right. I'll see you on e-mail. Bye." Her back to him, Abby put the phone down slowly.

Tad wondered uneasily what was going through Abby's mind. Since the Chicago-magazine fiasco, Abby had not had any interviews. Mainly, Tad felt, because she had insisted the headhunter tell all prospective employers she was expecting a child at the end of January. Abby wanted no more mix-ups or thwarted expectations on either side. Tad respected her enormously for that.

Feeling the sudden need to hold her, he closed the distance between them. "Yvonne got the job?" he guessed, taking Abby into his arms.

Abby traced the swell of her tummy with the flat of her hand in a protective deeply maternal gesture. "As an assistant managing editor. She's not coming back. They want her to start right away. I'm going to ship the things she left here back to New York." Abby paused, for the first time, her own mixed feelings about her friend's reentry into the magazine trade evident. Abby continued with a rueful smile, "Yvonne said to tell you she's sorry about the short notice."

Tad shrugged it off. "She always said it would be that way." *Abby had said the same thing.* At the time he'd told himself he could handle it. Now that the possibility was nearing, he was not so certain of that. Not nearly so certain.

Abby stepped closer. She rested her hand on his chest. "You okay?"

Tad nodded. "Sure," he said.

But inwardly he couldn't stop thinking about it.

And he was still thinking about it the next morning as he told the staff about Yvonne's departure and they tried to figure out how to divvy up the workload and compensate for her leaving.

"Well, I'm happy for her," Sonny said amiably, "but it's really going to leave us scrambling. Every edition leading up to Christmas is going to be jam-packed with photos and details of holiday events."

"Not to mention ads," Cindy said, looking just as worried as her younger colleague. "We've got, on average, an additional five pages of advertisements. I think the only merchant in town not advertising with us is Joe Don Jerome."

"His friend at the insurance agency isn't advertising, either," Raymond said.

"No. But Cullen is thinking about it," Cindy replied. "I ran into him at the grocery store last night. He said the number of new homeowner, life and health policies he was writing was down ten percent since he'd stopped placing ads in our paper. The new business was all going to a competitor who was still advertising with us."

"Nowell Haines told his wife the same thing," Sadie said. "She advised him to bring his business back to the *Blossom Weekly News,* but he said he couldn't."

Tad looked thoughtful. "Their loss," he said.

"I quite agree," Abby said. She couldn't believe that the Three Stooges, as Tad had dubbed the trio of businessmen, were still shooting themselves in the foot over Tad's decision to include consumer reporting and troubleshooting in the paper.

"Who's going to take over Yvonne's slot as Features editor?" Cindy asked.

Tad sized her up. "Actually I was thinking about asking you and hiring someone else to take over the advertising department."

Cindy beamed. "That would be great!"

"Can you sort of pull double duty until I get someone else in?" Tad asked. "I know it's the holidays—"

"No problem."

"Good. And speaking of holidays." Tad stood and disappeared into his office. He returned a moment later bearing five red envelopes. "I wanted to give you all your Christmas bonuses early in addition to the fifteen percent across-the-board raises you'll be getting as of January 1."

He handed out the envelopes. "I also wanted to let you know I've decided to expand the paper so we can go daily by next summer."

Another murmur of approval and excitement swept the group. "Furthermore," Tad went on, "I couldn't have done it without you."

The phone in his office rang. Still grinning from ear to ear, Cindy leaped up to get it. She returned promptly. "Tad, it's for you."

"Who is it?"

Cindy shrugged. "Some lady. She wouldn't give her name. She just said it was imperative she talk to you."

His expression concerned, Tad rose. When he came back, he had his jacket in hand. "I've got to go out for a bit," he announced to one and all. "Hold down the fort for me?"

"Sure," Raymond said.

"What was that about?" Sonny asked Abby.

Abby shrugged, hating to admit it, but feeling a little annoyed. "Darned if I know."

"Should I be jealous?" Abby asked hours later when Tad finally returned to the newspaper. Everyone else was out to lunch. Having eaten a little earlier— she got light-headed these days if she went too long between meals—she'd stayed behind to handle any walk-in business and the phones.

"Frustrated is more like it. That is, if you're sharing my feelings," Tad told her. He plucked their bagged lunch from the refrigerator in the coffee room and took Abby into his office to eat it.

She studied him curiously. "You were working on another troubleshooting story, weren't you?"

Tad nodded. "The same one I've been working on since I took over the paper."

"Joe Don's car dealership."

Tad unwrapped a turkey sandwich on rye and uncapped a thermos of piping hot minestrone soup. "Everyone complains about the quality of the cars, both new and used. And yet they still buy there because of the deal they can get."

"At least at first." Abby opened an individual carton of milk and peeled an orange for herself. "Then a lot of them go out of town to buy their cars."

"Right. Anyway, I've been sort of nosing around quietly, exchanging car-repair horror stories with the locals. Whenever I hear about anyone having anything atrocious happening, I find a way to bump into them and bring it up ever so casually, see if they'll talk about it. More often than not, they get this kind of scared look on their faces and clam up."

Tad wasn't the only one intrigued, Abby thought. Since he'd started investigating this in between all the many duties he had as owner, publisher and managing editor of the *Blossom Weekly News,* she'd become hooked, too. "That lady on the phone just now?" she prodded.

"An assistant over at the vet's. She's young, just out of high school, moved here from another town to start a life independent of her parents. The first thing she did was buy a used car from Joe Don." Tad scowled. "Currently said car is sitting in front of the garage apartment where she lives. The thirty-day warranty ran out on it and she can't afford to get it fixed. I tried to get her to talk about it the other day when I helped Sadie and Raymond take the pups to the vet for their checkup, but no go. I gave her my card, told her if she ever changed her mind, to give me a buzz—and she called this morning."

Abby leaned forward, her pulse racing. "And?"

Tad's frustration deepened visibly. "Like everybody else, when it came right down to it, she panicked and chickened out."

Abby shook her head while she continued peeling her orange. "That is so strange."

"Isn't it." Tad bit into his sandwich.

"After all this time—months—of working on this story, you still have no idea."

"None." Tad perked up. "But on the way back I saw a tow truck jumping Ernest Lee Scruggs's new pickup."

Abby furrowed her brow. "Again?" The pickup seemed to need jumping or had to be towed every other week, which was awfully odd since the owner was a mechanic.

Tad nodded. "Anyway, I stopped to see if I could lend a hand. Told him if he ever wanted to have a beer and trade stories about broken-down cars to give me a call."

"Think he'll take you up on it?"

Tad shrugged. "Hard to say. He's scared of something, too. He looked like he was getting awfully mad, though. When I left, he was kicking the tires on his truck."

"Oh, my."

"Oh, my is right." Tad gave her a once-over that swiftly left her feeling very sexy and very desirable. "So." He leaned back in his chair. "How are you feeling?"

Abby grinned, aware she'd never been happier even if she was beginning to get big as a house. "Pregnant. Very pregnant." And very loved.

"Oh, darlings, there you are!" Sadie burst in from lunch, Raymond behind her. They'd taken to eating over at her house so they could care for Belle, Buster and the puppies before coming back to work. "Raymond and I wanted to give you your Christmas present early." Sadie handed Tad and Abby an envelope, then watched with glee as they opened it together.

"C'MON NOW," Abby admonished Tad hours later in the classroom at the community college. "Be a sport."

"This is silly." Tad stared at the "baby" given to them by the instructor of the parenting class, started to attempt to pick it up to get it ready for its bath, then stepped back and shook his head as if to say, *No way*. He turned to her grimly, very much aware, as was Abby, that she'd already had her turn. "These are baby dolls."

"Lifelike baby dolls," Abby countered.

Tad braced his hands on his waist. "I do not need to practice bathing and diapering a baby doll."

"Obviously," Abby said, picking up their "baby" and handing it to him, "since you just taped that diaper to the baby's hip."

Tad glanced down at the doll, saw Abby was right. Frowning and grumbling something she was just as glad not to catch in its entirety, he put the "baby" back down on the table and ripped the adhesive tab off.

"You just ripped the baby's skin," Abby said dryly. "Little Will or Billie is now howling at the top of his or her lungs."

Tad grinned, enjoying her verbal jab as much as she'd enjoyed delivering it. He poked his thumbs through the belt loops of his jeans and retained his arrogant stance in front of the science-lab table. "No, he/she's not."

Abby arched a brow. "No?"

"Because you would be doing it," Tad said with a teasing grin. "Not me. And you—" he leaned forward to whisper sexily in her ear "—as you have so aptly demonstrated, are as much a pro at this as you are at everything else."

Pulse racing, spirits soaring, Abby drew back. "Flattery…"

Tad ran a hand lovingly over her tummy. "…will get me everywhere?"

Abby warmed beneath the tenderness of his touch and the feeling of the baby kicking deep inside her. "You wish!"

"Class." The teacher clapped her hands again. "Pay attention!"

Tad elbowed Abby lightly and gave her a look of mock sternness that said, *She's speaking to us.*

She gave him a look that said, *I know she is, and you, bad boy, better behave.*

They got through the rest of the class only because Tad decided to pay attention.

"That wasn't so bad, was it?" Abby said as they walked out into the cold clear December night.

Tad backed her up against the side of his Jeep and braced a hand on either side of her. Looking down at her, as if kissing her passionately was very much on his mind, he shrugged and replied, "Depends on how much humor you see in a soaped-up baby landing headfirst in the tub."

"Baby doll," Abby corrected, knowing how embarrassed Tad had looked about that. "And it was only your first attempt," she soothed as she rested both her hands against his chest.

His breath making frosty circles in the air, Tad gathered her close. He looked down at her and brushed the hair from her face. "What if I don't know what to do, Abby? What if I don't have that natural parenting thing that just tells you in here—" he thumped his chest "—what to do and say at any given moment."

Abby slipped her hands beneath the hem of his jacket and ran her hands up and down his back. "Then you read and study and learn," she said.

His quiet gaze said he wasn't sure that was all it would take. "Tad, we can do this," Abby encouraged softly, pressing ever closer. "We can be good parents."

"I know that." Tad opened the door and ushered her inside.

"Then…?" Abby asked after he'd circled around and climbed into the driver's seat.

Tad started the engine and gave it a moment to warm up. Hands resting on the steering wheel, he twisted to face Abby. The lamps from the parking lot bathed them in a gentle golden glow.

Blue eyes serious, he reached over, took her hand and confessed with unexpected candor, "It just hit me tonight. The enormity of what we're undertaking here. The knowledge that it might not be as simple or trouble-free as I thought it would."

Abby smiled, as mesmerized by his unexpected show of vulnerability as she was by his easygoing confidence and rugged good looks. "I was wondering when it would happen," she murmured, smiling, as other cars around them began to drive off.

Tad's brow furrowed. "What?"

Abby lightly touched his chest as she confessed playfully, "That you'd feel the anxiety I've been feeling all along."

Tad looked as relieved as she felt. "You never said anything."

"That's because most of the time I push those feelings away, just tell myself everything is going to be fine. But sometimes at night…sometimes—usually late at night or very early in the morning—I worry." Realizing they really were in the same boat, after all, Abby smiled at Tad. "Doc Harlan and Dr. Ellison both reassure me it's quite natural. So I know—" Abby took his hand and held it tightly "—it's going to be all right, Tad."

He nodded, accepting that. Then, still looking worried, he glanced at his watch, put the Jeep into gear. "So, what do you think? Is there anywhere we can get a baby doll this late at night?"

FROM THAT MOMENT ON, it was Tad's mission. On Christmas Eve he was still at it. "You've practiced enough, Tad." He'd bathed, diapered, fed and burped the baby doll every night without fail.

Tad bundled the doll in a blanket and returned it to the crib. "I just want to make sure I have everything down pat so that when we bring the baby home, I'll be an old pro," he said.

There was no need to worry about that, Abby thought, amused. He could change a diaper now in nothing flat. And he could give the baby doll a bath with his eyes shut. "Trust me," Abby said dryly as she took her husband into her arms for a lengthy yuletide kiss. "You're going to be as good at that as you are everything else."

Tad bent his head and returned her kiss even more languorously. Abby's heart was pounding when he let her go. "Now this is the way to spend Christmas Eve," he drawled.

Knowing they would make love later—probably again and again—Abby took him by the hand and led him downstairs to the tree. She was eager to give him his gift. "Ready to exchange gifts?"

He nodded.

At Abby's insistence, Tad went first. He was stunned when he saw the framed copy of the first edition of the *Blossom Weekly News* published and edited by the two of them. "It was an important day in our lives," she told him quietly. "I thought we should mark the occasion."

"As well we should," he said as he kissed her again.

He handed her her gift. Inside was a beautiful framed photograph of them together their first night in Paris and another of their wedding day. There was a third frame, one with no picture. "For the baby's first formal portrait," Tad said hoarsely.

Tears sparkled in Abby's eyes. She wreathed her arms around Tad's neck and kissed him soundly. "This is the best Christmas I've ever had."

"Me, too," he said thickly.

"Let's make a promise," Abby said urgently. "No matter what happens, let's spend every Christmas right here together. Let's make sure that our baby has his mom and his dad with him at Christmas."

"You have my word on it," Tad promised softly.

If he had his way, they'd never be apart again.

"SO WHEN ARE Sadie and Raymond going off on their real honeymoon?" Sonny asked the day after New Year's as the newspaper staff sifted through photos of homes. One had to be chosen for the next makeover project for the newspaper's Lifestyle section.

"They've decided to wait until after the puppies are weaned and our baby is born." In the meantime they'd spent their actual wedding night in Asheville, while the local vet had taken charge of Belle, Buster and the pups as his wedding gift to the new couple.

"I still get all misty thinking about their wedding on New Year's Eve," Cindy confessed as she held up a photo of a Cape Cod house in the country that needed a lot of work.

Abby knew exactly how Cindy felt. Watching the two lovebirds say their vows had made her tear up, too. Tad hadn't said much, but she'd known he was affected, too.

"Look at this one," Abby said, pointing out a sixties-style ranch home. "Think we could update this into something fresh and exciting?"

"It'd sure be a challenge," Sonny said.

"It'd also be something completely different from the rambling white elephant we just did," Abby mused.

"Where's Tad?"

"He took a gift basket of goodies and bottle of champagne over to Sadie's," Abby replied absently, still studying the ranch house. "He wanted it there when they got back."

The phone rang. Sonny went to get it. "Abby. For you!"

Hoping it was Frank at the paint store telling her he'd be happy to donate materials for the fix-up project once again in exchange for free mention of his store, Abby lifted the receiver. She was still on the phone, writing down details when Tad walked in. He took one look at her and said, "You look like you've seen a ghost."

It sort of felt that way. Aware all eyes were on her,

Abby shook off her lethargy and said, "Not at all. I'm just stunned." She glanced at the notes she'd made. "That was the headhunter who helped get Yvonne her job. She said *Southern Home and Garden* magazine in Atlanta is expanding their editorial staff and they want to interview me."

Tad cast a look at the faint hint of snow flurries coming down outside. "Now?"

Abby nodded, knowing the weather—and the threat of their first snow of the year—was the least of her problems. "I can't travel," she said. "I'm less than a month from my due date."

Tad was very still. His eyes never left her face. "So you're declining."

Abby nodded curtly, trying not to feel so relieved. "What choice do I have?" At least this time she didn't have to go all the way to Chicago to be more or less turned down at first sight.

The phone rang again. This time Cindy got it. "Abby." She nodded at the phone.

Aware of Tad's eyes on her, Abby picked up her extension. She listened intently, feeling once again like the wind had been knocked out of her. "You're kidding," she said slowly. "No. Well. Of course. Yes. Absolutely. Tomorrow." Abby hung up the phone. Everyone was still looking at her.

"Well?" Tad said, beginning to look a little impatient.

"That was the headhunter again." Abby swallowed, not sure what she felt. Elated. Excited. Scared. Upset. Stunned. With Tad still waiting, she drew a breath and announced calmly, "*Southern Home and Garden* is sending someone here to interview me."

Cindy grinned, unable to contain her excitement. "What are you going to wear?" she demanded.

"Beats the heck out of me," Abby said. "Absolutely nothing fits me these days except Tad's old shirts and my maternity slacks."

"We have time to drive to the maternity shop in Asheville before it closes," Tad said.

"Now?" Abby demanded, casting another look at the snow flurries.

"Sure," Tad said, his mood remarkably buoyant considering all that was at stake. He had no doubt he could keep her and the baby safe. But he could see Abby needed some convincing. He closed the distance between them and wrapped his arm around her shoulders. "I just heard the latest weather update from the National Weather Service," he told her gently. "No accumulation is expected, and it's still early in the day. I've plenty of experience driving in all kinds of weather and road conditions. And if we do run into bad weather, the Jeep has four-wheel drive."

Tad turned back to Sonny and Cindy. "You two can handle things here, can't you, while I go with Abby to purchase a power suit for her interview tomorrow?"

"Absolutely," Cindy and Sonny said in unison.

Tad smiled, went to the hook by the door and grabbed Abby's coat. "Let's go."

Abby lifted her hair off her collar with one hand, while he helped her on with her coat. As soon as they were outside on the sidewalk, flurries swirling around them, she turned to him and said, "You don't have to do this for me."

"I want to," Tad said, and to his surprise, he meant the words with all his heart. He hadn't been nearly supportive enough of her desire to go back to work in her field the last time and he still felt guilty as hell about that. He'd promised Abby he would never hold her back professionally if they married. No matter how difficult it was, no matter how much he didn't want her to take a job away from him, he intended to hold himself to that vow.

As it happened, luck continued to be with them. The weather held. And Abby found a beautiful cranberry red wool maternity dress and matching jacket in very short order. A long cream, navy and cranberry silk scarf drew attention away from her tummy.

By the time the interview took place at their completely redecorated home, she felt—and looked—like a million bucks. Knowing Tad was waiting to hear, Abby called him as soon as the Atlanta publisher left. He drove right over.

"Well?" he said, coming through the door, an exceptionally happy smile on his face as he paused to kiss her cheek. "Tell me everything."

Abby took his hand and led him over to the sofa. She kept her hand linked with his even after they sat down. "They were very impressed by my work on the Lifestyle section, as well as all my previous work."

"As they should be," Tad said.

Abby sat back against the cushions, looking every bit the capable career woman she'd been when he met her. "We agreed that the magazine needs a completely new approach and an updated look. So if I decided to take the job, I'd have carte blanche.''

As proud as he was, Tad felt himself beginning to panic. ''They offered it to you?''

Abby made a seesawing motion with her hand. ''They're still working out salary details and my need to commute back and forth from Atlanta on a weekly or biweekly basis with the headhunter representing me.'' She shrugged her shoulders. ''Whether or not we'll be able to come to an agreement, I don't know, but they are very interested.''

With effort Tad put his own concerns aside. At least she was willing to commute. At least she wasn't trying to cut him out of her life entirely. ''When would they want you to start?'' he asked casually, realizing all over again how very much was at stake.

''March.''

That was two months away. Tad enveloped her in a hug. ''Well, congratulations. I hope you get the job.'' However they needed to work it out, he decided, they would work it out, as long as she was willing to meet him halfway.

Abby drew back. Her cheeks were flushed, her eyes sparkling with delight and wonder. ''You mean that, don't you?'' she said happily.

Tad nodded, stunned to find he could put her happiness above his own. ''Yes, Abby, I do,'' he said quietly. ''I want you to experience everything this life has to offer. And if that job will make you happy, I'm all for it.''

ABBY HEARD NOTHING about the job until the following week when the publisher came in with an offer she found easy to refuse. "It's just not enough money, considering the commute," she told Tad as they got ready for bed that evening. "So I turned it down."

"Just like that?"

"We have to be practical here. It would take a lot of money and effort to maintain two homes for me to commute back and forth. I'll just keep looking."

Tad nodded. His feelings in turmoil, he climbed into bed beside her. He knew she was disappointed things hadn't worked out with *Southern Home and Garden* magazine, but he couldn't help but feel relieved, too. He did not want Abby that far away. He did not want their baby commuting between two different homes. But he also knew he had no more right to deprive Abby of her career dreams than she had to deprive him of his.

Beside him, Abby switched out the light, settled down into the feather ticking and let out a heartfelt groan.

Immediately concerned, Tad shifted onto his side. The softness of her hip collided with his. He touched her shoulder gently. "What is it?"

Abby grimaced and slid a hand beneath her waist. "My back again." She let out a gusty breath and shook her head. "I just can't get comfortable these days no matter what I do."

Tad knew she was tired of being pregnant. He took her hand, turned it palm up and kissed the middle of it. "It's only a couple more weeks."

Abby groaned again and peered at him from beneath her lashes. "Tell that to my aching muscles," she said as he reached beneath her and massaged where her hand had been.

"Maybe we should get rid of the feather ticking," Tad suggested thoughtfully, knowing that people with back problems often slept on harder—not softer—surfaces. "Try just lying on the extra-firm mattress without the ticking," he said.

Abby rolled toward him, her breasts and tummy colliding with his chest. "You wouldn't mind?"

Tad grinned and pressed a playful kiss to the tip of her nose. "I like the bed either way—it makes no difference to me. Besides, it's not like I'm going to get a lot of sleep if you're tossing and turning all night." He helped Abby to her feet.

"True," she said.

"Besides, this is all part and parcel of being an expectant dad." Tad turned the bedroom light back on. Insisting he needed no help, he made her sit in one of the chairs next to the window while he removed the sheets and blankets and the feather ticking that covered the mattress, then replaced the sheets and blankets. Finished, he helped Abby back to bed.

"Well?" he said as she settled slowly, gracefully onto her back.

She lay there a moment while he gently drew the covers to her waist. She made a comical face. "I still feel like a beached whale."

Tad chuckled as he got into bed. Abby had been saying that for months now, and nothing could have been further from the truth. Her skin was so luminous it glowed, and there was a fundamental warmth and tenderness about her, a certain serenity, that increased daily. "You look—" Tad paused to kiss her deeply then reluctantly pulled away "—like an incredibly beautiful expectant mother."

Abby ducked her head. "You're just saying that."

"No, Abby, I'm not. Right now you are the most beautiful woman in the world to me," he said huskily. He paused to kiss her again. Lifting his lips from hers, he whispered in a voice not to be denied, "Now roll over on your side."

"What!"

"I'm going to give you a back rub. Maybe that will help."

"At this point," she grumbled cantankerously enough to make him chuckle, "the only thing that will help is this baby being born."

Tad was getting anxious, too. But it wasn't time.

"Hush." He turned down the lights, turned on some soft music and slipped his hands beneath the hem of her gown. He knew—from the faint shadows beneath her eyes—she needed sleep—and a hefty dose of tender loving care.

"Close your eyes," he ordered softly.

Abby protested immediately, just as he'd known she would.

"Close your eyes, Abby."

With a sigh she did. Loving the silky feel of her skin beneath his hands, he kneaded the muscles of her back until she moaned. "That feels so good," she murmured, her whole body going languid. "It's even making me sleepy."

Tad grinned. Knowing she needed her rest now more than ever, he put his own desire on hold and kept up the gentle massage. "Just close your eyes and cuddle close."

Abby snuggled into her pillow contentedly. "You really are the best expectant dad a woman could ever ask for."

High praise from a tough customer, Tad thought, recalling that when Abby had first moved into this house she'd refused even to sleep in the same room with him. So who knew? Maybe this *would* work out. Maybe after the baby was born, Abby would decide not to leave, after all.

Chapter Twelve

The phone rang at four in the morning. Groaning, Tad reached for it while Abby got up for what seemed the millionth time that night to head for the bathroom. When she came back, she looked surprised to see him getting dressed. Her eyes gleaming with curiosity, she perched on the edge of the bed. "What's up?"

Tad grinned as he took in the mussed layers of golden-brown hair. Eight and a half months into her pregnancy, her breasts and tummy swollen with child, she had never been sexier or more desirable.

"Ernest Lee Scruggs has finally decided he's ready to talk to me about Joe Don's car dealership." Tad pocketed his tape recorder, notepad and pen, a cell phone and his flashlight as Abby bounded off the bed.

She wreathed her arms about his neck. "Be careful."

"Count on it." He paused to kiss Abby on the tip of his nose, then headed out into the cold.

As expected, Ernest Lee was waiting eagerly. He came out onto his front porch, a jug of moonshine in his hand. Tad greeted him and then hustled them both inside.

"See that pickup?" Ernest Lee pointed drunkenly out the window at his shiny red truck. "A thing of beauty is what it is, and it's also a worthless pile of manure."

Tad turned on his tape recorder, set it down in the middle of the kitchen table and pulled up a chair. "It never has run right, has it?"

"Nope." Ernest Lee dropped into the chair opposite Tad with a clumsy thud. "It sure as blazes hasn't. And you want to know why?" He pounded the kitchen table with his fist. "'Cause it ain't new! Joe Don Jerome rolled back the mileage on it."

Tad took out his notepad. "How'd you find this out?"

Ernest Lee hiccuped loudly. "I tracked down the serial numbers through the company that made it. When I said I was the original owner, they thought I was somebody else, so I did some more hunting on my own and found out that the reason Joe Don has so much trouble with so many of his cars is that he's been buying up all the known lemons on the market dirt cheap, rolling back the mileage a'fore they get to his place and then selling them as great deals. Only they aren't such good deals, are they—" Ernest Lee hiccuped again "—if they never run right from day one."

"Why doesn't anyone complain to the state attorney general?" Tad asked as he got up to make some coffee for the drunk mechanic.

"'Cause they can't." Ernest Lee's red-rimmed eyes filled with despair.

Tad leaned forward urgently. "Why not?"

Tears rolled down Ernest Lee's wind-burned cheeks. "'Cause they lied, that's why."

"Now we know the whole scam," Tad told Abby as soon as he got home some five hours later. "Joe Don Jerome sold the lemons to unsuspecting customers at what appeared to be cut-rate prices, Nowell Haines the banker encouraged customers to falsify through exaggeration or outright lies the information on their credit applications whenever necessary to push through the loans at a higher-than-market interest rate, and Cullen Marshall took care of the insurance. Together they made sure people got more expensive cars than they truthfully would have been qualified to purchase, and if anyone complained, they'd point out that they'd lied on their credit applications, and if found out, could go to jail for fraud."

Abby put aside the Lifestyle article she'd been editing while she waited for him and accompanied him to the kitchen.

"No wonder people were too scared to kick up a ruckus."

Tad helped himself to a bowl of the cinnamon-raisin oatmeal simmering on the stove. "Fortunately I now have the ammunition to stop them. I talked to the district attorney on my way home. He's going to launch a criminal investigation after he reads my article. He's not going to prosecute anyone who fudged on their credit application."

Abby sat opposite him. "That's wonderful, Tad."

Yeah, it was, he thought as he picked up her hand and kissed the back of it.

Just as suddenly Abby tensed. "Oh, no…"

"What?" Tad asked, baffled.

One hand on the tabletop, Abby levered herself upright. "Don't look now, but my water just broke."

"TAD, WILL YOU JUST calm down?" Abby said after putting on some dry clothing and telephoning the obstetrician.

"I'm calm."

Like an erupting volcano is calm, Abby thought. "It's going to be fine. My labor has barely started. The pains aren't even regular yet. We have plenty of time to get to the hospital." Plenty of time. She was not going to panic.

"That's good," Tad said. "Because I don't want you having our baby in the car en route to the hospital."

Abby smiled, amazed how calm she felt now that the moment was finally upon them. She'd thought she might fall apart. "All right. Just hang on while I get the articles I edited this morning while I was waiting for you. I want to drop them off at the newspaper on the way to the hospital. It'll just take a second."

Tad regarded her in exasperation. "Abby, I'm going to feel much better when I get you and the baby to the hospital over in Asheville."

"Then help me here." Abby collected the edited papers she'd left strewn across the living-room coffee table. "And we can leave all the sooner."

"CAN YOU BELIEVE she was worried about dropping off some work at the newspaper?" Tad asked Sadie and Raymond, who'd driven to the hospital to be with them. His adrenaline pumping, Tad paced the corridor floor as, inside the private labor room, the nurses prepped Abby for the birth.

Raymond smiled. "Sounds like Abby. Hardworking and practical to the bone. And she was right. It did just take a second. You had to drive right by the office, anyway. And you got her here in plenty of time."

Sadie patted Tad's arm and brought him back to the sofa to sit between her and Raymond. "Now, honey, you just calm down," she said, rubbing his back. "Everything is going to be fine."

Tad reminded his aunt and her husband tensely, "The baby isn't due for another two weeks." What if he or she wasn't quite ready? What if something goes wrong during the delivery? What if, what if...?

"Babies come early all the time, Tad," Aunt Sadie said as a nurse appeared, held up a sterile gown and cap and motioned Tad to come with her. "Everything's going to be fine," Sadie added reassuringly.

And for a time Abby's labor was textbook perfect, if a bit slow. Over the course of the next eight hours, she went from one stage to another, with nary a complaint. Handling the pain and the brand-new experience well, she even managed to joke with Tad and Dr. Ellison and the nurses. But as soon as their baby's head emerged, everything changed.

Tad saw it on the obstetrician's face even before the doctor stated urgently, "We've got a nuchal cord times two and it's tight."

The nurse's expression turned gravely serious, too.

She grabbed Abby's shoulders. "Stop pushing, Abby."

Perspiration streamed down Abby's face. "But I feel like I have to push," she protested breathlessly, still clutching Tad's hand and struggling to sit up, to see what was going on.

"Don't push," the nurse repeated. "The cord is wrapped around the baby's neck. The doctor has to release it. *Don't push.*"

"Tad," Abby whispered, looking to him for help. Tears of pain and terror streamed down her face.

"Hold on, Abby," Tad whispered against her ear. "I'm right here. I'm not going anywhere." He put his hands around her shoulders, and held her all the tighter, infusing her with strength and being careful not to dislodge her IV or get in anyone's way. "Everything's going to be fine," he repeated firmly. It had to be, he thought as a lump appeared in his throat and tears gathered in her eyes. They couldn't lose their baby. They couldn't.

Dr. Ellison swore. "I can't get it." He grabbed a pair of large bent-angle scissors from the sterile table. He struggled for what seemed to Tad like an eternity but was probably really more like half a minute—then abruptly exhaled in relief. "I got it." He placed the scissors down on the table. "Okay, push, Abby."

The nurse echoed Dr. Ellison. She lifted Abby's shoulders slightly. "Push, Abby, push!"

Abby gave it her all. Two pushes later the baby slid out.

But instead of the healthy pink or red they'd been led to expect in Lamaze class, their baby son was tiny and bluish-gray. And he wasn't crying and he wasn't moving. The silence in the cold and sterile delivery room was deafening. Quickly Dr. Ellison cut the cord. "Call the neonatal resuscitation team, stat!"

Abby's obstetrician carried the baby to a warming table with short glass walls and a bright light. The doctor and two nurses clustered there. Tad and Abby could see and hear the frantic activity as the nurses and doctor rubbed the baby vigorously with towels, trying to get him to wake up and breathe on his own. "Do you have a heart rate?"

The nurse replied, "One hundred and falling."

"No spontaneous respirations," Dr. Ellison reported grimly. "Let's bag him."

Clinging to each other, Tad and Abby watched as an oxygen mask was fit over their son's face. The nurse began to squeeze the bag ever so slightly, and at that point a new medical team rushed in.

"What's the story?" the doctor asked and Abby's obstetrician filled him in.

"We had good fetal heart tones up until the moment of delivery," Dr. Ellison added.

"Keep up the manual stimulation. Let's get ready to intubate and prepare a dose of epinephrine." One nurse scrambled to get the epinephrine, the other the intubation tube. With his thumbs the pediatrician opened the baby's mouth, inserted a silver instrument and tilted the baby's head back so he could see down the throat. He put the tube in, pulled out the silver scope, put on his stethoscope, listened to both sides of the baby's chest. "Good aeration," the pediatrician reported briskly. "Heart rate?"

"Sixty and falling."

One nurse put the epinephrine down the breathing tube. The other continued with the chest compressions.

"Heart rate's going up. Eighty. Ninety. It's over a hundred."

"We're getting spontaneous respirations."

Thank God, Tad thought. He noted with relief their baby's chest was at last moving on its own.

Still clinging to each other, Tad and Abby watched, barely daring to breathe. They knew, although doing better, their son was not yet out of danger.

"Heart rate?" the pediatrician asked.

"One hundred twenty and strong."

Tears of joy streamed down Abby's and Tad's faces as they saw their baby's feet and hands were at last moving, too.

"Well, he looks like he's coming around," the pediatrician said with satisfaction. "Let's try to extubate him and see how he does." With the nurses' assistance, the pediatrician removed the tube. As soon as he did, the baby let out a lusty cry that echoed throughout the room.

Tad and Abby laughed and cried and hugged each other all at once. Tad knew the sound of their son exercising his tiny lungs for the very first time was the most beautiful sound in the world. And he knew he'd remember it the rest of his life, as would Abby. And one day, when their son was much older, a teenager maybe, they'd tell him what a scare he'd given them.

The nurses smiled. "Let's get him a dry blanket." They removed the blanket beneath him and slid in another, then put a white knit cap on his head. All the while their baby—who was now a healthy pink—continued to cry and carry on as if furious at being yanked from Abby's warm womb into this cold world.

"Okay, let's get him over to the special-care nursery where I can keep an eye on him," the pediatrician told the nurses assisting him.

The nurses transferred the baby to a glass-covered incubator and wheeled him out. The doctor headed for Abby and Tad, introduced himself as the neonatologist and briefly explained what would happen. "Your baby's breathing on his own now and his heart is beating, but we need to keep a very close eye on him for the next few hours, so I'll be moving him to the special-care nursery." The doctor's eyes were kind. "Depending on how he does, we'll decide whether we can move him out to the regular mother-baby nursery or if we need to keep him here and do some testing." He held up a cautionary hand. "Most babies who suffer this sort of insult recover completely and there are no residual damages, but we won't know exactly how your baby's going to do until he gets through the next few hours."

The nurse looked at Tad. "When you're ready, we'll take you over and show you where it is and how you can visit your son."

ABBY, EXHAUSTED from the birth, stayed awake just long enough to get stitched up and be moved to a private room. Then she fell asleep, her hand clutching Tad's, tears of joy and relief still rolling down her face.

Tad knew Abby believed the worst was over. He wished he felt the same. Deciding to check on the baby again—hoping that would waylay his anxiety—he left the room and headed down the hall to the special-care nursery. As he neared the glassed-in area, he saw Doc Harlan—who'd told Tad he'd be by to check on Abby and the baby—inside, consulting with the nurses and the neonatologist.

Tad moved closer to the window. Little William was in a warming bed. He was dressed in just a diaper and his color was still good. He was motionless again, but this time it was because he was sleeping. Tad noted he had a full head of black hair and looked a lot like Abby. As Tad thought about what had almost happened back there in the delivery room, guilt assailed him anew. He didn't care what anyone said. He knew it was his fault Abby had delivered early. They'd both been pushing hard at the newspaper. Too hard, he now saw.

When Doc finished consulting with the neonatologist, he strode out into the hall. "How's Abby?"

Tad swallowed hard around the ache that had been in his throat since things had first started to go wrong. "Sleeping." *Please, God, don't let her wake up to bad news.* "How's baby William doing?"

Doc clapped an immensely comforting hand on Tad's shoulder and confided gently, "They've done two tests on the baby to see how much oxygen is circulating in his blood—which tells you how well he's breathing. The first one, taken right after he was revived, was not as good as we'd like to see. However, it was consistent with the type of trauma the baby suffered at the time of delivery.

"He seemed to be breathing well on his own, so the pediatrician held off on reintubation and repeated the test twenty minutes later. The second test showed marked improvement, and the pediatrician feels comfortable just observing the baby in the special-care nursery for the next twelve to twenty-four hours.

"If William continues to breathe easily, then Abby will be able to come in and start feeding him in the next few hours. But if he's struggling for air or breathing too fast," Doc cautioned, "we'll have to hold off on starting feeding and do follow-up testing."

Tad regarded Doc warily. "Doesn't the baby need to eat?"

Doc nodded. "If we can't feed him, we'll start an IV and feed him that way for the time being." Doc went on to explain that babies breathed through their mouths only, so the pediatrician didn't want to do anything that would make it harder for William to breathe.

The fear gripping Tad's heart squeezed a little more. More than anything he wanted to protect Abby and his son. "You're worried about my son, aren't you?" he asked grimly.

"Some, yes," Doc admitted honestly. "But William's a fighter, Tad, and he's holding his own for the moment. There's a lot to be said for that." Doc studied Tad with a physician's eye. "I wish I could say you looked as good."

Taking Tad by the arm, Doc led him down the hall in the direction of Abby's room. "You've had a really rough time of it, too, haven't you, son?" he asked compassionately as every wrong thing Tad had ever done came back to haunt him with crushing speed.

Years ago he'd let his kid brother down, with an error in judgment that had ended up costing Billy his life. Now, years later, he'd done it again, this time with his wife and son. And he was just as powerless to do anything about it after the fact. Instead, he had to wait it out and see if his son was going to be okay. The way Billy hadn't been.

With effort Tad pushed the torturous memories away. His dreams for the future fading faster than a shooting star, he knew he had to unburden himself. And who better to talk to than Doc, who'd often said that in his thirty-some years as a healer he'd seen and heard it all?

"I never should have pressured Abby to move here. But I did because—God help me—I wanted her with me. Not just as the mother to my child but because I wanted her to make my dream hers."

"Sharing a dream can bring a couple closer together," Doc said gently.

"But it wasn't just that," Tad said grimly, his shame mounting. "I needed her skills, her insight, to make the paper what it is today." Tad shoved a hand through his hair. "I couldn't have garnered anywhere near the success without her input." And therein lay the trap he'd created for them. "Don't you see, Doc? I'm the one who got her excited about newspaper work. Not enough to want to do it forever of course— I don't think that's possible—but enough to want to put in way too many hours." *Like she had that very morning,* Tad thought guiltily. "And now, because of that, our baby is here early, and I can't shake the feeling that in my selfish need to have everything my way I might have gotten us into a bad situation that I can't fix.'' What if—because of his damned selfishness and self-centeredness—things went wrong again and he and Abby lost their son? Tad had read between the lines enough to know that although William was stable, he was not out of danger yet.

The silence that fell between the two men was more indicting than any tribunal. Hand on Tad's arm, Doc directed Tad past Abby's hospital room to a deserted waiting room a little farther down the hall. Once there, he propelled Tad onto one of the sofas and made him sit.

"The last thing Abby needs is to hear you talking like this," Doc told him gruffly.

"Maybe," Tad allowed grimly, ashamed. He wished like hell he'd had something more noble to report. "But it's all true. I took advantage of Abby at a real low point in her life." *Was this—Will's condition—punishment for that?*

Doc folded his arms. "Abby strikes me as a young woman who knows her own mind. She wouldn't have come to Blossom with you if she didn't want to be here."

That wasn't quite true, Tad thought uncomfortably, as pain and regret tightened like a vice around his heart. He had backed her into a corner when she lost her job at *Trend,* and he knew it, even if no one else here did. Until now he'd believed he'd do it all over again in a flash if it meant he and Abby could have the chance to make their marriage a real one and be together again, but now he wasn't so sure he hadn't brought this all on them himself! He swallowed hard. If anything happened to their baby, if he was at fault, he knew he would never forgive himself. And neither would Abby.

Doc moved to the bank of windows and stood opposite Tad. "As far as the baby coming early goes, that could have happened if she hadn't worked at all. So you needn't blame yourself about that." Doc paused, trying to see if he was getting through. "Look, son, you and Abby and the baby have all been through a lot today. It's going to take time to recover. Talking to Abby about any of your doubts or regrets about past misdeeds is not going to do any of you any good, particularly at this juncture, so I want you to promise me you'll let that go for now," Doc said firmly. "Save it for later, after William is home, if you must discuss it."

Doc seemed to think by then it would no longer be necessary.

"Right now, just concentrate on getting some rest yourself. And helping Abby and baby William do the same. It wouldn't hurt you to get something to eat, too. Not to mention a shower, shave and fresh set of clothes." Doc placed an arm around Tad's shoulders. "So here's what we're going to do...."

Chapter Thirteen

Abby awoke the following morning, not sure how long she'd been asleep, only knowing that every part of her ached with the need to be with Tad and see her baby again. Shakily she tried to sit up, only to discover she still had an IV in her arm and was woozy as all get out. Worse was the fuzzy memory of Tad talking to Doc Harlan, telling him he regretted ever bringing her to North Carolina. Or had that been a nightmare? Abby wondered, confused.

Closing her eyes, she sank back against the pillows. And that was when she heard it, the quiet heavy footsteps, then Tad's voice, low and urgent, and the brisk purposeful voice of the neonatologist.

Tad and William's pediatrician came into the room. To Abby's surprise, Tad was showered and shaved. He even looked as if he'd had some rest. But there was a distant regret-filled look in his blue eyes that hadn't been there before she went to sleep—which made her think that her memory hadn't been a nightmare at all. And there was something else going on here, too, she thought. Otherwise, the faces of both men wouldn't look quite so reluctant and grim, and she wouldn't be feeling quite so panicked.

"Hello, Abby," the pediatrician said gently.

Abby swallowed around the lump in her throat as every self-protective instinct she had snapped immediately into place. "How's the baby doing?" she asked as Tad sat beside her on the edge of the bed and took her hand.

William's pediatrician smiled at her, but the expression in his eyes was grave. "Abby, I'm a little bit concerned about him. He seemed to recover from the initial birth incident quite well, and we checked some tests on his blood to see if he was getting enough oxygen, and those looked good. But since that time he's started to breathe a little fast again and his temperature dropped a bit."

"I don't understand." Abby shot Tad a fearful look before turning back to William's pediatrician. "What does that mean?"

"When you or I get sick, we get a fever. When a baby this young gets sick, sometimes the temp goes down a tiny bit, instead of up," he explained, his serious expression telling her everything she didn't want to hear. "The first thing we do when that happens is check the baby's blood sugar and infection count. William's blood sugar was fine. But his infection count showed too many of the cells that indicate he might be getting sick."

The pediatrician went on to explain they'd ordered a chest X ray, which had looked normal, and then drawn blood for cultures. "In the meantime we've started William on antibiotics and IV fluids."

Abby struggled against the panic that threatened to envelop her. "When can I see him?" She had to get to William, let him know they were there.

"Right away. As for feeding, as long as his respiratory rate reminds high, as I've explained to Tad, I can't allow you to breastfeed him. We'll give William all the nutrition he needs through an IV so that we don't hinder his breathing."

They were doing everything they could. She had to have faith. Abby drew an unsteady breath and worked to keep her voice even. "How long is he going to be in the hospital?"

"If the blood cultures remain negative, his breathing slows to a normal rate, and he continues to do well, then he can probably go home in seventy-two hours. If the cultures are positive, William will have to stay here in the special-care nursery anywhere from ten to twenty-one days."

Still struggling to understand, Abby asked, "Did he get sick because he was born early? Or was he born early because he was already sick?"

"Most of the time these infections just happen, and we're unable to relate it to any specific event if there's no infection in the mother. You, Abby, have shown no signs of fever or infection, so we'll probably never know why this occurred."

Abby could deal with that. As long as William got well. And he would get well, she thought fiercely. She and Tad would see to it.

William's pediatrician talked to them some more, promised to come back to see them again that evening, then left to continue his rounds. Together, Tad and

Abby walked down to the special-care nursery. A nurse showed them how to scrub their hands for several minutes with a rough bristly brush and some brown antiseptic-smelling soap, then ushered them in.

Abby teared up when she got her first good look at her son. He was so beautiful. He had a head of black hair, long-lashed eyes, rosebud lips and one heck of a determined chin. He was nineteen inches long and weighed six pounds five ounces, according to the identification card on the outside of his isolette. He was lying on his back in the warming bed clad in just a diaper. An IV line had been inserted into his foot, and a clear plastic helmet had been placed over his head. Abby felt frightened and reassured all at once. He was alive, and as long as he was alive, he had a chance to pull through.

Her heart pounding, she glanced at the nurse. "What's the helmet for?"

"That's an 'oxy hood.' We're giving him a little extra oxygen to help him breathe."

Abby leaned against Tad, aware she'd never needed his strength and determination more than she did at that moment. "He's so tiny," she whispered. "So defenseless." She wished she could hold him.

Tad nodded and tightened his grip on her. "But he's one heck of a fighter, Abby. The doctors have said so."

THE DAYS THAT FOLLOWED were indisputably the roughest in Abby's entire life. As the pediatrician had suspected, William had a positive blood culture that confirmed the presence of an infection in his tiny body. A second chest X ray also showed a small pneumonia in his lungs, and another weighing showed a loss of three ounces. They continued the IV and the antibiotics, and prayed the powerful medicine, combined with the essential nutrition, warming bed and oxy hood, would do the trick. And all the while Abby and Tad paced and prayed.

Twelve hours after being on antibiotics, William's breathing improved somewhat. A second blood culture showed the same bug that the first culture had. Convinced they'd selected the right medicine, William's pediatrician continued the antiobiotic, and within thirty-six hours of the baby's first becoming sick, a very grateful and blissfully happy Abby was able to hold him in her arms. And, taken off oxygen, William was able to eat for the first time. Hours later, his IV fluids were discontinued and he was moved to a crib.

Tad and Abby both had reason to rejoice when repeat blood cultures, drawn several days later, were negative. It meant, William's pediatrician explained, that they had suppressed the bug. Nevertheless, William had to finish a fourteen-day course of antibiotics.

During that time Abby was discharged from the hospital.

Abby's parents—notified by Sadie—sent telegrams and flowers to the hospital, expressing their good wishes, but—otherwise engrossed in their work—did not offer to come and visit or help out. Tad felt badly for Abby. Surely, he thought, if ever there was a time when a grown woman needed her parents, this was it. But Abby wasn't surprised. She told him she'd expected as much and not to worry about it. *She* wasn't going to. Instead, she focused her every thought, her every ounce of energy, on helping their infant son get well. As did Tad. Until finally, day by day, William improved, and they heard the news they'd been waiting to hear.

"You can take your baby home."

Tears of joy streamed down Abby's face as she looked at the infant in her arms. A huge knot of emotion grew in her throat, making speech impossible. Tad kissed her forehead and his son's tiny fist in turn, and for a few minutes he too seemed unable to speak. Finally he thanked William's pediatrician profusely for all he'd done.

"Anytime," the doctor said with a smile and a wink. "And maybe next time," he said, playfully hinting there might be other newborns of Tad and Abby's for him to take care of, "the whole thing will go a lot easier."

Next time. Abby jerked in a quick breath at the thought.

Would there be a next time? Another pregnancy?

She faced Tad awkwardly, wondering where they went from here. Their agreement only covered the period until their baby's birth. Now William was here. He was finally out of danger. And the future loomed ahead of them uncertainly.

The doctor left, and a heavy silence fell between Tad and Abby. At last Tad braced his hands on his hips, then offered matter-of-factly, "I'll go down to the business office and take care of the paperwork necessary to sign Will out."

Abby nodded. "I'll get our things together and wait for you here."

ALTHOUGH WILL SLEPT peacefully the whole time, the forty-five-minute ride home seemed interminable. Abby felt odd, sitting in back, while Tad sat in front and drove. Odder still was hearing about the newspaper. Although Tad was still very much caught up in the goings-on in the office, it seemed ages since she'd worked there. Even longer since she and Tad had shared anything remotely like the fiercely passionate relationship they'd once enjoyed. *It's not my imagination,* Abby thought as she stared out at the cold blustery February day. The two of them were united in their love and concern for their child. But as for everything else…

Tad had been keeping a very tight rein on his emotions and withholding every bit as much as he said since the birth of their child. She knew he loved their baby, too, and had been devastated by little Will's illness. But it was more than that. She didn't know how or why it had happened, but there was an emotional wall between them now, keeping them apart. A wall she couldn't ever see herself scaling.

Maybe, though, she thought dispiritedly, she shouldn't be surprised by that. He'd married her on a whim, because of the passionate nature of their whirlwind love affair, and stayed married to her because of the baby and because of the paper. Now the baby had been born and the newspaper was on solid ground. Tad had to realize, as did she, that it was time they thought about going their separate ways again, just as they had once promised each other they would.

As Tad turned the Jeep into the drive, Abby sighed. The only problem was she wasn't sure she wanted to leave, even to go back to work in the magazine field. Given a choice, she would much rather work on getting their relationship back to the happy state it had been in before Will's birth. Unfortunately she couldn't do it alone. And right now she wasn't sure Tad was all that driven to help her.

No sooner had he cut the engine, than Sadie and Raymond were rushing out the door. They brought the baby in. Sadie had the house warm and the cradle waiting. For a few minutes they oohed and aahed over the still-peacefully sleeping William. Then Sadie, remembering an urgent telephone message for Abby, abruptly went to get it.

Abby left to return the call, then rejoined the group several minutes later, still in a state of shock. "The editor-in-chief of *Southern Home and Garden* magazine has just quit to take a job in London. They've offered me the position." Abby named a salary that was twice what she'd made at *Trend*.

"What are you going to do?" Sadie asked.

"I don't know and I don't have much time to decide. They'd need me to start in six weeks, and they want an answer within forty-eight hours." Abby swallowed and looked at Tad. "If I don't take it, they want to start a full-fledged search."

"Congratulations," Tad said with what sounded like real enthusiasm. He hugged her warmly, clearly impressed. "That's a huge career leap."

"Yes," Abby agreed woodenly, "it is."

Sadie and Raymond looked at each other and stood. "I'm sure you two want to discuss this alone." Sadie kissed Abby's cheek, as did Raymond. Both offered their congratulations.

"Thanks," Abby said, knowing now what she hadn't known before Will's birth—and Tad still didn't know—that she couldn't take a job that would take her away from her baby, even for a few days at a time.

William was only going to be young once; she wanted to cherish this time with him. And she wanted to find a way to rebuild her marriage to Tad, to get over this crazy distance between them, however—why ever—it had come about. But only, she thought, if he was willing to meet her halfway.

Sadie and Raymond left quietly, and Tad went to get the bottle of champagne they'd received as a gift in honor of William's homecoming. While she watched, dread weakening her knees, he searched the kitchen cupboard for two glasses. Finding them, he set them down on the counter. "I don't see how you can turn this job down."

Just tell me you love me and want to stay married to me forever, and watch how fast I react. "The job is in Atlanta," Abby reminded him, putting aside the crushing hurt she felt and carefully gauging his reaction. *His needs and desires were just as important as hers. This had to be about what he wanted, too.*

His expression impassive, Tad shrugged. Meeting her glance, he said gently, "It's only an hour and a half flight to Atlanta. We can figure out a way to share the care of Will and both still have what we want in our careers.''

Abby thought back to the promise they'd made to stay together only until after the baby was born. Then the nightmarish conversation in the hospital. What was it she'd thought she'd overheard Tad say to Doc Harlan? *I never should have pressured Abby to move here…but I did because… I needed her help in making the paper what it is today… And now that our baby is here… I can't shake the feeling that…I might have gotten us into a bad situation…*

She hadn't wanted to face it then, or ask him if he'd had second thoughts about the marriage. It had been just too painful. Now she had no choice.

Having seen her parents' bitterness and disillusionment at the end of every one of their many marriages, she'd rather she and Tad end their marriage while they were still friends. Like it or not, she told herself firmly, following his cues, he was doing them all a favor by reacting this way. This job was the graceful way out for both of them.

''So it's true. Abby is leaving the *Blossom Weekly News,*'' Cindy said sadly the next morning.

Tad put the finishing touches on the ad for Abby's replacement. ''The opportunity is incredible.'' *And I'm the last person in the world who should stand in her way.* Hadn't he promised himself, when Billy died, that he would never be responsible for depriving anyone of the life they should have had again? In the background Sadie and Raymond exchanged concerned glances. Catching them, Tad frowned.

"But she just had your baby!" Sonny protested with all the youthful naïveté of a recent college grad.

Secretly Tad had hoped Abby would want to stay there with him, especially after all they'd been through together, building the paper to its current level of success. But, he reminded himself sternly, Abby had been honest with him from the start, telling him that, as much as she wanted to be fair about the baby and give their child a mother and father he could count on, she was not going to sacrifice the career she'd spent the past ten years building for his dreams of a permanent home and life in North Carolina.

Besides, if she didn't want to continue their marriage by now, she never would. Tad didn't want to lose Abby altogether. The only way he could keep her in his life without the acrimony of divorce, as in her parents' relationship, or the coldness and strain and unspoken resentments in his own parents' marriage was to muster all his courage and let her go gracefully. So that was, he thought resolutely, exactly what he was going to do.

ABBY WAS IN THE KITCHEN when Tad came in the back door, a cardboard box of her belongings in his arms. Raindrops dampened his shoulders and glistened in his hair, and his cheeks were rosy from the cold March air. He also looked like he'd had as rough a day as she had, trying to explain to everyone why they were splitting up. "Where do you want these?" he asked.

Abby struggled to hide her melancholy. "Dining room, I guess."

Tad carried them in there, set them down gently and then returned.

"Is Will sleeping?"

Abby nodded, wishing this wasn't so awkward. "Yes. I just put him down."

Tad made several more trips. By the time he'd finished, he'd carried in six boxes that were filled to overflowing. Abby surveyed the jumbled mess. "I had no idea I had so much stuff at the newspaper."

Tad shrugged out of his coat and looped it over the back of a chair. "So, when are you going to Atlanta to hunt for a place to live?" he asked casually.

"Personnel is going to call me tomorrow after they've received my signed employment contract." Which she still hadn't sent. "I'll set up a house-hunting trip then."

"But you're expecting it to be when?" Tad pressed.

He sure was anxious to get rid of her, Abby thought irritably. She shrugged. "Next week sometime—at least that's what I hope." Studying the slightly aggravated, very distant light in Tad's eyes, Abby thought maybe he was right. Maybe the sooner she wrapped up the details on this, the better.

Tad poured himself a cup of freshly brewed coffee. "Will you be leaving Will here?"

"For that particular trip, yes." Abby turned away from the stack of thank-you letters she'd been writing. She tried not to think about how difficult it would be to be separated from William even for a few hours, never mind a few days. She studied Tad. "Unless you want me to take him with me."

"No." Tad lifted his cup to his lips. "I'd like to

take care of him here. I can grab a couple of days off from the paper.''

Another awkward silence fell between them. Finally Abby shook her head. ''I feel like I should say something to ease the tension between us,'' she said quietly.

Tad turned and stared out at the bleak March day. The sky was gray. A light rain was falling and had been all day. ''It's hard to be comfortable when a marriage is splitting up.''

''True,'' Abby allowed, irked that he could take this in stride so much more easily than she could, when it had been she all along who'd insisted they stay together only until after the birth.

Aware he was now watching her as carefully as she'd been watching him, Abby stubbornly marshaled her pride and steeled herself not to cry. Hearing the clothes dryer buzz, signaling the end of the cycle, she headed into the utility room. ''Although I guess we should have known that our romance was way too passionate to last, at least the level it was in Paris.'' It was just too bad, Abby thought as she pulled a load of warm baby clothes from the dryer, that she'd wanted it to be that way forever.

Tad watched her carry the clothes into the kitchen. She sat down in a chair and began to fold them. ''I don't know about that. Our sex life here was pretty damn passionate,'' Tad said matter-of-factly, ''at least when you were pregnant.''

So much so, Abby thought, that she'd allowed herself to be completely fooled about the direction of their future.

''That's because we were both romanticizing the

pregnancy and awaiting the birth of our baby,'' she told him as she neatly folded a blue print sleeper. ''Now William's here and it's a different kind of joy we're feeling. One that is a lot more…parental.'' Abby drew a bolstering breath as she turned a tiny undershirt right side out and stacked that, too. ''Anyway, I love my career and know it will sustain me through life's ups and downs, just as the newspaper will ground you in any number of ways. And,'' Abby continued pragmatically, warming to the task of getting out of this marriage with at least her pride intact, ''it'll be easier for William this way.''

Easier for all three of us, she amended silently.

Abby returned to the laundry. She plucked the damp clothes from the washer and tossed them into the dryer. ''Perhaps it was the impulsive way we married or the wonder of expecting our first child together, but whatever the case, you and I romanticized marriage to a ridiculous degree. And marriage isn't a fairy tale,'' she concluded as she switched on the dryer and returned to Tad's side. ''People just don't live happily ever after these days.''

Tad finished the last of his coffee and set the mug down with a thud. ''You're right about that,'' he said gruffly.

Abby looked at him, her heart sinking. If only he knew, she thought, how very much she wished he would argue with her about this, tell her she was all wrong, that marriages did last, and theirs could, too. Because she wanted to live happily ever after with him, and William, and maybe even have another child or two. But she couldn't do it alone, she thought, studying his squared shoulders and girded thighs. She couldn't do it at all without his help. And that, she realized reluctantly, was obviously not going to come.

"I'm going back down to the paper," Tad said curtly, picking up his coat. He looked at her like he had the hounds of hell on his heels. "If anyone needs me—" he was already striding out into the rain and the cold "—I'll be there."

Chapter Fourteen

"I couldn't believe it when Abby told me you'd gone back to the office tonight. But then I couldn't believe it when she told me she was taking that job in Atlanta, either."

Tad swiveled away from his computer screen and faced his aunt with exasperation. It had been one heck of a day. The last thing he needed was familial interference. "Aunt Sadie, you know I love you—" he began irritably.

"I love you, too." His aunt paced, waving her arms excitedly. "But that doesn't mean the two of you aren't the most stubborn shortsighted people I've ever seen. Furthermore, Tad McFarlane, I never thought I'd see the day when you'd be afraid to go after what you want! But here it is, anyway!"

"I'm not afraid," Tad said grimly. Grabbing his mug, he went over to pour more coffee into it. "I'm keeping a promise I made to Abby." *Even if it was costing him dearly.* He'd told her he understood her devotion to her career—and he did. He'd told her he'd support her decision to go back to work as a magazine editor as soon as the baby was born—and he had. The fact that it had come just weeks after William's birth was a shock, but that did not in any way negate the promise he'd made. And now it was up to him to honor that promise. It didn't matter if it felt like his heart had literally been ripped in two.

Sadie perched on the edge of his desk. Her frown deepening, she followed his gaze, then demanded, "Will you stop looking at Abby's formal letter of resignation and listen to me? You're going to end up looking as mournful as Buster on a bad day for the rest of your life if you aren't careful."

Figuring this conversation had gone on long enough, Tad tore his eyes from Abby's letter and gave his aunt a warning glance. "Don't you think you're exaggerating just a bit?" he said dryly. After all, it wasn't as if he and Abby would never see each other again. They'd agreed to rear their son together. They would likely see each other all the time. So what if it wasn't quite the same? So what if he might not ever make love to her again or hold her through the night or enjoy the morning sunrise and the first cup of coffee of the day with her? She was going to be happy. She was returning to work she loved almost more than life. And for that reason he had to put his own selfish concerns aside and be happy for her.

"No, I do not think I'm exaggerating a bit. And quite frankly I'm furious with you. I never thought you'd let life pass you by the way I did for so many years. But I was lucky. I found Raymond and fell in love and married him."

Tad smiled at his aunt gently. "And I'm happy for you, Aunt Sadie."

"I know you are, honey." Sadie watched him kick back in his chair. "But think of all the time I wasted earlier in my life by being so shortsighted and foolish and picky and afraid to really invest myself in any one relationship." She paused, her expression mirroring the sadness he felt deep inside. "You and Abby have a child, Tad. You have a marriage. Don't let either of them go."

"I HAVE TO TELL YOU, Abby," Yvonne said as Abby tried for the hundredth time to put the signed employment contract into the envelope that would be express-mailed to Atlanta first thing the next morning, right after she had spoken to the publisher and accepted the job. "The magazine-business rumor mill is going crazy! Is it true? Are you going to be the new editor-in-chief of *Southern Home and Garden* magazine?"

Abby finally put the employment contract down and switched the telephone to her other ear. "They've asked and given me forty-eight hours to decide." Briefly Abby filled Yvonne in on all the perks that came with the job. "If I accept, I'll have to cut my maternity leave a little short and head for Atlanta right away, but they'll let me bring the baby to work for the first year." Abby paced over to the bassinet, where William slept soundly.

"Wow."

Yeah, wow, Abby thought as she lightly, lovingly smoothed William's soft cheek. The job was a dream. The perks were incredible. After ten years of working nonstop for just such an opportunity, she ought to be walking on air. But instead, all she could think was that she was leaving Tad and taking their baby with her, and that Tad was more than willing to have her go.

Not that that should've been a surprise to her, though. She'd known from the outset that Tad's dream of one day owning and running his own newspaper had meant more to him than she did. The two of them had split up less than twenty-four hours after they'd first tied the knot for just that reason. Had it not been for the fact that she was carrying his baby, they never would have lived together and stayed together for all those months.

"You don't sound excited."

Tears blurring her eyes, Abby paced away from the bassinet. "I'm not."

"Because of the baby?" Yvonne prodded gently.

"It's everything," Abby said, and then to her horror, burst into sobs.

"Oh, honey," Yvonne clucked sympathetically.

"It's hormones," Abby sniffed, trying to stifle her tears with her fist. "Postpartum ones this time." That had to be it. She could not be falling apart just because the marriage she'd never for one minute really expected to last was breaking up.

"Well, you know what they say," Yvonne said. "Pregnancy is supposed to be one long roller-coaster ride. And you had one heck of a time, seeing William through his illness and waiting for him to get better."

"You'll get no argument there." Abby plucked a tissue from the box and blew her nose. Her life with Tad had been a roller-coaster ride from start to finish.

And she was so sorry it was over. She'd gotten to like—no, love—having Tad in her life.

There was a brief silence on the other end of the line. "How is Tad taking all this?" Yvonne asked gently.

Abby swallowed around the growing knot of emotion in her throat and tried to get a grip on herself. "He doesn't seem to care what I do either way."

"Now, Abby, I am sure that's not true!"

Abby thought about Tad's immediate assumption she would take the job in Atlanta, never mind that their baby had just been born and they'd have to live in two different cities. If that wasn't pushing her out the door with both hands, if that wasn't letting her know her days as his wife were over, she didn't know what was. "Unfortunately it is."

"Then steal a page from his book and seduce him into changing his mind," Yvonne said, practical as ever.

Abby flushed. "He never seduced *me* into anything!"

"I beg to differ. Any man who convinces a woman to marry him during a whirlwind weekend romance in Paris has also *seduced* her into wanting what he wants."

"Not really," Abby murmured wistfully, as she thought back to the weekend that had so changed her life. "To tell you the truth, I wanted all that, anyway," Abby confided. "The husband, the home, the baby. A personal life aside from my work." And for a brief time, she'd had it.

"Aha! I *thought* you were a closet romantic."

Abby massaged her temples. "Yeah, well, I was always afraid to admit it for fear I'd get it all, then have it taken away." She hadn't wanted to feel deeply or let herself be vulnerable or love a man more than life. But she had.

"And you did have it all with Tad, didn't you?" Yvonne asked gently.

Suddenly the lump was back in Abby's throat, bigtime. "You saw us together. You know we did."

"Then what are you doing talking to me," Yvonne demanded in exasperation, "when you could be going after what you really want, right this instant?"

HALF AN HOUR LATER Abby was headed for the phone again when the doorbell rang. Sadie and Raymond stood on the other side. "I was just going to call you," Abby said as she fastened her earrings.

Sadie cast an admiring glance at the sexy black cocktail dress Abby hadn't worn since that fateful weekend in Paris. "You were?"

Abby paused to slip on a pair of heels. "Yep." She searched through the front-hall closet for a suitable wrap. "I need a baby-sitter. Pronto."

Raymond helped Sadie with her raincoat and took off his. "William asleep?"

Abby nodded. "And he's just been fed and diapered."

"Sounds like we're all set, then," Raymond said. Because Tad had the Jeep, Raymond handed Abby the keys to his sedan.

"Might we ask where you're going?" Sadie asked.

Abby looked Sadie square in the eye. "To find that

husband of mine. He and I have some straightening out to do.''

IT WAS TEN in the evening and Tad was still toying with the wording on the newspaper advertisement he was composing when the door opened and shut. In stormed Abby, looking incredibly beautiful and loaded for bear.

Slim as the day he'd met her, thanks in no small part to the stress of the past few weeks, the only change in her willowy form was the added lusciousness of her breasts.

Pausing long enough to hang her coat on the rack next to the front door, she strode toward him resolutely, her high heels clicking on the polished wooden floor. Her expression both defiant and determined, she reached in front of him, picked up her letter of resignation, ripped it up with a flourish and then dropped the pieces of it in front of him.

Tad stared at her, aware she'd never looked more feisty or beautiful than she did at that very minute, in the short and sassy black cocktail dress.

His heart pounding, he looked at the papers she'd so dramatically shredded in front of him, then back at her face. He hoped like heck this all meant what he hoped it did. But with Abby, and the way her moods had been going up and down lately, there was no telling.

He sat back in his chair, determined to play this every bit as mysteriously as his wife. Blue eyes sparkling with unbridled mischief—and challenge that matched her own—he looked her up and down slowly, his eyes lingering on the fullness of her breasts and the slenderness of her hips, before once again returning to her face. "Mind telling me what the meaning of that little gesture was?" he drawled lazily.

"I'll tell you what the meaning was," Abby said as she dropped unceremoniously into his lap and wreathed her arms about his neck. "You are not pushing me out of your life, Tad McFarlane. I am here to stay."

"Oh, yeah?" Tad shot back, liking the unabashedly amorous light in her golden-brown eyes. It felt so good to have her in his arms again. He'd missed holding her and making love to her so much.

"Oh, yeah," Abby echoed as all the hopes and dreams he had once had for them and thought were dead surged to new life. "Because I realized tonight that the months we've spent together have taught me something."

"And that would be?" Tad prodded, realizing he never wanted to let Abby go. And yet he knew there was still so much they had to clear up before they could go on. As he looked into her eyes, he realized she knew it, too.

Abby rubbed her hands thoughtfully across the soft cotton fabric of his shirt, molding her trembling palms to the muscles of his chest. "That I have to go after my marriage and a life and a love with you with the same tenacity and faith and commitment I've always given my career."

Tad rubbed his thumb across her face, tracing the shape of her cheek and jaw. "I have to say I'm all for that," he murmured as he bent his head to kiss her.

Then he drew back. "But before we rush ahead and recommit to each other, there are some things we have to talk about."

"I agree," Abby said quickly, a determined edge to her tone. "And first on the agenda is the job, Tad. Before I came over here, I turned down the job at *Southern Home and Garden*. And I told the headhunter I'm withdrawing from the job search permanently."

Tad tensed. "I told you before, Abby—I don't ever again want to be responsible for robbing someone else of the life he or she was meant to have." He cupped her hands in his. "I know how much your career has always meant to you, and I don't want you to look back later and regret passing up this opportunity."

Abby gazed deep into his eyes. "Is that why you told Doc in the hospital you regretted having me move here and work on the paper?" She briefly explained what she'd heard.

Tad grimaced. "I realized that night how selfish and self-centered I'd been. I felt guilty about forcing my dreams on you and wanting you with me—not just during the pregnancy but for all time—no matter what the cost to you."

Abby moved closer in a drift of perfume. "What did Doc say to all that?"

Tad stared into her long-lashed golden-brown eyes. "He told me you wouldn't have been here with me if you didn't want to be."

Abby's lips curved softly. "Doc's right, you know. Baby or no baby, I never would have stayed married to you all those months if I hadn't loved you or hoped a miracle would happen and we'd find a way—with time—to work everything out.'' Abby paused, still studying him, gauging his reaction. ''But there's one thing I don't understand. If you felt that way, why didn't you just tell me you wanted me to stay here rather than go to Atlanta?''

Tad regarded Abby seriously. ''Because I wanted you to make the decision about your future based on what you needed in terms of your career and your life, not on what I needed. I felt it was only fair, since we spent most of last year chasing *my* dreams.''

When Abby heard that, she knew Tad really had changed, as had she. Both of them for the better. ''And if I had chosen the job in Atlanta? What then?''

Tad turned his swivel chair to the left and directed Abby's attention to the computer screen on his desk. Aloud she read, '' 'For Sale. Thriving newspaper in Blossom, North Carolina—' '' She turned to him in amazement.

''That's as far as I got,'' he said, ''but you get the gist.''

She looked at him, stunned. ''You were going to sell the newspaper?''

Tad nodded, feeling a lump in his throat the size of a walnut. ''And follow you to Atlanta. And, if necessary, win your heart and your attention and your love all over again. Because as Sadie pointed out,'' he told Abby gruffly, looking deep into her eyes, ''our love for each other is worth fighting for.'' He held Abby close and stroked her hair. ''So if you want to call the publisher, tell him you've talked to me and

I've agreed to move, and you want to take the job, after all, then it's absolutely fine with me.''

"Oh, Tad. Thank you." Abby embraced him. "That means so much to me. But... I don't want to do that.''

He studied her face carefully. "You're sure?"

Abby nodded. "I realized as soon as I thought about what it would be like to take such a challenging high-pressure job that it wasn't something I could do without working twelve- to sixteen-hour days. And while that would have been fine while I was still a single woman, now I'm a mom and a wife, and I want to be with my family a lot more. Plus—'' her lips lifted in an affectionate grin ''—word has it that the editor-in-chief of the *Blossom Weekly News* is a *very* understanding guy. He's so understanding, in fact," Abby continued, "that he lets his wife work at home whenever she wants or bring their baby to work so the baby can be with the two of them as much as possible.''

Tad grinned and sifted a hand through her hair. "Funny," he drawled, his eyes sparkling mischievously too, "I'd heard exactly the same thing.''

"So it's a deal?'' Abby wreathed her arms about his neck. "We'll stay here, stay married and continue to build the *Blossom Weekly News* into the finest newspaper North Carolina has ever seen?''

"Agreed.'' Tad kissed her fiercely. "But only on one condition,'' he said.

Abby cuddled against him, content. "Anything.''

Tad cupped a hand beneath her chin. "This whole misunderstanding has made me realize that I have to talk about things. Not gloss over our problems or run from them the way my parents did after my brother's death. Because my parents and I should have talked about things. Not just after Billy's death, but all along, even if it was painful. Instead, we kept it all bottled up inside because we didn't want to hurt one another. And we ended up hurting one another all the more in the process by becoming permanently emotionally estranged. And then I did the same thing in my marriage to you, in my attempts to protect you. When all my silence on the truly difficult emotional issues really did was end up hurting you," he said softly.

"You weren't the only one who was afraid." Abby drew a ragged breath and looked at him with serious eyes. "I said my vows, never really believing it could or would last. And I held a part of myself—the most vulnerable part of myself—from you all along. Only when I was about to lose you did I realize I had a lot more to give than I thought." She leaned forward to kiss him tenderly. "I love you with all my heart and soul, and I always will."

He held her tenderly and looked deep into her eyes. "And I love you with every fiber of my being." He tugged her closer and indulged in a long steamy kiss that left them both feeling very content, glowing and alive. "Don't ever doubt that."

Abby's spirits soared and she knew there was only one thing left to say. "Then I, Abby Kildaire McFarlane, once again take thee, Tad, to be my lawfully wedded husband…"

"And I, Tad McFarlane, once again take thee, Abby, to be my lawfully wedded wife…"

"Forever…" Abby said softly.

"And ever…" Tad agreed.

"And from this day forward, I promise to keep the lines of communication open between us, speak always what is in my heart and on my mind. And I expect you, dear husband, to do the same."

"I think I can handle that," he replied.

Abby kissed Tad soundly once again. "Good," she said, cuddling against him, "'cause we have a long and happy life ahead of us."

"And maybe," Tad said as he kissed his way down the slope of her neck, "given a little time, maybe even another baby or two."

Abby kissed the strong column of his throat. "William would like that, I'm sure."

"As would Sadie and Raymond." Tad sighed, content.

Abby drew back. "Think we should go home and tell them the good news?"

"Absolutely." Tad nodded vigorously. "But first—" Tad kissed her "—you and I have some catching up to do."

And they did.

**SEXY, POWERFUL MEN NEED
EXTRAORDINARY WOMEN WHEN THEY'RE**

Destined for Love

Take a walk on the wild side this October
when three bestselling authors weave wondrous stories
about heroines who use their extraspecial abilities to
achieve the magic and wonder of love!

HATFIELD AND McCOY
by HEATHER GRAHAM POZZESSERE

LIGHTNING STRIKES
by KATHLEEN KORBEL

MYSTERY LOVER
by ANNETTE BROADRICK

Available October 1998
wherever Harlequin and Silhouette books are sold.

HARLEQUIN®
Makes any time special ™

Silhouette®

Look us up on-line at: http://www.romance.net   PSBR1098

COMING NEXT MONTH

#749 IF WISHES WERE...DADDIES by Jo Leigh
Three Coins in a Fountain
Jessica Needham wished to be left alone, particularly by Nick Carlucci—
but she was having his baby. She'd convinced herself he'd never need to
know—right up until she opened her door to find Nick on the other
side....

#750 SIGN ME, SPEECHLESS IN SEATTLE by Emily Dalton
As the title star of the popular column "Ask Aunt Tilly," Mathilda McKinney
dispensed advice to the lovelorn and the troubled. But who would advise
Mathilda, now that drop-dead-gorgeous duke Julian Rothwell was steamed
at her counsel—and demanded Tilly herself as payment!

#751 SHE'S HAVING HIS BABY by Linda Randall Wisdom
Accidental Dads
Caitlin O'Hara and Jake Roberts. They went together like peanut butter
and jelly. Friends since the first day of kindergarten, they shared everything,
including Friday-night pizza and war stories from the romance trenches.
But there were some things you didn't even ask your best friend—like "Can
you make me pregnant?" Or did you?

#752 DOORSTEP DADDY by Linda Cajio
The Holiday Heart
Richard Holiday: Single, sexy—and up to his ears in dirty diapers and
raging hormones, toddlers, teenagers and kids in between! But was he ready
to give up his bachelorhood? The three happy children made his house feel
like a real home.... The only thing missing was a wife....

AVAILABLE THIS MONTH:

Look us up on-line at: http://www.romance.net